SURFMEN

To Nina Muzze,
My "Other" Parents

SUREMEN

BY

C. T. MARSHALL

www.Fireshippress.com

i

SURFMEN by CT Marshall

ISBN-13: 978-1-61179-287-4 (Paperback)
ISBN -978-1-61179-288-1 (e-book)

BISAC Subject Headings:
FIC014000 Fiction Historical
FIC 0147000 Fiction Sea Stories
FIC001000 Fiction Action

Cover work by Christine Horner

Address all correspondence to:
Fireship Press, LLC
P.O. Box 68412
Tucson, AZ 85737
Or visit our website at:
www.fireshippress.com

DEDICATION

To all the brave men and women that face the sea so that we may live.

ACKNOWLEDGEMENTS

Surfmen has been nearly a decade in the making, a wicked long process. Good historical fiction is a bit of a war of attrition, meaning a ton of time spent with the two "R"s, reading and research. I'd like to extend a very special thank-you to great historians everywhere. Without your diligence, historical fiction wouldn't exist; it would be plain fiction.

There have been dozens of historical works written about the United States Lifesaving Service, but four specifically that were paramount in creating <u>Surfmen</u>. These four in no particular order are <u>The U.S. Life-Saving Service: Heroes, Rescues and Architecture of the Early Coast Guard</u> by Ralph Shanks and Wick York; <u>The Lifesavers, a Story of the United States Life-Saving Service</u> by James Otis; <u>That Others Might Live</u> by Dennis L. Noble; and <u>Ship Ashore, The U.S. Lifesavers of Coastal North Carolina</u> by Joe Mobley. Without these four books and the hard work of their authors, <u>Surfmen</u> wouldn't exist.

I'd also like to thank the staff and members of the US lifesaving Service Heritage Association. The USLSSHA and their publication, <u>The Wreck and Rescue Journal</u>, relayed scores of stories about the Lifesaving Service, and truly helped me know and understand these very real heroes of the sea.

If someone is willing to put in the time and miles, there are lifesaving and maritime museums up and down the East Coast. Throughout the last 7 or 8 years, I've visited too many to specifically mention. Each of these museums is unique, and thanks to their dedicated staff, with each visit my respect for the lifesavers grew.

I would specifically like to thank James Charlet and Linda Malloy of the Chicamacomico Lifesaving Station Historic Site in Rodanthe, NC. The Chicamacomico Station is the largest, most complete USLSS complex in the nation. Over the course of multiple visits, the staff of Chicamacomico graciously answered my questions, and their programs allowed me to breathe life into the characters in this work.

One of the first versions of Surfmen got sent to my good friend and fellow writer, Todd Sapre. Todd's insight launched a ton of re-writes, and ultimately helped steer <u>Surfmen</u> to its present course.

As to the nuts and bolts of the written word, I'd like to specifically thank Carolyn Marshall, Alan Rinzler, and Chris Paige. A career English and Spanish teacher (and my wife), Carolyn suffered through years of chapter by chapter and line by line edits with <u>Surfmen</u>. Alan Rinzler not only edited the work, but really helped transform the story. Chris Paige is the editor extraordinaire at Fireship Press, and is so talented that at times I struggled to discern her words from my own. <u>Surfmen</u> wouldn't have gotten off the ground without all of your red pens and your advice.

I'd like to extend a special thanks to Bill Hammond, author of <u>A Matter of Honor</u>, <u>A Call to Arms</u>, <u>For Love of Country</u>, and <u>The Power and the Glory</u>. Bill is the preeminent historical novelist of this day and age, and in 2012 won Best Historical Fiction honors for both <u>A Call to Arms</u> and <u>The Power and the Glory</u>. Bill read an early version of <u>Surfmen</u>, and his kind words pushed the final story to fruition.

Lastly, I'd really like to thank the men and women of the United States military. All branches in some way, shape, or form share DNA with the United States Lifesaving Service. As Jack Nicholson's character Colonel Jessup boldly states in <u>A Few Good Men</u>, "We sleep under the very blanket of the protection that you provide." Thank you for your service.

CHAPTER 1

November 1848
Diamond Shoals, off the coast of North Carolina

The fierce and howling wind drowned out the screams of the dying. The sea lashed the stranded ship, crashing over the rails before rolling across the deck to disappear into the foam below. Her bow rode low in the water, waterlogged in the pounding rain and cloaked in salt spray. Her keel was wedged, twisted and broken in the strong grip of sea and sand. Mangled lines mingled with tattered sails and crushed timbers in the swirling torrent that swept her decks.

Amid the wrecked spars and crumpled sails, a young boy and his mother clung to the precarious protection of the companionway bulkhead. Both were soaked through, their flesh puffy and wrinkled from long exposure to the water and salt that washed over them from all sides. The cold had long since sent icy fingers through their skin and penetrated deep into their bones. Their clothes of broadcloth, fine wool and silk were shredded, exposing bare flesh to the storm.

The mother's long brown hair was knotted and unkempt; it hung limply around a once beautiful face that had been shattered by splinters when the mizzenmast had snapped during the onslaught of the storm. Furrows from nose to ear showed the white of her cheekbone through her torn skin.

"It's all right....all right...all right...shhhhh." Her mouth was pressed tightly against her son's ear. She had draped herself across his shoulder and back, trying to protect him from the ravages of sea and storm.

The boy's knees were drawn up under his chin. His frail arms were wrapped tightly around them. His heavy breeches

1

were torn from knee to hip on his left side and his left leg was black with bruises and swollen. At some point he'd lost a shoe, and his big toe stuck from the stocking. His other heavy brogan was a stone at the end of his leg. It was so soaked and the leather so swollen that his foot was immovable beneath him.

Hours before he had, for the first time, seen a man die. Just before the mainmast had toppled, Mr. Whittle, the first mate, had been crushed when the bindings securing a large stack of heavy lumber had let go. Mr. Whittle had screamed. It wasn't a long scream; the stack plunged down and buried him right on the deck. For a few, horrible moments Mr. Whittle's bare feet poking out from under the stack had twitched in the rain.

The boy turned his eyes to his mother. Her ragged dress had once been grand. It was the dress that she had worn at the farewell party in Charleston before their journey. Now it was torn from shoulder to bodice. It alternately opened and closed, playing peek-a-boo with her right breast and the tip of her right nipple. She clutched it closed, modest even now.

The boy stared into his mother's eyes.

"Where's Father?" he shouted against the scream of the wind.

His mother stared bleakly across the deck, refusing to meet his gaze as the storm raged on. It could have been midday or midnight; the dark gray that cloaked the ship was unforgiving. Only the brief snatches of lightning exposed the wreck in sharp relief.

"Where's Father?" he whispered a second time.

His mother met his eyes. Hers were dull flat and gray. "He went to...to...to get help," she mouthed against the wind.

She couldn't say the lie aloud. And he knew it to be a lie. At seven, he was old enough to know that. He had watched his father battle the sea. He had seen him among the other men, and he had seen them all flung over the rail, one by one. His father had been among the last alive, but a great wave had taken him over the rail into the swirling sea below. The boy

2

knew that there was no help to be found there. There, the sea pursued the ship with foam-flecked lips.

His mother stared about, bleak and hopeless. "I'm going to try and find..." The wind and sea choked her words as a fresh wave washed the deck.

She turned her head slightly to the boy. "...try and find Father."

The boy shuddered at the thought. His only comfort was in her presence, but he knew better than to argue. His nurse had taught him that when he was little. He swallowed hard and clenched his teeth in an effort to clamp down on the uncontrollable chatter. He glanced furtively at his mother and tried to be brave.

"Be brave, my love." She kissed him on the cheek and struggled to her feet.

The deck heaved and tossed, and his mother staggered across the deck and against the rail. She clung for a moment, then started to work her way hand over hand toward the forecastle.

The boy watched her struggle toward the bow. His knuckles whitened from the grip on his own shins. The boy glared at the roiling water, commanding the sea to stop rolling the boat, willing his mother forward.

She was gone before she made it.

A towering wave swept the deck. There was no scream. One minute she had been staggering along the rail, the next minute she was gone. She didn't make a sound. He was alone.

"Mother?" the boy questioned the wind. There was no response.

He would have wept, but no tears came. The wind, sky and sea had long since drained his tears. He blinked hard. Once. Twice. But each time he opened his eyes, he was still alone. He hurt.

He felt the change before he heard it. With a low groan, the ship tilted toward the water, and he slid sideways into the rail.

3

He scrambled to grab a large wooden cleat. The groaning continued, rising in pitch and volume, adding a new element to the symphony of sound produced by the storm. A large jellyfish slid across the deck. Its rough tentacles slapped against his exposed thigh, and a long angry red welt magically appeared. He regarded this new injury with cold detachment. It was like looking at a picture in a book; his pain was spent. He clung to the cleat and squeezed his eyes closed.

The first day after they'd left Charleston, Captain Daniels had let him steer the ship. High atop the quarterdeck, he was king of the world. The three masts had born snow-white sails, and the ship had responded eagerly under the wheel. The Captain had treated him like a man grown. He had shown him the compass and the charts. Mr. Whittle, the first mate, had been a wealth of information as well. He had drawn their course with his finger for him in the captain's cabin.

"Here's where we're headed, Tiger," Mr. Whittle had said, placing his right forefinger on a point labeled Baltimore, Maryland. Mr. Whittle called him "Tiger", and the boy thought it to be an exceptional nickname. He had seen a picture of a tiger in school, and thought tigers were tough and sleek with big teeth and a mean growl.

Mr. Whittle had then placed his left middle finger on Charleston, South Carolina. "And here's where we're coming from."

The boy concentrated on his fingers. "That does not seem very far," he said, glancing up at Mr. Whittle.

Mr. Whittle stifled a laugh. "Further than you think, lad." He slowly traced the route up the coast from Charleston and stopped midway.

"What's that say, Tiger?"

"Ocracoke," the boy answered eagerly. He was an exceptional reader.

"Well done!" Mr. Whittle traced out a semicircle with his finger and continued north.

The boy frowned in concentration, "Wait...Mr. Whittle? Why don't we go straight along the coast there?" The boy touched the edge of Ocracoke.

"Don't miss a trick, do you lad?" Mr. Whittle grinned. "What's that say along the coast there?"

"Diamond Shoals," the boy responded quickly.

"Right again, Tiger!" Mr. Whittle ruffled his hair.

The boy's father had entered the cabin unnoticed, and spoke from behind the two bent over the chart. "What's a shoal, son?"

The boy turned quickly to his father, and snapped up straight. "Shallow water, sir," he answered.

Mr. Whittle had also turned to the boy's father. He swept off his cap and stood twisting it in his hands. "Beg your pardon, Sir. I was showing the lad our course."

"It's quite all right, Mr. Whittle. I'm pleased that he's showing an interest. He's not keeping you from your duties?" the boy's father questioned, frowning.

The boy glanced at Mr. Whittle. His father commanded respect. He was an important man.

"No, Sir," Mr. Whittle responded, "He's no trouble at all. He's an excellent reader. Probably reads better'n me."

"Well...he's attended school and been tutored extensively, Mr. Whittle," the boy's father said disdainfully, adjusting his immaculate topcoat. He turned on his heel, and spoke over his shoulder, "You may proceed, Mr. Whittle." He strode from the cabin.

The boy glanced at Mr. Whittle. "Sorry, Mr. Whittle...I, uh, didn't want to get you in trouble...Father, he's..."

Mr. Whittle laughed aloud, and set his cap back on his head at a jaunty angle.

"'Tis all right, lad." He drew a pipe from his breast pocket and began to stuff it with tobacco from a small leather pouch that he kept tucked behind his expansive waistband. Taking a wooden box of matches from a wall shelf, he struck one on the table.

"Your father is a wealthy man, lad," he spoke around the stem of the pipe as he carefully stoked it to life. "He owns more ships than I've ever crewed...and that's sayin' something."

Mr. Whittle exhaled a perfect smoke ring and looked down at the boy. "Including this one." His face broke into a grin. "Where were we?"

"Diamond Shoals," the boy answered quickly, smiling back.

"Right. Why do you think we'd go around a shoal, Tiger?"

The boy looked back at the map. "The water's not deep enough for our boat?" he guessed.

Mr. Whittle's head was wreathed in smoke. It smelled good, spicier than a wood fire. The boy breathed deeply.

"Right again. Well done." Mr. Whittle clapped him on the shoulder. "Shoals and reefs have undone many a ship, lad. Especially in this stretch of water. Mostly during the storm season though, not this time of year."

"We'll be all right going around then?" the boy asked.

Mr. Whittle burst out laughing. He laughed a lot. "Course we will, Tiger. I've served with Cap'n Daniels for seven years, lad. He's never been wrong yet."

Shuddering, the boy opened his eyes, dispelling the memory. The deck was still heaved over. He was still alone. Captain Daniels was wrong. Mr. Whittle was wrong. Sometimes the storms come early.

The wind had calmed a little. He was sure that either he had finally gone deaf or the roaring had lessened. The sea still crashed over the deck, though, and every few minutes he had to tighten his grip against the rail to keep his position as the sea swirled around him. A faint popping had been going on for several minutes before he registered it. It sounded kind of like the fireworks that he'd seen in Charleston, he thought, but it was getting louder. A distinct creaking added emphasis. He watched dully as the boards across the main deck began to flip into the air. First one side would stick up with a pop, then there was a shrieking creak, and several feet of board would flip into the air. The boy stared as the deck let go in growing sections and was replaced by swirling seas, and then the sea reached his feet.

The boy's stocking foot was washed by a wave, and when it retreated his big toe was underwater. The water had him by his ankle...his knee. He glanced up to see the forecastle ripped away. Then he too was gone, torn away and swept underwater.

The sea pressed his chest like an iron, and there was no air. His eyes were open, but he couldn't see. It was a world of green. A piece of lumber swirled by and raked him across the cheek, taking a bite out of his skin and turning the green to red before his eyes. He could feel the sea pulling him down. He glanced down. Maybe Mother and Father had hold of his feet. He was so tired.

A strong pull on his hair lifted him up and snapped his eyes back open. He was out of the water, but he couldn't cough. His battered leg dragged against something hard and made him cry out in pain. He screwed up his eyes and tried to focus. Something pushed his mouth open and jammed down his throat. He felt the bile rise in his gut, and retched violently. Seawater spewed out and covered the sleeve of his torn tunic. He drew a ragged breath, and began to cry.

Through the tears, he saw a shirtless man. He was soot black, and only his yellow teeth were plainly visible in the dim light. The man reached forward and wedged him into a corner of a small skiff. The boy struggled to speak, but only coughed again. The yellow teeth grinned.

The man fought to steady the pitching skiff. The waves battled to turn it across the sea, but the black man had years of practice. The muscles of his broad chest and forearms stretched taut as he leaned into the oars and deftly steered the small craft away from the wreckage. The boy watched numbly as a body spiraled past, and looked again to the man.

"Are you the...devil?" the boy managed weakly, his vision blurred.

The black man grunted a short laugh. "No, suh! Got you afore he could come." The man negotiated a huge wave, and then continued, "I'm Jacob, but who might you be is the question." The man called Jacob pulled the oars and forced the small skiff toward shore.

"T—Thom—Thomas," sputtered the boy and squeezed his eyes shut.

CHAPTER 2
November 1848
Ocracoke Island, North Carolina

"Thomas, Cap'n," Jacob took a swallow of tea, his voice nearly drowned out by the hammering rain on the shake roof above. "Said his name was Thomas, afore he passed out," Jacob finished, and glanced at the boy.

Thomas murmured in his sleep on the lap of a large woman, who sat in a rocking chair between Jacob and the cast iron stove at the far end of the room. A heavy woolen blanked draped the unusual pair: the pale boy and the mahogany woman. Thomas's slight frame was almost hidden amidst the folds of the blanket and Rose's ample bosom. Rose rocked him gently and murmured soothingly in her native Lumbee tongue. The stove's door was open, the coals glowed a dull red, and a hiss could still be heard from the kettle on its top. The kitchen was warm and snug, its two windows black from the wash of the storm. A yellowish light was cast from a small hurricane lantern in the center of the table. The remaining lanterns remained unlit on their wall hooks, forgotten when Jacob had appeared from the belly of the storm.

The man that Jacob had addressed sat on the opposite bench across the scarred table. Thoughtfully, he leaned forward, ignited a wooden match from the lamp, and lit his pipe. The flare of the match showed his features in stark relief. The coarse hair of his heavy gray-flecked whiskers hid his mouth, matching the heavy brow and shock of thick black hair above. His eyes were alive in the glow of the match, sea-blue and thoughtful.

9

"Could you see the name of the boat?" Captain McGuire asked Jacob. His voice deep and resonant. It was a voice accustomed to command.

Jacob shook his head and frowned in the dim light. "No, suh. Lucky I got in and out as it was."

Captain McGuire nodded. He'd thought as much. He shared a long look with Jacob. Very few men would have attempted such a rescue in this weather. On the best of days, Diamond Shoals and the near shore waters of Ocracoke Island were fierce; during a storm they were terrifying. The captain drew on his pipe and turned his eyes to the boy. Rose was still rocking him gently, holding him tightly against her round belly, heavy with child. Rose had been a beautiful girl and had grown into a beautiful woman. She'd married Jacob two years before; Captain McGuire had made the introduction. Though she didn't share Jacob's pitch-black skin, the Lumbee had different thoughts concerning race. They'd intermarried with whites and blacks since the first colonization of the Outer Banks. She felt Captain McGuire's eyes and raised her own from the nest of Thomas's tangled hair. She flashed a brief smile.

The boy stirred in her arms and burrowed more deeply into the protection offered by Rose. They'd peeled off his wet clothes and bandaged his cuts and abrasions; under the heavy wool of the blanket he was naked as a newborn.

"How old you figure, Jako?" The captain asked quietly, his eyes never leaving the boy and Rose.

"Seven...eight maybe, Cap'n," Jacob answered in the same low voice. He cleared his throat uncomfortably.

Captain McGuire turned his eyes to Jacob. He drew his pipe from between his teeth and blew a stream of smoke at the low ceiling.

Jacob held the captain's gaze. "No other survivors, I'm thinking."

Captain James McGuire nodded thoughtfully. Both men knew what that meant. At seven or eight, the boy was too young to be a cabin boy; chances were that the youngster hadn't been traveling alone.

Thomas opened his eyes, and blinked hard in the dim light. He didn't know the room, or the two men across the table. His eyes widened as he recognized Jacob from the sea, and he bit down hard on his lip to avoid crying. Even so, his body racked with the effort, and he drew a ragged breath. His lungs still burned with salt.

"He's awake," murmured Rose.

Captain McGuire leaned forward and smiled at the boy. "I hear your name's Thomas, lad?" he asked gently.

The man's deep voice reminded him of Captain Daniels, and he nodded warily.

"Well, I'm James McGuire," he pointed at the woman holding him, "and that's Rose."

The boy looked up and met Rose's eyes. They were soft and kind. She smelled faintly of wood smoke, and he felt her arms tight around him. He looked at the black man suspiciously.

The Captain's eyes wrinkled in mirth. "Don't worry lad, that's Jacob. He's the one who..." the Captain's voice trailed off. "Who helped you," he finished weakly.

Thomas sniffed, but kept his eyes on the black man. "I thought," he started and coughed. He drew another ragged breath. "I thought," his voice growing stronger, "he was the devil."

James leaned back with a chuckle. "No, Thomas. He's a friend. A friend of mine." The Captain leaned in once more, "We'd all like to be friends of yours. Would that be all right?"

Jacob smiled and nodded encouragement. Thomas felt Rose's hug tighten.

Thomas nodded slowly. "I guess so, Mr. McGuire."

"Good, Thomas, good. Now, I've got to ask you some questions. Some questions to help you. All right?"

The boy nodded again.

James leaned back and relit his pipe, rolling the stem into the corner of his mouth. "Do you have a second name, Thomas? I have a second name: McGuire. But some people don't, like Jacob. How about you?"

Thomas nodded, "I have three names, Mr. McGuire, Thomas Charles Hooper."

James smiled back, "That's fine. How old might you be, Thomas?"

"I'm seven."

"Seven, boy? You're older than we thought," Captain McGuire smiled through the half-truth. "And, where are you from?"

Thomas glanced up at Rose, "I'm from Charleston, South Carolina."

"Well, that's fine, Thomas. I've been to Charleston half a hundred times. It's a beautiful town. You see, I've got a ship. I'm a sea captain, and I travel all over. Right now, you're in a town called Ocracoke, on an island in North Carolina. That's where we live."

James took a long breath and looked up at Rose. Rose's eyes told her concern.

"Do you remember Jacob helping you earlier this evening?"

The boy nodded and glanced again at Jacob.

"Do you remember anything else about this evening?"

The boy nodded again and held his breath.

"What ship were you on, Thomas?"

Thomas blinked hard, the memories a jumble. "I think it's called the *Innesvale*, Mr. McGuire."

James glanced at Jacob, and the two shook heads as one. Neither one knew her. James turned his eyes again to Thomas, "Good, Thomas, good job remembering. Were there other passengers, Thomas?"

Thomas started to cry slow tears, but his voice remained strong. "No, sir. Just me, my mother, and my father. Have you seen them, Captain McGuire?"

James pulled on his pipe and ran his hand through his hair. "No, lad, I can't say that I have." He forced a smile. "But we're going to see if we can't help you find them. What's your father's name?"

Thomas swallowed hard. "Charles Hooper."

"Very well, Thomas. That's all the questions for now. Rose will fix you up a bed in the house, and we'll see if we can't help you. Is that all right?"

Thomas nodded, and shut his eyes to the memories.

CHAPTER 3

August 1851
Ocracoke Island, North Carolina

The night was black, and Thomas stared out the room's only window from the comfort of his covers. He felt rather than heard the distant roll of thunder, and waited for the next streak of lightning out across the water at Skipper's Point. Absently, he wiped the sleep from his eyes and strained to hear the voices of Jacob and Captain McGuire floating down the hallway through the half-open door.

"I don't know what else to do, Jako."

"Nothin' much you can do, Cap," Jacob responded.

"He's got no other relatives still alive. I've contacted his father's attorney, the one settling the affairs for Hooper Trading. It seems Hooper Trading was on the losing end of a series of unfortunate events. They have a stack of bills, and a stack of creditors. There's no room for a boy."

"I know, Cap'n, you told me that before," Jacob interrupted.

James stayed the interruption with an outstretched hand, waving Jacob off. "I know...I know. But, if we send him back to Charleston, he'd be a ward of the state. I can't do that to the lad."

Jacob nodded in vehement agreement. "He's been doing good here, Cap. It's a hell of a thing that he went through, and the boy ain't had a moment's complaint."

James lit his pipe and rolled it to the corner of his mouth. "We aren't kin, Jacob."

Jacob smiled at the captain and wiped his mouth with the back of a strong black hand. "Don't see how that matters much, Cap."

James's mouth twitched with the dawn of a smile. "I know, Jacob, but to some it might."

Jacob shot a sidelong glance at the captain. "Didn't think you gave a damn what other people thought, Cap."

James's smile broadened and he exhaled a cloud of smoke at the ceiling. "Most times you're right about that, Jako."

Jacob had been Captain McGuire's first mate on two different ships. He'd come aboard in the West Indies when James was still a cabin boy of thirteen, and had never left. Of similar age, he and Captain McGuire had grown up together. They'd shared salt and storms with a deck beneath their feet for thirty years. Five years ago, Jacob had approached James. He'd been ready to leave the sea for the land, ready to put down roots and start a family. James had reluctantly agreed, and kept him on to keep watch over his home and hearth on Ocracoke. With the death of James's first and only wife in childbirth more than a decade past, Jacob and Rose were the only family he'd likely ever know.

"You know, Jacob, this isn't just up to me, it affects you and Rose, too. I'll be at sea. You and Rose will be here. It's got to be all our decision."

Jacob nodded in thought. He'd long since made up his mind regarding young Thomas. "Aye, Cap'n. You know Rose's mind. Ever since the first night, she's figured the boy to be hers. Even after Della was born." Jacob flashed a yellowed smile at Captain McGuire. "I think you'd be hard pressed to get him away from her, now."

James chuckled. "I'm sure you're right about that, Jacob."

Jacob continued, "So if no one will have him..."

In his room, Thomas shoved the pillow over his ears and began to cry. He'd heard only pieces, and the gist was that no one would have him. He sobbed quietly.

"It's all right, Tom," a small voice whispered in the dark.

Thomas opened his eyes to Della as she pulled back the coverlet and crawled in to bed with him.

"Don' cry, Tom," the small girl planted a sloppy kiss on the bridge of his nose and swiped up some of the tears.

Thomas grinned in spite of himself. Della, with her three-year-old wisdom and wild brown hair, burrowed herself up next to him on the bed and yawned sleepily.

"You plan on sleeping here, Della?" Thomas asked in a whisper.

"Yup," the little girl nodded, "you're my best boy and you're sad. Mommy always sleeps with me when I'm sad." She opened one big brown eye and squinted at Thomas. "You ain't got a mommy, though, Tom."

Thomas sobered and gently patted Della's mop of brown hair. "No, Della, I don't."

"Yes you do, Thomas," James said from the doorway. "You've all the family you'll ever need, if you'll have us."

Thomas sucked in his breath.

Della patted Thomas's arm. "See, Tom. Now, quiet down and go to sleep."

He did.

CHAPTER 4
July, 1855
Ocracoke Island, North Carolina

"Thomas...Thomas," Thomas fought against the flashes of nightmarish memories. He could hear the voice, but sleep still held him. The lilt of the voice was familiar. It sounded like spice and sea spray.

"Come, Thomas." The voice was low and insistent.

Thomas sat upright with a start, promptly colliding with the man who had been bent over him.

"Umph," the man grunted, rearing back. "Settle down and stop thrashing the bed." He rubbed his forehead with the heel of a rough hand.

The dim light of a candle illuminated the room, and Thomas shook off the sleep and pushed the ragged dark hair out of his eyes. He smiled sideways at his awakener, and tossed his feet over the side of the aging four-poster bed, disengaging his legs from the tangle of sweaty white sheets.

"Sorry, Jacob!" He grabbed the man's outstretched hand, pulled himself to his feet, and flashed a quick grin. "I was just dreaming of you."

Jacob had aged little in seven years. His bristly black hair had become streaked with white, but the hard muscle of his chest, shoulders and forearms remained. Rising from his seat at the side of the bed, Jacob went to the room's solitary window.

"The Cap'n's back," Jacob said over his shoulder as he drew the curtains open. The window beyond was cracked open, and a faint chill breeze stirred the curtains. Jacob threw the window wide. The room immediately freshened with the salty breeze.

Thomas's eyes widened in surprise. "When, Jacob?"

Jacob turned and strode to the door. He scooped up the pitcher of water and the washbasin that stood on the floor in the narrow hall. He returned and placed the two items on the small table under the window. Thomas didn't push for an answer. He knew Jacob had heard him. It was simply his nature to think things through before answering.

"Jes' a few hours back. Middle o' the night. I knew that you'd want to be up and about when he woke up," Jacob finally answered as he pulled a clean towel from the shelf next to the door and folded it carefully next to the washbasin.

Thomas stretched. He was bare-chested, and it felt good standing in the chill morning air. It was still dark outside. The far eastern horizon was just starting to glow, but it wouldn't be full daylight for another hour.

"Wash up, Tom. I'll see ya out in the kitchen. Rose'll be startin' breakfast soon." Jacob turned to leave.

Thomas lightly slapped Jacob on his bare shoulder. "Not if I see you first!"

Jacob staggered as if the light slap had undone him. He pretended to moan.

Thomas played along with the charade and went to slap him again. He raised his hand, but instantly Jacob had his wrist in an iron grip. With blinding speed, Jacob flipped him sideways back onto the bed. He'd somehow rolled him over his hip. Thomas hadn't even seen him start to move. Thomas spun when he landed, ready to continue, but Jacob was gone, the door closing softly behind him.

Thomas smiled. One day he'd catch Jacob off guard, but he had a feeling that that day was a long way off. He stretched again and turned to the orders at hand.

He filled the basin from the pitcher carefully, not wanting to clean up a spill today. Shutting his eyes, he shoved his face into the water. It was ice-cold. He counted in his head as he shook to and fro under water. At the count of ninety he came up sputtering and gulping air. Not bad for first thing in the morning. Jacob must have strained the water from the rain barrel next to the porch. It wasn't salty at all. He shivered and carefully eyed the basin. Most of the time there were little green wigglers, and a face full of mosquito larvae was no way to start a morning. He reached for the bar of lye soap that lay next to the pitcher. Whistling tunelessly, he began to lather himself from fingertips to armpits. Once, when he'd first come to live with the captain, he'd ignored Jacob's morning wash ritual. Jacob hadn't said a word, and a younger Thomas had reveled in his rebelliousness. The next morning he was awoken when the pitcher of water splashed over his head. Jacob had set to him then with a bar of soap, and Jacob was a very strong man. He'd never skipped the ritual since.

Thomas reached out and closed the window to use it as a mirror. With stiff fingers he raked out his hair. It was dark brown, in this light almost black, and wavy as it dried. He scrutinized himself in his window mirror. The Cap'n was home, and he wanted to look his best. His eyes were blue-green like the sea. Jacob said that the sea had turned them that color when he'd almost drowned as a boy. The beginning of a few whiskers crept sparsely toward his chin. He regarded these delightedly.

Thomas puffed up his thin chest and flexed the muscles of his arms and chest. He was of medium build. He was neither barrel-chested and stout like the captain, nor wiry and strong like Jacob. Thomas inspected his freshly scrubbed hands. They were brown from the sun and had become hard from work. The calluses that stitched his palms were white and flat. Fishing lines, thick sails, and oaken oars took a toll on the hands.

The sky had brightened. He glanced himself up and down one last time, and threw the window open again. Carefully he dumped the washbasin out the window, and it splashed onto the ground below. He turned to the shelf beside his door and neatly hung the damp towel on the wooden bar on the underside of the shelf. Rose had placed a clean shirt on the corner of his bed sometime during the night. His thoughts elsewhere, Thomas pulled the shirt over his head.

Good old Rose. Rarely did Thomas or Jacob ever wear shirts, but she always had a clean shirt waiting when Captain McGuire returned. In Rose's eyes, it wouldn't do to greet the man of the house half-dressed. The Cap never questioned the shirts, but Thomas had seen him smirking every time Jacob scratched his chest uncomfortably. Jacob had once thrown his shirt out the window. He called it a damnable thing. Rose had been so mad that she had chased him around the kitchen table and foyer with a straw broom for a half-hour. Jacob thought it was great sport, and had laughed heartily until she'd run out of steam. Thomas never knew exactly what happened afterward, but the next day a contrite Jacob worked the washbasin while Rose fanned herself on the porch in the captain's rocker.

Thomas studied his trousers. Captain McGuire had brought the trousers from New York last spring, and they still fit fairly well. Thomas always kept them rolled to mid-calf. It was easier than walking around with wet trouser legs.

Lastly, Thomas regarded his leather shoes on the wooden floor beneath the shelf. Thomas sighed. He hated shoes. He could still remember being little and his mother requiring him to always wear heavy brogans. They sure made your feet ache. Rose would think it proper to wear shoes this morning. He chewed his cheek thoughtfully. The Cap wouldn't care. He was a ship's captain; nobody wore shoes on the whole boat but him.

Thomas smiled broadly. Cap was back. With a backward glance at the shoes, he slipped out the door and sprinted down the hallway toward the kitchen, running headlong into Della.

"Tom!" Della straightened her skirt, exasperated, and spoke in a hushed voice, "Watch where you're going!"

Thomas flashed the girl a quick grin and scooped her up, swinging her in a half circle. "Come along, Della. The Cap'n's back."

"I know, Thomas," she giggled, "why do you think I've got on a dress! Now put me down."

Thomas drew himself to his full height. "Of course, my lady," he said formally.

Della promptly punched him in the shoulder. "Silly."

Thomas pretended to be shocked and rubbed his shoulder in mock pain. Della grinned and the two started down the hallway together.

"Thanks, Tom," Della shot him a glance, "For the other day, I mean."

Thomas returned the glance. "Don't worry about it, Della. You're my best girl. Nobody messes with my best girl."

Thomas remembered the scene vividly. He'd turned the corner in town to find three boys heckling Della, Madame Sardaine's French book in the mud at her feet.

"Which are ya, Della, an Injun or a nigger?" the first was saying when Thomas rounded the corner.

"Ha ha! I think she's both," the second had joined in.

Thomas had heard enough. He'd waded into the three, punching the first boy square in the ear, and the second right on the point of his nose. The third had broken and run.

Thomas scooped up the book and handed it back to Della. "Wanna go skip rocks, D?" he'd asked gently.

Della had wiped the tears away and had taken Thomas's hand.

They were almost to the water's edge before Della said anything. "Thanks, Tom."

Thomas grinned at the younger girl. "Don't pay them any attention, D."

Della nodded, and squinted out at the bay. "Look, Tom...did you see him?"

Thomas studied the water. "See what?"

"There," Della pointed. A river otter had just broken the surface. As they watched he rolled over onto his back and worked at a clam between his small paws and razor sharp teeth.

"Otters are my favorite," Della smiled, the boys forgotten.

Thomas grinned back. "They're one of mine, too, D."

Thomas broke from his reverie, took Della's hand, and the two raced for the kitchen.

Captain James McGuire lay on his bed fully clothed, and smiled into his beard. He had awakened when he'd heard Jacob tussling with Thomas in the room next door. He heard Thomas slip past his door and stifled a laugh at the sound of bare feet slapping the floorboards on the way to the kitchen. Rose would be angry about the shoes.

Quietly, he swung his legs over the edge of the enormous bed and took off his heavy boots and socks. A show of solidarity. The boy was growing up.

Carefully, James drew a long wooden pipe from his linen shirt pocket. He opened a small wooden box on the bedside table and withdrew a pinch of finely shredded light brown tobacco. He lit a wooden match on his thumbnail with the ease of long practice and drew deeply. He grunted in satisfaction. Brazil or St. Kitts. He couldn't remember where the tobacco had come from. Either way, it was delicious. Much better than the shag tobacco that he kept aboard the ship. He fingered the gray streaks in his beard and rose slowly to his feet. His gaze softened as he glanced at the faded tintype of his dear departed Leigh Ann. She'd died in childbirth many years ago, and with her was lost his only child. He smiled in spite of his melancholy. That was, of course, until Thomas had come into their lives. James rolled his shoulders and the muscles groaned against the stretch. He was getting old to be at sea for months at a time. But the cargos were rich, and nothing held sway over his heart and soul like the sea. He smiled again. Except maybe Thomas.

James stretched and stared out the open window, stroking the bowl of his pipe. Thomas had been a welcome addition to their little family. James grinned at the thought: the boy had come to them without a father, and now he had two.

Chewing the edge of his moustache thoughtfully, Captain McGuire studied the view from his window. The narrow passage of water at Springer's Point lay still in the morning light, and the harbor beyond was beginning to awaken with the first of the day's activity. Squinting, he could make out the barren masts of his ship and two others moored directly offshore. As a boy, Ocracoke had seen a bustling trade along "The Ditch" at Cockle Creek. Ships of every conceivable shape and size had entered the sound here, and the trade was good. The storm of '46 had changed that though. It had reopened Hatteras, and sanded in much of the deep water around Ocracoke.

James straightened his shirt and finished his pipe. He carefully rapped the ashes into a metal dish on his bedside table. He dropped the pipe back into his shirt pocket and started for the kitchen building next to the house.

The scene through the low slung door of the kitchen shack warmed James's heart, and his eyes danced with pleasure. Rose was scolding Thomas and pointing at his feet. Jacob was astride one of the benches at the table behind Rose and mimicking her moves. Thomas was staring at the floor stifling his laughter at Jacob's charades, and that only fanned the fire in Rose's scolding. Della was slicing slab bacon into a large skillet.

"Master Thomas, I declare, what in the world be gettin' into you?" Rose continued to shake a finger up into Thomas's face.

"Don't you pay that no-account Jacob no nevermind. He's a bright one, he is. An old wampus cat." She spun to glare at Jacob.

They all registered James's presence at once. Rose's words died on her lips, and she bustled to the wood stove to pour him a cup of yaupon tea. Della grinned broadly. Jacob leapt to his feet and clasped his dear friend on the forearm above the wrist. The two gripped tightly for a moment.

"Welcome home, Cap'n," Jacob whispered.

"Grand to see you, Jacob," James answered, laughter dancing in his eyes. "Is Rose giving you a hard time?"

Rose swept over, the fresh tea steaming in a blue chipped mug in her outstretched hand. "Lord, Cap'n, it's good to see you. Don't pay attention to this crowd. All they done is loaf since you left. The only ones that've been busy are Della and me."

James held Thomas in his best fierce Captain's gaze. "That true, boy?"

Thomas looked from one to another. "That's not true, Cap!" he exclaimed.

Captain James McGuire wrapped his adopted son in a huge bear hug, lifting him off the ground. "Don't worry, lad. I know that Jacob can't lay about. He's afraid he'll grow roots like one of the trees in the yard."

Thomas hugged his adopted father fiercely for a moment before pushing away. "What news from Boston, Cap?" he asked excitedly.

James dropped into the single chair at the head of the table and took a long draft of the home brewed tea. He clenched his teeth at the bitter bite at the back of his tongue. "God, how I miss you all when I'm away. The yaupon's divine, Rose."

He shifted in his seat and gestured for Thomas to take the bench at his right hand. "The news is the same as always, my boy. The suppliers want to charge more, and the merchants want to buy for less. The Abolitionists want to free the slaves. More of the same, I suppose. Have you kept Jacob out of trouble?"

Jacob smiled wryly. The smell of frying bacon filled the small building as Della stoked the small cook stove. Rose removed a pan loaf of thick white bread from the stove's single drawer, and placed it on the table along with a crock of freshly churned butter. Thomas stared at the fresh bread longingly, and looked to the barrel of flour next to the woodstove. White bread was a treat that Rose only made upon the captain's return. Most breakfasts were of salted fish or turtle.

"We fished steady, Cap'n..." Jacob began.

"The porpoise hunting's been grand, Cap," Thomas interrupted, his voice bubbling with excitement. "Pilot whales, too. Why, last month..."

James looked at Thomas. "Hold on, son," he said gently, "you've interrupted Jacob. He doesn't speak much as it is. Let him finish."

Thomas grinned shamefacedly and mumbled, "Sorry, Jacob."

"S'all right, Tom. The boy's right, Cap'n. He's come quite a hand on the oars and the pole. Can take the surf goin' out better'n most men I seen," Jacob grinned sideways at Thomas. "He's gettin' tough, too."

James turned back to Thomas. "Have you kept up your reading in my absence, son?"

"Yes, Cap," Thomas replied quickly. "I finished the Chaucer and am halfway through Shakespeare's Sonnets." He nodded to indicate Della. "We've been acting out some of the plays."

James drew forth the pipe in his pocket, and a pouch of tobacco. Absently, James filled the pipe and clenched it between his teeth. He drew open the firebox door and lit a splint of wood in the coals. Holding it to his pipe, he drew and exhaled softly toward the ceiling.

"The language in the Chaucer is tough, Thomas. Are you prepared to speak of the stories over dinner tonight?" he queried.

"Of course, Cap," Thomas replied eagerly.

Captain McGuire turned toward Della, "And you, Della? Are you studying?"

Della lifted her chin. "Of course, Captain. I read better than Thomas half the time."

The Captain threw his head back and guffawed. "And... *Comment votre français arrive-t-il*, Thomas?"

"My French is coming along fine," Thomas grinned. "*La Madame Sardaine a ete une grande aide.*"

"Excellent, Thomas, Madame Sardaine has a great many talents, of which being a linguist is only one." James smiled knowingly and drew again on his pipe. Many a sailor knew of her other talents, but that was still a year or two in the future for young Thomas.

"How about the charts and numbers, Thomas? Have you done what I'd left for you?" James continued.

"Well," Thomas began. "Not as much, Cap. The charts are confusing."

"Then I'd better help you, son." James grinned around the stem of his pipe.

Thomas's eyes widened in excitement. "I'd like that, Cap. I really would."

Jacob placed the platter of cooked bacon on the table and swung a leg over the bench. He was looking inquiringly at James. "What are the charts for, Cap'n?"

James was in a grand mood. His family was gathered close. The air smelled like fresh bread, sizzling bacon, wood smoke, and pipe smoke. It was a great day to be alive.

"Well, Jacob," he said drawing a last deep lungful of rich smoke, "Thomas has to know the charts if he's to go along on the next voyage as a cabin boy and work his way to Captain, and one day own his own ship..." his voice trailed off, rich with emotion.

Thomas's mouth hung open in disbelief. "Cap?" he questioned. He was afraid that he'd heard wrong.

James turned his eyes to Thomas and looked deep into their blue-green depths. "What would you name your ship, Thomas?" he asked quietly.

Thomas basked in the glow from the Cap's eyes. He slowly turned his eyes to Della.

"It will be the *Otter*," he whispered.

Jesse." He grinned again. "Stop chewing on that nasty old cigar and let's find a place to talk."

The two men moved through the gathering crowd toward the restaurant adjacent to the lobby. Senators, Representatives, and those seeking an audience were clustered throughout the lobby, and Congressman Cox stopped a half-dozen times for a handshake, a hello, or a nodded acknowledgment.

Jesse Yeates studied his fellow politician as they made their way through the gathering crowd toward the restaurant. Cox was short of stature, but long on political experience. His thin face was accented by a long brushy goatee and matching sideburns. His dark hair had become streaked with gray over the last few years, but he hadn't slowed with age. He was a force to be reckoned with, and his influence extended far beyond the floor of the House.

The two men were shown to their seats in the large restaurant by a tall, thin, impeccable black man.

"How about that corner table, Sam?" Sunset suggested, moving away from the offered seats. He waggled his thick eyebrows suggestively. "I don't want these other men to hear me whisper sweet nothings to Congressman Yeates."

"Of course, Mr. Cox," Sam replied dryly and gestured for the two men to follow. "This way, gentlemen."

As they took their seats, Sunset drew a folded newspaper from his inside jacket pocket and cleared his throat. With his free hand he withdrew a pair of half-moon reading spectacles, then dropped into the chair opposite Jesse.

Sunset began reading aloud. "And I quote...'Shortly after the men of the Lifesaving Service appeared, but failed to render any assistance to those on board'...blah-blah...'It is asserted emphatically that, had the members of the Lifesaving Service been at the scene of the wreck early in the morning, nearly every soul could have been saved'...blah-blah..."

Yeates growled in warning, but Cox stayed the interruption with a motion of his hand.

Sunset continued, "Captain Anker says that at the time the *Metropolis* was beached, there would have been little or no loss of life, had the Lifesaving Service rendered the expected assistance."

Sunset looked up at the red-faced Jesse Yeates. "Is this how your Tarheel constituents handle all the shipwrecks along your shores?" he grinned.

Jesse slammed his hand on the table hard enough to slosh coffee onto his saucer. An impeccably dressed gentleman at a nearby table looked their way.

"Damnit, Cox. These goddamn Yankee newspapermen!" Yeates exploded.

Sunset Cox kept grinning. "Now hold on, Major." He held up the newspaper. "The *Times* was better than some. The Boston papers claim that your good folks along the Outer Banks plundered the bodies as they washed ashore."

"Murderous slander, Cox. Ninety dead, and all the newspapermen want is to incite hatred against the very people that even as we speak are probably sheltering the survivors under their own humble roofs!" Yeates shoved back from the table forcibly. "I've heard enough of the papers. What's your game, Cox?"

Sunset Cox stirred his coffee. He was enjoying baiting Yeates. The two had known each other since the Democratic Convention in '74. Four years was a lifetime, on Capitol Hill. He carefully removed his glasses and squinted at Yeates.

Cox adeptly changed the course of the conversation. "How many of the counties do you represent on that long stretch of sand?"

Yeates eyes narrowed perceptibly. "All of them, Sunset." He paused; the redness in his face was beginning to abate. "But, I think that you already knew that."

"Hmm." Representative Cox leaned back from the table to allow Sam to refill his coffee. "Thank you, Sam. Your coffee's the best in Washington."

Sam regarded the congressman coolly, and nodded slightly. "I'll let the kitchen know your thoughts, sir," he said as he turned to assist his other guests.

Sunset Cox squinted again at Jesse Yeates. "J.J.... are you aware that our dear Secretary of the Treasury will be ordering an official inquiry into the events surrounding the *Metropolis* disaster, as it regards not only the Lifesaving Service in general, but most specifically an inquiry into the operations along coastal North Carolina?"

Jesse Yeates studied Congressman Cox. The man was a strategist beyond compare and, in this unsettled political climate, a key player to have on your side.

"No," Yeates said slowly, "I can't say that I was. However I'm not surprised. The *Huron* went to pieces off of my shores only weeks ago and, what with the *Metropolis*, I imagine that there is some strong pressure coming from both inside and outside the Hill."

Sunset smiled, and took a sip of his coffee. "J.J., do you have any idea how many people are estimated to have been saved by our dear Revenue Marine Division's efforts since 1871?"

Yeates shrugged noncommittally. The information had been presented during the beginning of this year's session, but it was just one more in the sea of reports that came through the Senate.

Cox leaned towards Yeates and locked eyes with the younger statesman. "Four thousand, six hundred and fifty. They rendered assistance to four hundred seven distressed vessels, and saved over six million dollars in property," he said quietly.

Yeates eyes widened. These were large numbers. "But, Sunset," he began, picking up the paper from the middle of the table where Sunset had let it lay, "Nobody ever seems to care who or how many were saved...only those that were lost."

Cox shook his head and ground his teeth. "I do, J.J."

Yeates softened his tone. "As do I, my friend."

Sunset stared straight into Jesse's eyes. "Were you aware, Congressman Yeates, that Aaron Sargent, the representative from California, is already preparing legislation to turn the Lifesaving Service over to the Navy?"

Jesse Yeates ground his teeth at the news. As a career Army man, albeit on the losing side, he held a natural mistrust for the Navy. Though they only had a handful of lifesaving stations in coastal Carolina, the measure would mean jobs for non-natives. Such news was never good for a politician in an election year.

Cox leaned back in his chair and crossed his left knee over his right. Absently, he touched the crease in his suit pants. Yeates took a long sip of coffee, but it had grown cold, and he grimaced. The ever-attentive Sam was at his elbow instantly.

"Another cup, Sir?" Sam asked politely

Yeates dismissed him with a wave of his hand. His mind was racing, "Two questions, Sunset. One, why would the Navy do a better job than Revenue Marine and the Department of the Treasury? Two, how does the great State of New York fit into this?" Sunset Cox believed wholeheartedly in effectively representing his constituency.

Sunset chuckled, and looked up from his trouser leg. "To the point, eh, J.J.? As to your first question, I don't believe that the great United States Navy would do a better job than the Revenue Marine Division. Then again, I don't think the Revenue Marine Division's doing a great job, either." Sunset took a long sip of his coffee. "I think that the Lifesaving Service should be on its own, self-governing if you will, with Treasury's oversight, of course." Sunset's eyes narrowed at Yeates. "As to the second question... I'll ask a question of my own: how many Lifesaving Stations are on the Carolina Coast, J.J.?"

"Seven," Yeates responded, puzzled.

Sunset continued, "That's right. Only seven stations supporting one of the most dangerous stretches of water along the Atlantic Seaboard. Those stations spread over how many miles?"

"I'm not certain." Yeates shifted uncomfortably. "Over 100, though," he added.

"Not enough, don't you think?" Cox questioned gently.

Yeates was puzzled, and the furrow between his eyebrows deepened.

"No offense, Sunset," Yeates said coolly, "but I've always thought of you as a strategist," Yeates paused continuing to study his counterpart, "not a philanthropist."

Sunset Cox brightened and his eyes crinkled with humor. "Sometimes, my stern friend, sometimes, you can be both."

Yeates growled a short laugh. Sunset Cox was finally going to get around to the point of this meeting. Cox uncrossed his legs and leaned into Yeates. He placed his elbows on his knees and let his hands dangle between his legs.

"How many of your constituents does the Federal Government employ at those seven Lifesaving Stations on the Outer Banks?" Cox queried.

Yeates mouth twitched in a half smile. Here was the Samuel Sunset Cox that some said had more power than President Hayes.

"As I recall, each station has a Keeper and six surfmen," he answered.

Cox smiled, still leaning in to his colleague. "That and more. That's currently forty-two government checks in an area that you represent. Suppose legislation under an independent US Lifesaving Service were to be passed for an additional fifteen to twenty Lifesaving Stations on those barren sands. Maybe one hundred twenty new jobs. Suppose that same legislation required the use of local men for local expertise."

Cox reached across the table and took a sip of coffee. His excitement was palpable. Yeates let the man continue without interruption.

"Suppose that those new stations would need cooks, caretakers, laundresses?" Cox continued to smile. "And of course, those new stations would need to be built by local builders. There'd need to be men available to categorize the items washed ashore. There'd need to be..."

Yeates stayed the economics lesson with a raised hand. "I get it. I get it, Sunset. But, I ask again, what does New York gain in helping my constituents in North Carolina, and when would you foresee such legislation being introduced?"

Sunset Cox rose from his chair, stuck out his small belly and hooked his thumbs on his waistband. "Good day, Congressman Yeates,"

He turned to leave. "I've already introduced it—last year in the House." He glanced over his shoulder at Yeates. "New York is a coastal state, too."

With those words, Congressman Sunset Cox left Congressman Yeates at his table with a lot to think about.

CHAPTER 6
March 1878
Washington, DC

The broad doors to the Willard Hall at the Willard Hotel were open to the early spring night on F Street in Washington, DC. The room was filled with well-dressed men, brandy, and cigar smoke. A celebration of sorts was under way. Many a casual passerby in the street below paused and strained to look up the broad stairs and across the wide veranda to catch a glimpse of the powerful men within.

In the vague light of a street lamp a solitary man stood twisting his bowler hat in his hands. He glanced toward the doors and the tinkle of glassware and muted laughter. He rubbed a thick hand through his receding dark brown hair, and nervously fingered his sweeping handlebar moustache.

Sumner Kimball had been in government service for seventeen years. He was a good leader, a tough Mainer and an adept campaigner, but he still wasn't comfortable with the pomp and circumstance. Tonight's gathering was in his honor and that certainly didn't help. After seven years of struggling to handle lifesaving efforts under the Revenue Marine Division as well as his other duties, he had just hours ago been honored with the position of General Superintendent of the new United States Lifesaving Service. He'd been granted the position by President Hayes, and confirmed by many of the same men at this very gathering.

The past several weeks had been a whirlwind for Kimball and the Lifesaving Service. Republican and Democrat, South and North, old enemies and new friends had united in a single common goal for the first time since the war, and the old

Lifesaving Service was cast aside. Though Kimball honestly thought that his small department had done great deeds over the past decade, there had still been a wholesale loss of life and property up and down the coast as a result of too few men and too little management. The old service had been branded as only marginally effective on the floors of both House and Senate, and the new United States Lifesaving Service had risen from the ashes. The revisions of the past several weeks and months had left Kimball exhausted and apprehensive. As of this moment, he was no longer under the protection afforded by the Department of the Treasury, and, more than ever, he was personally responsible for the men, buildings and equipment of the entire Lifesaving Service. President Hayes had told Kimball, "You will not fail," and Kimball had accepted the order without question. The responsibility was dizzying.

Kimball settled the bowler back onto his head with resolve, smoothing his best suit over the slight bulge of his wide belly, and started up the steps. He nodded to the black porter stationed at the top of the staircase and paused just outside the door. As he let his eyes adjust to the bright light from within, he surveyed the room.

He spotted Representative Yeates deep in conversation with Senator John Brown Gordon of Georgia. Yeates had his jaw clamped shut on the butt of one of his trademark unlit cigars, and was nodding emphatically to his counterpart. Sumner couldn't suppress a slight grin. He'd been in the gallery after the *Metropolis* disaster when the competing lifesaving bills had been read on the floor. Mr. Yeates had been one of the first to speak. Sumner grinned more broadly at the memory; Yeates had personally challenged any man in the room, should they have additional remarks to make criticizing lifesaving efforts or anything else in the Tarheel state. There had been an uproar. A man like Yeates wasn't challenging those men to a debate. The challenge he'd issued required a matched set of dueling pistols.

Congressman Sunset Cox joined Yeates and Gordon. At Sunset's side was a tall, slim gentleman in full naval regalia. The men shook hands all around. Sumner edged through the open door to hear the conversation more clearly.

"Who's this, Sunset?" Yeates raised an eyebrow at Congressman Cox.

"Gentlemen," Sunset began smoothly, "Allow me to introduce Admiral David Dixon Porter."

Sumner gasped at the audacity of Cox from the safety of the door. He was introducing the commanding Union admiral that had effectively blockaded the entire South to Yeates and Gordon, two of the fiercest officers of the Confederacy. Cox was grinning ear to ear and obviously loving every minute of it.

"Gentlemen." Admiral Porter gave a slight bow and extended his hand in greeting.

Yeates's face had purpled and he glared sidelong at Cox. He looked at the man's outstretched hand and ground his teeth together in indecision.

Senator Gordon smiled politely and stepped past Yeates, taking the outstretched hand. "You'll have to excuse Mr. Yeates, Admiral," he glanced at Yeates. "Many of his family are from Wilmington, and old habits die hard."

Admiral Porter nodded affably. "It's all right, Mr. Gordon. I'm just glad I was at sea when the 31st North Carolina marched."

Sunset Cox stifled a laugh, and Senator Gordon guffawed. The effect was contagious, and within seconds the small group was laughing heartily. Even Congressman Yeates.

Sumner Kimball glanced around the rest of the gathering. Two score Senators and Congressmen were gathered in small groups around the large hall. Assorted aides and hangers on buzzed busily on the outskirts of the small groups. He'd seen this kind of gathering before, and the names might change but the types of faces never did.

He felt a touch on his arm and turned to the man that had approached unnoticed.

"Ahh. The man of the hour," the man said quietly, protecting his privacy. "Welcome, Mr. Kimball." He extended a hand in greeting.

Sumner took the hand and smiled warily. "Good evening, Senator Burleigh."

Senator Burleigh nodded and shook his hand heartily with the ease of long association. He was the incumbent senator from Kimball's own state of Maine, and the two had met on several occasions.

"Congratulations on the appointment, Mr. Kimball. I know that you'll continue to represent Lifesaving Service in a manner suited to a Mainer." Senator Burleigh grinned, but the smile didn't reach his eyes.

"Thank you Senator." Sumner felt his first test. Senator Burleigh was well known for his political shenanigans. Burleigh was smoking an expensive black cigar and he rolled it to the corner of his mouth as he reached into his suit pocket and withdrew a slip of folded paper. Without a word, he handed the slip to Sumner.

Sumner's pale blue eyes narrowed. "What's this, Senator?" he questioned.

Senator Burleigh smiled around the cigar, his head wreathed in smoke.

"It's a name, Mr. Kimball," he said quietly. "You see, since the war, my nephew has had a tough time getting work. I would consider it to be a personal favor should he find employment as a superintendent or keeper with your new Lifesaving Service. He was a true Maine hero at Gettysburg with the 17th Maine."

Sumner unfolded the paper and glanced at the name without reading it. He looked back to Senator Burleigh. "Does he have experience with the surf, then, Senator?" he asked politely.

At the question, Senator Burleigh shifted his feet and said quietly, "I've no earthly idea, Mr. Kimball." He drew heavily on the cigar and said flatly, "I don't really care. I do know, however, that he's got a wife and family that need a government check."

Sumner locked eyes with the Senator. "Well, Senator, I care. The men of the Lifesaving Service need to be the very best men in the surf, regardless of who their uncles might be. Good day, Mr. Burleigh."

Sumner refolded the paper and handed it back to the Senator. Without a backward glance, his heart racing, Sumner turned from the Senator and strode into the room toward the knot of men surrounding Congressman Cox. Behind him, Senator Burleigh's face had reddened, then paled under his shock of white hair.

Sunset Cox had watched the little scene from the corner of his eye, only half-listening to the swirl of conversation around him. He smiled widely; it had begun.

"Gentlemen," Sunset said to his companions, "let me introduce Sumner Kimball, the General Superintendent of our great Nation's first official Lifesaving Service." He grabbed Sumner by the arm, pulling him to the center of the small group.

The men clapped him on the back and several shook hands. The introductions and greetings were jumbled and confused. A full snifter of brandy was shoved into his hand.

Sunset leaned close to Sumner's ear. "I see that our good Senator Burleigh has already greeted you," Sunset whispered. "Was it a brother or a cousin, Mr. Kimball?"

Sumner Kimball removed his bowler hat and took a long sip of the finest brandy that he'd ever tasted.

"A nephew," he replied flatly without turning to look at the Congressman.

"Hah!" Mr. Cox barked and squeezed his shoulder. "Are you ready, Mr. Kimball?"

"As ready as I'll get," Sumner replied, draining his brandy and handing the glass and his bowler to a passing steward.

Cox grinned, again, and took the younger man by the arm. He half escorted, half dragged Kimball to the front of the room, weaving through the gathered knots of congressmen, senators, and policymakers.

"Gentlemen," Sunset Cox ordered the room's attention in a booming voice. "Gentlemen!"

Conversations stilled around the room and eyes turned to Cox and Kimball in the front. Sumner twitched and shifted his weight from foot to foot.

Cox waited until all eyes were on him. Several men had taken their seats. He slowly drew several sheets of paper from his pocket and gathered the men's eyes like an experienced teamster gathered the reigns.

He cleared his throat. "Gentlemen, I'd like to introduce the General Superintendent of our nation's Lifesaving Service, Mr. Sumner Increase Kimball." His voice boomed in the large hall.

There was general applause and more than one raised his voice in a hearty "Bravo!" Cox stilled the applause with raised hands. He still clutched the sheaf of paper.

"But first," he continued, "I'd like to read a few words that were written by Mr. Kimball when he first got involved with the Lifesaving Service. Former Secretary of the Treasury, George Boutwell, was good enough to copy this for me." He turned slightly to Kimball. "He thought that these eloquent words spoke volumes for our new man."

Sumner rolled his eyes at the politician and waited patiently with the rest of the room.

Sunset continued his oratory. "And I quote, 'Mr. Secretary, I shall accept your offer upon one condition. If you will stand by me, after I have convinced you that I am right, I shall attempt to bring about the reforms you desire. But I want to warn you that the pressure will be tremendous. Congressmen will come to you in long processions and will attempt to convince you that I am wrong, and that the Service is being ruined. It will require an uncommon display of backbone on your part, but if you will stand firm and refer all complaints to me I promise you that I shall put the Service where you want it and where it ought to be.'"

The room applauded politely.

Congressman Cox folded the papers carefully; all side conversations had ceased. The room collectively leaned forward expectantly.

Cox continued in a softer voice, "Gentlemen, for too long the Lifesaving Service has fought charges of political favoritism. Mr. Kimball has borne this unfortunate yoke for seven years. Under the new Service, this stops. He has the final say. It is his reputation on the line."

The crowd of politicians murmured and more than one exchanged a sidelong glance.

Senator Burleigh rose from his seat. "Congressman Cox," he demanded, "What assurances are there that good, God-fearing men, who have our true interests at heart, will be in positions of power under this system? How can we be certain—"

Sunset Cox interrupted gently, "Like your nephew, George?"

Burleigh's face reddened and he glared over Cox at Kimball. He turned, snapped his hat onto his head from the table in front of him, and strode from the room.

Cox fixed the others with his pale blue eyes, roving from one to the next.

Mr. Kimball stepped forward next to Sunset Cox and spoke emphatically. "Our true concern is to assure the saving of lives, gentlemen, and though that may be uncomfortable for some of you, that is the true nature of the Service. To that end, we need to find and hire the very best men in each area for the Service. It will be my personal charge to locate these men, verify that they are well trained and well equipped, and continue to protect lives along the coast of our nation."

"Like they were protected aboard *Metropolis* and *Huron*, Kimball?" The speaker was a fat, red-faced Congressman from the state of Vermont. He hadn't taken a seat with the rest.

Congressman Yeates roved the back of the room behind the seated men, chewing his cigar forcibly. At these words, he stopped and turned to the speaker.

"You can stop right there, Buck," he called warningly from the rear of the room. "The *Huron* and *Metropolis* went down with great loss of life off *my* state, North Carolina, where we have only seven stations to cover more than one hundred miles of dangerous coast. How much coastline do you have in Vermont? "

The fat Congressman turned to Yeates. His lips thinned as he readied an angry retort, but he was prevented by Sunset Cox.

Sunset held up his hands. "Gentlemen, gentlemen. My esteemed colleague from North Carolina has a valid point. Fifteen of the thirty newly-appropriated stations will be on his coast. That's half, Gentlemen."

The fat Congressman turned from the room while Sunset was speaking and followed Senator Burleigh through the open door.

Sunset Cox turned again to Sumner Kimball. "On that subject, Mr. Kimball, I think we'd all like to know, and especially Congressman Yeates, where you plan to locate these stations along that most dangerous shoreline?"

Kimball smiled, hitting his stride. "The coastline of North Carolina is one of the most dangerous, that's true, and through the new stations I truly believe that we will avoid the tragic events surrounding *Metropolis* and *Huron*. We will immediately begin construction on over half of the new stations. These new stations will be closer together. Additionally, we will be defining a new training regimen that will assure that those tragic events will not be duplicated."

Yeates spoke again from the rear of the room. "What about Cape Hatteras, Kimball? It's the furthest outpost before you hit

the outlying islands, and in the shadow of Diamond Shoals."
Yeates removed the cigar from his mouth. "Very dangerous
water."

Sumner smiled at Yeates. "I agree, Congressman Yeates."
He spoke carefully. "That outpost is difficult, and will require
commanding keepership. To that end, I've placed a
superintendent in District Six who is familiar with many of the
locals and will be assisting me in the placement of keepers all
along the Outer Banks. We've spoken on several occasions, and
he's given me a short list of adept men to fill these positions,
but we haven't arrived at a conclusion regarding the Cape
Hatteras station."

Yeates brow knitted in thought. "The small ports along the
Outer Banks are full of competent men."

"Gentlemen," Admiral David Dixon Porter spoke from his
seat in the corner of the room. All eyes turned to the Admiral,
and he stirred his tea thoughtfully.

He raised his eyes to the politicians. "I believe that I have a
suggestion."

Cox exchanged a look with Yeates. This was a surprise.
Kimball raised his eyebrows as well.

Admiral Porter continued quietly, "How about Captain
Thomas Hooper?"

Sunset Cox stroked his goatee to cover his surprise.
"Captain Thomas Hooper?" he questioned the Admiral. "Of the
Otter?"

Admiral Porter smiled at the looks of consternation around
the room, and locked eyes with Sumner Kimball. "Yes," he said
softly.

In the rear of the room, Yeates whistled softly between
clenched teeth, staring in astonishment at the Admiral. "No
offense, Admiral, but you'd be the last person that I thought
would suggest that name," he spoke flatly.

The Admiral turned in his seat and looked straight at
Congressman Yeates. "We're talking about the need for an

extremely competent man from the area, are we not, Mr. Yeates?"

Sumner Kimball watched the scene thoughtfully. "Sorry, gentlemen, I'm not familiar with the name."

Yeates took the cigar from his mouth and spat tobacco juice into the spittoon next to the door, never breaking eye contact with the Admiral. "You see, Mr. Kimball, the *Otter* and Captain Thomas Hooper were the plague of the Union blockade during the war. I believe that he broke through Admiral Porter's lines on a half-dozen occasions to resupply Wilmington and Charleston. I think that I could safely say that Captain Hooper was the bane of Admiral Porter's existence for six long years. I believe, in fact, that Admiral Porter at one time even offered a significant bounty for information leading to his capture."

Admiral Porter smiled gently and took a sip of tea. "It was nine times, Congressman," he corrected. "Make no mistake, Mr. Yeates, he was once my mortal enemy, and you are absolutely correct." He paused and sipped his tea again, "But he is the man for the job."

Sunset Cox cleared his throat at the front of the room and looked to Sumner Kimball. "Well, finally a surprise, Sumner. Captain Hooper may be worth a look."

The moment had passed between Yeates and Porter. Congressman Yeates turned his attention toward Sumner. "Mr. Kimball, I'd better come along when you make that offer."

Sumner wrinkled his brow. "Why is that, Mr. Yeates?"

Congressman Jesse Yeates chuckled. "Well, Mr. Kimball, you may run the new Lifesaving Service, but..." He drew another cigar from his pocket, stuck it in his mouth, and rolled it to the corner of his jaw. "...you're still a Yankee."

CHAPTER 7
July 1878
Beaufort, NC

The streets of Beaufort, North Carolina were crowded in the late summer sun. Teamsters hustled and whistled heavy wagons in a steady jostle on the muddy streets, and more than one passerby glanced up at the suited solitary man on the railway platform.

Superintendent Kimball felt the glances from the passersby below. The natives of coastal North Carolina had proven to be a curious sort over the past few months. Not unlike the people of coastal Maine, he smiled to himself. Tight communities were always suspicious of outsiders, and Sumner Kimball was certainly an outsider here. All he had to do was open his mouth and speak.

"Good day, Mr. Kimball," a heavyset man murmured in passing from the seat of a spring wagon. The street was a ribbon of sand and choked with the afternoon's bustle.

Sumner tipped his neat bowler to the man and nodded in greeting with a faint smile. He was wearing them down. On his first trip through the area, no man would have said hello. The locals up and down the Outer Banks had come to realize, however, that the new Lifesaving Stations represented jobs and regular government checks. Sumner smiled again; the prospect of prosperity had changed more than one attitude.

Idly, Sumner drew a small gold watch from his vest pocket. The trains of the Atlantic and North Carolina were traditionally on time, and he hadn't much longer to wait. It didn't ease his mind. He was impatient for his guest to arrive; he stamped his sleepy left foot on the walk. Patience was not one of his strong suits.

All in all, his new stations along the Carolina coast were coming along very well. Already his local men had four of the seven stations that stretched across Cape Hatteras built. He'd personally seen to their complete outfitting, and the stations simply awaited their full staff of occupants for the coming storm season. He had begged, borrowed, and stolen the finest equipment for the stations, and was confident that the North Carolina coast would test that same equipment in the months ahead.

Sumner chewed the edge of his prodigious moustache absently. The only station that wasn't ready on that end was Cape Hatteras. He'd approached several men with the keepership, but, on hearing the location of the station, everyone, to a man, had made their excuses. Hopefully, that would change with the arrival of his visitor.

The sharp whistle of the next train broke his reverie, and Mr. Kimball straightened, removed his bowler, and ran his fingers through his dark hair. He hoped he was presentable.

The train wheezed to a stop. There weren't many passengers. A pretty young woman hurried by Sumner, a boy of eight or nine clinging desperately to her skirts. The trickle of the remaining passengers flowed by and around Sumner Kimball, and the porters dragged heavy trunks and small valises to and fro across the platform.

Sumner continued to stare at the steps as the last of the passengers found their way to the platform, and to the street beyond. His smile diminished and was replaced by a light frown. His eyebrows knit together in concern.

Sumner Kimball twitched the corners of his moustache. His guest didn't appear to be aboard. Uncertainly, he took a step toward the unloading train.

A heavy hand grabbed his left shoulder, and half-spun him around.

"Who you huntin', Kimball," the voice was a low growl in his ear.

Sumner turned, his frown broadening into a wide grin. "I'm waiting for you, Congressman Yeates. I thought that I'd missed you. Can I help you with your luggage?"

Yeates grinned and let go of his arm. "You almost did miss me, Lifesaving Man," Yeates continued grinning and extended his hand in greeting. "I got off the back of the train. As to luggage," he held up a small valise, "this is it."

Sumner shook his hand firmly, his left hand going to the man's forearm. "I sincerely appreciate your coming. How was the trip?"

Yeates snorted, rearing back his burly frame and twisting the kinks out with a stretch. "Goddamn trains, I'd just as soon ride a horse." The congressman laughed loudly and shook his heavy beard.

Kimball smiled again. Congressman Yeates certainly said exactly what he thought. Unfortunately, the word from Washington said that he wasn't long for Congress for that very reason.

"Well, Sumner, let's find a place to camp." Yeates took Sumner by the elbow and led the way down the stairs to the street below.

Sumner smoothly took the lead. "This way, Congressman," he suggested. "I've made arrangements for a room at the Biddemont house, where I've stayed the last several nights. There's a place to wash up and a beautiful view of the Beaufort Inlet."

"Excellent." Yeates patted his arm. "I stink of American politics, don't I?" he grinned.

Sumner's eyes widened, but he knew the man was just toying with him. Last year, he might've risen to that remark with a stammered apology. "I can't say, sir, the salt air has me not smelling much," he answered.

Yeates roared with deep laughter and clapped the younger man on the shoulder again. Hard. "Well said, my friend. Now, where are you hiding this Shittemont House?" he asked as they continued down the street.

Sumner's eyes crinkled at the misnomer. "Biddemont, sir. It's just ahead."

Yeates eyes narrowed intentionally at Sumner. "Not Quaker owned, is it?" he growled.

Sumner smiled, "No sir. All the brandy you can handle. Let's have a glass after dinner on the porch, or pizer, as I've come to call it."

Yeates grinned again. "Let's."

Dinner at the Biddemont house was a grand affair and lengthy. Mrs. Biddemont was so excited to have a real congressman staying under her roof that she had pulled out all the stops. There was roast duckling, an exquisite turtle stew flavored with sherry, steamed clams and oysters, and a dark rich salt-cured ham from the Biddemont's own smokehouse.

Most of the city council stopped in to the Biddemont to pay homage to Yeates, as the landlady had spread word of her important guest throughout town. Many of the townspeople as well had crowded the porch to catch a glimpse of a real, live Congressman. The plates had been cleared, and the brandy had come out. Yeates had offered a toast to nearly everything and everyone in Beaufort. Sumner's face was flushed unevenly from the influence of strong drink, but Yeates still rumbled on. Beneath the wide table, Sumner glanced at his pocket watch. The hour was late, and getting later.

"...and so, Mrs. Biddemont. I thank you again for the fine meal, and," Yeates stood, "of course, your exceptional hospitality."

Mrs. Biddemont was on the verge of tears, and she nodded happily. "Of course, Congressman Yeates. You will always be welcome in our house."

J.J. Yeates upended the last of his brandy and smiled again. "Now, I must beg your leave, Madam, and you, gentlemen. My colleague Mr. Kimball needs his rest, and we've much to do on the morrow."

Sumner scrambled to his feet to join the Congressman. "I thank you as well, Mrs. Biddemont, Everything was simply delicious."

Mrs. Biddemont smiled and nodded to Sumner. "Of course, Mr. Kimball, it's always a pleasure," she spoke quietly.

Yeates drew a thick black cigar from his jacket pocket and stepped through the parlor onto the long low porch. It was dark outside, and Mr. Kimball bumped the doorjamb as he followed.

Sumner's eyes adjusted to the gloom away from the lamplight, and he drew a stool over to where Mr. Yeates sat in the porch's single rocking chair. Sumner fumbled for a match in his front vest pocket, and reached to move the globe of the outside lamp with his other hand.

Yeates stayed his hand with a hiss. "Don't do that, my young friend. Else we'll have the rest of the county here to visit."

Sumner nodded and laced his fingers in his lap. "Of course, you're right of course, Congressman."

Yeates barely suppressed a belch. "That woman can sure cook, eh, Sumner?"

Sumner smiled. The congressman was backlit by the street lamps below. He made a hulking shadow, the thick cigar waggling furiously as he chewed away.

Yeates removed the cigar and spat into the street. "So, Sumner, tell me a story," he said gently, and replaced the stub of the cigar.

"Sir?" Sumner asked guardedly in the dim light.

Yeates stifled a chuckle. "Don't play poker with me, Kimball," he growled around his cigar. "I believe that you've got a progress report to Congress coming up, and, knowing you both personally and by reputation, I doubt that you're unprepared."

Sumner smiled, "No, sir." He squinted at Yeates in the dim light. "I've already prepared the report and I've a copy for you to share with Congressman Cox. Shall I go and get it?"

Yeates smirked. "Just the highlights, my friend. I'll leave the heavy reading to my colleagues up North."

Sumner brushed his hand through his hair and began. "Everything is coming along very well, sir. After my appointment last year, we saw the completion of eleven stations along your shores. This added to the original seven stations built in '74. So, now we've got eighteen total that stretch from Jones Hill to the North, and we've just completed Durant's, overlooking the inlet between Hatteras and Ocracoke Islands."

Mrs. Biddemont appeared with an ornate silver tea service, and poured a cup for both men. Without speaking she scurried back into the house.

Sumner carefully deposited two lumps of white sugar into his tea. Yeates was staring out into the empty street. Sumner carefully stirred his tea and took a small sip.

"Anyway," Sumner continued, "we've been progressing fairly well."

Yeates grunted and turned to look at Kimball. "How about men and equipment?"

Sumner smiled. "The men experienced several fierce storms last year. And the rough hurricane season was hard on both the new and old keepers and men... but they coped fairly well."

Yeates's cigar had disappeared, but his jaw continued to work absently. "I've heard that the new Beach Apparatus has worked very well up and down the coast. Are we using the Lyle gun and breeches buoy down here as well?"

Sumner squirmed. "Not at all the stations, sir. We've got several new guns ordered and are waiting."

Yeates regarded Sumner coolly. "The Lyle gun can fire a grapple six hundred and fifty yards, and that means that we can save that many more lives without the keepers and men putting themselves at risk in the surf."

Sumner rolled his eyes. "I know, sir. I located the gun personally."

Yeates stared at the man. "Well then. Get more."

Sumner nodded. "I'll send a letter to Captain Lyle—after all, he invented the gun—and tell him we need to be completely outfitted within the next two months."

Yeates leaned back in his chair, satisfied. "Right then." He squinted again at Kimball. "When will you have the remaining stations up and running?"

Sumner squirmed in his seat again. "Hard to tell, sir. There are only six stations left to build under the current appropriations."

Yeates stared at Kimball. "Make it a priority, Sumner. I don't want those appropriated dollars to disappear into some other agency's pocket."

Kimball nodded slowly. Point taken.

"How about the Cape?" Yeates leaned toward Kimball.

"Under construction now, Congressman. I believe that we'll have it ready for next season. We'd started construction, but lost everything in last winter's biggest 'cane." Sumner added hesitantly, "But we still haven't men or a keeper for that station."

Yeates drew a long black cigar from his inside jacket pocket and licked the end before squeezing it into the corner of his mouth. "Why not?" he grunted.

"Well, sir, honestly, no one will take that duty. I've got a long list for most of the stations, but the surf at Cape Hatteras is some of the most treacherous along the Banks." Sumner looked Yeates directly in the eye in the dim light. "I'd hoped that maybe you could help with that, based on our meeting at the Willard. I've sent word on three occasions to Thomas Hooper with no response. Frankly, I'm at a loss."

Yeates marveled again at the openness of the younger man. Few politicians ever admitted ass much. "What's on our itinerary for tomorrow morning? Where are we headed?"

Sumner regained his footing. He was on well-traveled ground. "I've arranged for a local boatman to run us up to Hatteras Island tomorrow, sir. I'd like to show you how our construction is progressing there. Then I'd like to tour the stations to the North clear up to..."

Congressman Yeates interrupted, smiling, "We'll get a look at the new stations soon enough, Mr. Kimball. I'm here to help, not just draw up a report."

Sumner was confused. "Sir?" he questioned.

Congressman Yeates spit again into the street and rose to his feet. "First, let's head further South, my young friend, down to Ocracoke Island."

Sumner nodded slowly, and Yeates continued. "First...you need a keeper." He paused and studied the superintendent. "A surfman."

CHAPTER 8
July 1878
Ocracoke, NC

Dawn found the two men aboard a large skiff under a square-cut sail bound for Ocracoke. Their captain, John Evans, crouched at the tiller and regarded the unusual pair. He'd grumbled this morning over the change in course, but, he reflected, Ocracoke was closer and his price was the same. He turned the skiff slightly with an experienced hand to keep her in the deeper water and take full advantage of the wind. He'd worked for Kimball before, and, though a Yankee and a bit of a dandy, he seemed to be a fine man. Evans smiled to himself. At least he paid well.

Kimball sat on the forward bench seat with his hands firmly on his knees. He had his back squarely toward where they were headed as he reflected on whence they'd come. It wasn't hot yet, but it would be, and he could feel the sweat beginning under his black bowler hat and beneath his heavy suit. He frowned enviously at Congressman Yeates, who lounged on the center bench. Yeates had met him on the porch that morning in simple pants tucked into long deerskin boots, and a cotton tunic stretched across his broad shoulders and heavy chest. The tunic was open at the collar to reveal a large chest with black hair that sprouted unevenly through the opening. Yeates snored softly. He'd leaned back the instant that the skiff had pushed off. Kimball gritted his teeth. It really wasn't appropriate attire or behavior, he thought, but you couldn't suggest such a thing to a standing U.S. Congressman, especially one as gruff as Jesse Yeates.

Sumner gazed out across the water. Yeates's words of last night fluttered at the back of Sumner's mind like a moth at a candle. Surfman. A very apt term for just the man that he needed at Cape Hatteras Station.

He looked again at the snoring Congressman, and started abruptly at seeing that the man's eyes were wide open. Congressman Yeates smiled and winked at Sumner, abruptly sitting up and swinging his feet over the bench to face the man.

"Damnit, Kimball, you look hot," Yeates chided, and he reached for the rolled up blanket that he'd been using for a pillow. From inside the roll, he pulled a long cigar and studied it in the morning sun.

Sumner frowned at the Congressman. The man had read his mind. He pulled off his bowler irritably and brushed a hand through his sweaty hair. Yeates chuckled softly and stuck the cigar in the corner of his mouth.

He grinned again at Sumner. "Sorry to have changed your carefully prepared itinerary, Kimball."

Sumner studied the Congressman. He doubted if he was sorry at all.

Yeates stretched his arms over his head and continued, "But I think you need my help with more than just looking at partially constructed stations and reading lengthy reports. Wouldn't you agree?"

"It's just that the men of the Northern stations are expecting us, sir," Kimball responded sourly.

Yeates leaned forward, resting with forearms on his knees and folding his hands. "I know...I know, my friend. We'll have a poke at Thomas Hooper first, though. The Carolina way—face to face," Yeates finished with a grin.

Sumner hadn't changed positions and his back was seizing up. He stared at the Congressman. "I certainly appreciate it, sir," he said, returning Yeates's grin with a sly smile of his own, "but he hasn't responded to any of my inquiries. I just don't know if he's interested."

Jesse Yeates continued to smile. "Oh, Mr. Kimball, he's interested. He just doesn't know it yet." Without another word to Kimball, Yeates swung his legs over the bench, ducked under the small sail and engaged the boatman in a deep conversation about the tides, currents, and fish, leaving Sumner to stew in his own thoughts—and heavy clothes.

By the time the skiff bumped into the wharf at Cockles Creek on Ocracoke, midday had come and gone, and Sumner had finally removed his jacket. He paid the boatman from a large leather wallet and made a note of the cost in a small leather-bound book. The two men walked side by side into the sleepy town. A small naked boy and his skirted older sister were jumping into the water off the edge of the pier. The pair stepped aside, their eyes downcast, to allow the two men to pass.

"I've found the locals on Ocracoke to be a clannish lot, Congressman," Sumner murmured as they walked.

Yeates eyebrows knitted together. "You need to speak the language, Kimball." He turned back to the pair of children and got down on one knee. He dropped his blanket roll between himself and the two children. Carefully, he withdrew one of his long black cigars from the folds and held it up. Sumner smiled in spite of himself. He'd often wondered how this gruff, tough Major had gotten elected to public office. He shouldn't have wondered. The boy's eyes followed the cigar hungrily, and met Yeates's eyes from beneath a mop of light brown hair.

"Son, where can I find the home of Captain Hooper?" he asked gently. His accent had thickened, and Sumner had to turn away to hide his smile.

The boy grabbed the cigar from Yeates's hand, smiling crookedly through his two missing front teeth. "Last hummock looking o'er Skipper's Row, Sir," the boy answered quickly. His sister's face had reddened in anger, and Sumner thought that he was probably in for a thrashing when they left.

Yeates rose to his feet, slung his blanket roll over his shoulder and started up the road. With a last glance at the children, Kimball hurried to follow.

The small hummock with its cover of live oaks was pretty easy to find, and the search only cost one more cigar. At the end of a haphazard row of houses, two live oaks grew gnarled and twisted at the corners of a very neat whitewashed cottage and a miscellaneous smattering of additional buildings. The cottage and sandy yard were striking in appearance. The two men hadn't seen a single other painted dwelling, nor one nearly as well kept. The boards and timbers of the buildings were an unusual collection of salvaged lumber and salvaged ships' timbers, but each had been cunningly sculpted to fit the next by knowing hands.

In the center of the yard, an older black man squatted over a set of nets, mending them with a heavy needle held in coarse brown hands. His hair was streaked with white and he had his back to the two men. He didn't look up.

Sumner made as if to speak, but stopped abruptly at a glare from Yeates.

The black man was shirtless, and his back was very black from prolonged exposure to the sun and wind. Age had sagged the backs of his arms a bit, and he had three rolls of extra skin on the back of his neck. A seabird cried overhead, and the breeze whispered in the leaves of the oaks.

"Not here," the black man's voice broke the stillness. He hadn't turned around or stood. His voice was strong despite his age.

"Sir?" Kimball questioned with raised eyebrows.

The man spun in his squatted position to face the two men. His feet were scarred, and the toes were spread wide from the absence of shoes. He squinted up at the men in the sun. His eyes were yellowed with age, and the bristly hair on his chest was snow white.

"Unlest you be here to see me...which you ain't...he's not here," the man stated flatly. His hands hadn't faltered without his eyes on the net, and they worked quickly in, out, and over the heavy mesh.

Kimball glanced at Yeates uncertainly, and shifted his weight from foot to foot. Yeates dropped his blanket roll and began to reach for his stash.

The black man snorted, and held the net up to the sun. "Save your cigars, mister," he shrugged. "Don' smoke."

Yeates tugged his heavy beard and grinned. Sumner's eyes narrowed. Word traveled fast. Now what?

The man rose to his feet, carefully folding the mended net. He placed his hands on the small of his back and arched, facing the sun. He smirked over yellow teeth at Sumner Kimball.

"You must be Kimball," he stated. It wasn't a question. Word certainly did travel fast.

Sumner quickly recovered his wits. "Yes sir, but I'm afraid that you have the advantage." Sumner extended a hand to the older man.

The man looked at the outstretched hand, reached down, and gathered the folded net in his arms. Without another word, he turned with the net to the storage shed on the right hand side of the yard. Kimball looked at Yeates and shrugged. Yeates made a slight motion with his hand. They'd wait him out. Several minutes ticked by, and the two men stood in the yard sweating. The man returned with another net and unceremoniously dumped it onto the ground.

"Still here, huh?" he asked. The man turned again to his work.

Sumner side-stepped closer to Yeates and whispered softly, "Waste of time, Mr. Yeates."

The old man had his back to them again, carefully working over the torn net. "Major Yeates?" he asked without turning "J.J. Yeates?" His hands had stilled in their dance through the webbing.

Yeates drew a black cigar from his blanket roll and put it in his mouth. "That's right," he responded.

The black man stood again and stretched a second time. "It's hot. Les' git in the shade." He motioned for the two to follow and led them to the wide roofed porch between the house and the kitchen building. He dropped into one of the two chairs, and gestured for Yeates to take the other. He vaguely gestured for Kimball to find a seat somewhere. It wasn't his concern.

"Sorry to hear about the 31st, Major." The man wiped the sweat from his eyes with a heavily calloused palm.

Yeates chewed hard on his stub of his cigar and rubbed his thick black beard. "Well, friend, that war, as with all others, had to come to an end." Yeates withdrew his cigar and spit into the sand of the yard. "Just thought that the outcome would be different, that's all."

The man nodded, lost in memories, and after a long pause continued, "Name's Jacob. Why ya need Cap'n Tom?"

Kimball leaned forward from his precarious perch on the boardwalk between the two buildings where he'd folded his coat on his lap.

"Well, Jacob," Yeates began, "Mr. Kimball is the top man in the Lifesaving Service, and he's in need of a keeper for the Cape Hatteras Station."

Jacob smiled. "Lotsa men want to be keepers, Major. That government pay goes a long way round here. Doubt you need Cap'n Tom."

Kimball spoke up for the first time. "No one wants the Cape Hatteras duty, Mr. Jacob," he said frankly.

Jacob chuckled, "You're right there, Mr. Kimball. You ever seen the surf off the Cape in a storm?"

Kimball's face reddened. "No, Mr. Jacob, I haven't, but I need to find a man who can handle it."

Jacob turned his head toward the western shore. His yellowish eyes faded in the wash of the setting sun, and no one spoke. Kimball took Yeates's lead and waited patiently. The shadows grew long, and the seabirds cried on their way to roost. Jacob had turned to the ghosts of his past.

Finally he turned his head back to the two men. "I'll be settin' out some salted mackerel and fresh water. You can sleep on the pizer," he said with resolution, to the large porch. "I'll take you to him at daybreak."

Jacob had said what needed to be said. He rose and entered the house.

CHAPTER 9
July 1878
Hatteras, NC

The next morning they set sail...again. Jacob had roused them long before daylight, and had handed them each a tin cup of the fierce yaupon tea. Sumner grimaced at the memory. It was a bitter taste, but a favorite among the locals. He'd been forcing it down for months on end, and would certainly appreciate a good cup of English tea with honey and a mite of fresh cream.

The day wasn't hot, at least. A thick fog had rolled in from the West across the sound late last night, and he'd hardly slept at all on the open porch. Sumner glanced at his traveling companions in the stern of the small skiff. Yeates seemed to have slept well; he had been regaling Jacob with stories from the War since they'd pushed off from Skipper's Row. At least one of them was in a good mood.

Sumner had resumed his position from yesterday in the center of the small craft with his hands braced on his knees. He'd taken a few minutes this morning to brush some life back into the suit coat that had served as his only blanket last night. At least he wasn't sweating today. He warmed to the thought; Yeates might be envious of his heavy suit today if it started to rain. He shifted his seat. It was difficult to get comfortable, and this morning's sea was much more unsettled than yesterday's. Each time they pushed over a wave, the bow banged hard into the next. Jacob seemed unconcerned, though, and handled the small skiff with the ease of long practice. Sumner grudgingly admitted to himself that a less experienced man at the tiller would have made the ride much rougher.

"...those years on the march took their toll, though, Jacob," Yeates seemed to be winding down at last and his newest unlit cigar was down to a mere stub between his clenched teeth.

Jacob nodded, his yellowed eyes flicking constantly from wave to sail to wave, his hand effortlessly guiding the tiller arm. Kimball smiled inwardly. He wondered if Jacob had heard enough. He'd certainly had little to say.

Sumner turned his attention forward. The fog had settled in for the day, and the stiff breeze carried a hint of rain. This was certainly bleak. If Jacob jumped ship, they'd be in a fix. He had no idea where the land started and the water stopped.

"Cap'n's fish camp is just ahead," Jacob said confidently. "'Scuse me, Mr. Kimball, let me strike that sail." Jacob pushed past Kimball in a low crouch and dropped the sail. He returned to the stern and drew a long push pole from inside the gunwale with practiced ease.

Sumner glanced over the side as Jacob began poling them toward their destination. A variety of seabirds stood atop prominent sandbars alonside the skiff. He frowned slightly, but Jacob clearly knew his way through the bars; he kept them in the deepest water so they didn't run aground. He looked again to Jacob, and Jacob smiled at his discomfort.

"Don' worry, Mr. Kimball." Jacob continued smiling and spoke in a low voice, "I know the way."

Mr. Kimball nodded, and returned a forced smile. At least the waves had abated. He turned his head to look forward, but all he could see was fog and mist. Puzzled, he glanced back at Jacob.

Yeates caught his eye from his seat in the stern next to Jacob. He, too, grinned at Sumner and pointed back toward the bow. Sumner followed his outstretched finger. In the filtered light, a shadow loomed out of the fog ahead.

Sumner could make out two rickety piers standing in the shallow water. He squinted into the fog beyond. The piers led to a long, low-roofed structure, barely distinct in the swirling mist.

As they bumped into the closer of the two piers, he could make out long waving salt grass stirring in the breeze. It was as if an ancient wizard had made the structure appear and float over the water. The mists shifted and he caught sight of the building.

"Welcome to the Hooper fish house," Jacob said quietly, and slid the push pole back to its resting space along the gunwale. He casually flipped a rope over, snared a piling on the edge of the pier, and drew the skiff as tightly against it as the lapping waves would allow. He made no move to exit the skiff, and settled back against the gunwale and tiller. Jacob smiled at the men awaiting his lead and canted his head toward the dim lamplight coming from within.

Yeates smiled at Jacob, stood and turned to Kimball. "Shall we, Mr. Kimball?" he spoke as he swung to the pier.

Sumner got unsteadily to his feet and scrambled after the congressman. He turned to Jacob. "Ah...," his voice trailed off uncertainly, his eyebrows arched and almost met the brim of his black bowler. "Mr. Jacob, will you be joining us as well?"

Jacob scratched his jaw. "No suh, I've met Cap'n Tom before."

Congressman Yeates chuckled. "Come on, Mr. Kimball," he said, tugging the man's arm, "I believe that Jacob thinks we should handle this one ourselves." Sumner turned and followed Yeates toward the dim lamp light ahead.

"Watch yourself, Sumner," Yeates grunted, stepping over a pair of missing boards on the walkway.

Sumner gingerly stepped over the gaping hole and looked up at the building ahead. As they made their way toward shore, the fog wasn't as thick and swirled uncertainly. Since coming to the Banks, he'd visited many fish camps and fish houses along the sound. They had all been small affairs, shacks really, on precarious stilts allowing for skiff access. None had resembled the structure ahead.

Twin piers ran hundreds of feet into the black water of the Sound. They were making their way up the right hand side, but there was easily room enough between the two to have several skiffs side by side. The water between was deep black and flowed with a slight current. The piers ran into a large low building, one on each side. The building was long and rectangular with a pitched roof. In an area where a fish shack that measured eight feet by ten feet was large, this one was enormous. It must have run sixty feet on the longer sides, and had to be thirty or forty feet wide. As they drew nearer, they could hear low voices from within. The steady pounding of a wooden mallet sounded from the large opening between the piers.

Yeates stopped and grunted. He pointed at a painted sign that hung facing the water on one of the heavy pilings. Sumner read over his shoulder. "Hooper Fish House." And in smaller letters underneath. "If no one is about...Wait." Yeates flashed a quick grin over his shoulder at Kimball as he headed for the gaping door.

A large windmill stood over the building turning at a decent rate in the breeze. Sumner was thoughtful. He hadn't seen many windmills in the area. He'd never seen one with pieces of old sail stretched as blades. It was very progressive thinking. He hurried to catch up with Yeates.

The rhythmic pounding of the wooden mallet grew louder in the close confines of the building. The piers ended abruptly ten feet in, and two steps led to a long, wide-planked floor. Sumner studied the dim interior. A long trough ran down one side of the building and spilled water into the sound below. The trough was filled with barrels, and the water that coursed around the barrels ran with a steady current. Sumner nodded to himself. That explained the windmill; it was pumping the cool water of the Sound into the troughs, making the fish house into a giant springhouse. Assorted nets were draped neatly along the far wall, and empty barrels were stacked floor to ceiling in the far corner. Close by the stack of barrels, a huge wooden box was built on the floor and overflowed with salt. Three men worked in the dim light from two oil lamps hanging from the low rafters. This was an operation.

An older man sat tipped back in a chair against the wall at the top of the steps. He seemed to be asleep. His low cap was pulled down over his eyes. Three other men had their backs to the new arrivals and were packing salted fish into barrels. All three were stripped to the waist and barefoot. The largest of the three swung the wooden mallet, pounding lids onto the barrels that the other two wrestled into position. It was hot, close work. The two men glanced at each other indecisively. What now?

"Help you, gentlemen?" the man in the tipped back chair asked. He didn't raise the brim of his hat, and his hands remained folded over his thin belly.

Yeates pulled a long cigar from the breast pocket on his cotton shirt, examined it closely, and clamped it in the corner of his mouth. He rolled it to the other side of his jaw and spoke around the butt, "We're searching for Cap'n Hooper. Is he about?"

The man in the chair reached up and scratched his scraggly gray beard but made no move to lift his hat. A slight lopsided grin played at the corner of his mouth. "He's about six foot, I'd say, more or less."

Yeates studied the older man carefully, his beard stirred as his jaw clamped shut around his cigar. He was obviously used to a different sort of treatment. Kimball smiled in spite of himself.

Kimball studied the three men working with the barrels. None had even turned. He could see sweat standing out on the man swinging the mallet despite this morning's damp chill. His back was tanned like shoe leather, broad and evenly muscled. Wavy brown hair hung to his shoulders. Occasionally he grunted to one of the other two men, but few words were evidently needed. These men were well acquainted with the work at hand and each other.

Yeates's heavy brows had knit together. "I'm Congressman Jesse..."

The man sat the chair legs down carefully and removed his hat. He looked up at Yeates and Kimball out of one good eye. The other eye was blue and dead. "Know who you are, Congressman," he interrupted and looked over Yeates's shoulder at Kimball. "You too, Mr. Kimball." He adjusted the hat on his head, and looked over their shoulders. "Morning to you, Mr. Etheridge," he said loudly.

Sumner glanced over his shoulder. Two watermen were poling a small heavily burdened skiff under the overhang of the building. The man in the bow raised a hand in greeting as he tied up along the pier. The second man stowed the long push pole. Without a word, the pair began wrestling heavy barrels from the skiff up onto the pier.

"Get 'em into the trough to cool down, boys, and this time don't forget to get your name on 'em." The man hadn't moved from his seat, and he looked again at Congressman Yeates.

The three men who had been salting and packing mullet came down to help the new arrivals get their barrels out of the skiff and into processing.

The one called Mr. Etheridge grunted around the stem of a long homemade pipe as they lifted the barrels from the flat bottom of the skiff. "Morning, G.W.," he nodded to the seated man and turned to the three helping with the barrels on the deck above. "Morning, Cap'n Hooper."

Yeates's eyes sharpened, and he and Sumner exchanged another glance.

"Morning, Mr. Etheridge." The speaker was the man that had been seating the barrel lids with the wooden mallet. He swung the heavy barrels into the trough with a grunt. He stepped away from the trough, and turned squarely to Yeates and Sumner.

The man shook out his shoulder length brown hair and knotted a quick ponytail. He drew a handkerchief from behind

72

his wide belt and mopped the sweat from his face and neck. He wiped his hands carefully, folded the handkerchief and put it away. Sumner studied the man as he cleaned himself up. A short beard shrouded his chin and lower cheeks. His shirtless torso was well muscled and his feet were bare to the weather. Sumner glanced at the feet again. His toes were spread wide; this man didn't wear shoes much. The man's pants might once have been brown, but were faded to the color of sand and rolled to just beneath the knee. A wide porpoise-hide belt wrapped his narrow waist and was punctuated by a porpoise-hide sheath that held a large whalebone-hilted knife. Sumner glanced quickly at Yeates, who appeared to be studying the man as well. He looked back at the man and met his eyes.

Captain Thomas Hooper was smiling at him. The smile was tight-lipped, and Sumner glimpsed a storm brewing behind the fierce blue-green eyes. "Gentlemen," Thomas said crisply.

Yeates stepped forward and held out his hand. "Captain Hooper?"

Thomas Hooper shook the offered hand. "I am, Mr. Yeates." He glanced at Sumner. "Mr. Kimball, I presume?" Sumner nodded, and shook hands after Congressman Yeates. The handshake was short and firm.

Thomas Hooper drew a long-stemmed pipe from his back pocket and carefully packed it with tobacco from a small leather pouch. The overflow water from the trough splashed into the dark water below, and the pause lengthened and became uncomfortable. Yeates produced a thick wooden match from somewhere and handed it to Captain Hooper. Hooper took the match and struck it off his thumbnail. He methodically stoked the pipe and squinted through the smoke at the two men.

"Surprised you-all found the place." Thomas removed the pipe and spat onto the board floor.

Sumner glanced at Yeates out of the corners of his eyes.

"I brung 'em." A voice spoke from behind Yeates and Kimball. Thomas looked over the two men at the speaker. None had noticed Jacob leaning against the heavy timber that anchored the corner of the building.

"Thank you, Jacob," Thomas said through clenched teeth. Sumner doubted that he was thankful.

Jacob smiled slowly. "My pleasure, Cap'n Tom."

"Sir." Yeates stepped forward. "We've come on urgent business. Your country is in need..."

Thomas drew deeply on his pipe and blew smoke toward the exposed rafters. "I know why you've come, Congressman. I've read multiple letters and fielded several inquiries from Mr. Kimball." Thomas allowed a shadow of a smile. "He is persistent." He nodded toward Sumner.

Kimball smiled at Thomas acknowledging the compliment. "Thank you, Sir."

Thomas removed the pipe stem from his mouth and rubbed his short beard. "Nevertheless, I'm not interested." He choked the pipe out with a calloused thumb and dropped it back into the pouch hanging from his belt. "You've had a long trip for nothing." Thomas began to turn back toward the men at the trough.

Yeates reached out and lightly touched his arm, staying the turn. "Captain Hooper, you're exactly right. We've had a long trip. I beg of you, sir, have the courtesy to hear out Mr. Kimball. His is a sworn duty to protect lives throughout the States. At least hear what the man has to say."

Thomas locked eyes with the Congressman. After a long minute, he glanced down at the Congressman's hand on his arm. Abruptly, Yeates let his hand fall away, and nodded at Thomas. Yeates's eyebrows were raised, and politics were forgotten. This was an appeal, man to man—North Carolinian to North Carolinian. Thomas nodded slightly and spoke to the seated man, "G.W., please see to Mr. Etheridge's catch." He turned his head to the watermen. "G.W. will fill out your chit, Mr. Etheridge. We'll be loaded on the morrow, and sail no later than week's end. I'll send a runner on our return with your portion."

The watermen nodded as one. Obviously the man held enormous trust with his neighbors. Times had been tough since the war, and cash money was scarce. Yet these two watermen offered their catch to Captain Hooper with only a vague promise of payment. Sumner looked at Captain Hooper with growing respect. G.W. produced a wide, thick black leather book and the stub of a worn pencil. He heaved himself to his feet and went to Mr. Etheridge and his companion. He would conclude today's business, not Captain Hooper.

Thomas Hooper toed a small barrel over. He sat on the top of the barrel and gestured vaguely toward G.W.'s abandoned chair. There was one chair and two men. Both Yeates and Kimball remained standing. Thomas fingered his pipe, but didn't stuff and light it. He held it aloft for the two men to see.

"This pipe belonged to Captain James McGuire." He squinted at the two men. "He was my adopted father. Did you know him, Congressman Yeates?"

Yeates and Kimball exchanged a look, and J.J. Yeates slowly shook his head.

"He was the finest man I ever knew," Thomas continued. His blue green eyes had taken on a faraway look, the storm that had been brewing behind them lessened. "When I was a boy, he told me that each man, each day, has a choice." He locked eyes with Sumner. "It's a man's choice what he will become, what he will do." He sighed and added quietly, "And, gentlemen, I've already made my choices." He drew the tobacco pouch from his belt and carefully stuffed the pipe.

Yeates cleared his throat. "We know, Captain Hooper. We know the choices you've made. I've family in Wilkesboro that wouldn't be alive today had it not been for the food that you smuggled aboard the *Otter*." He looked at Kimball out of the corners of his eyes. It was time for the young man to plead his case.

Sumner spoke quietly, staring directly into the eyes of the captain. "Captain Hooper, the new lifesaving station at Cape Hatteras is to protect the most dangerous shoreline on the Eastern Seaboard. I know why there are no volunteers. I need a man that can keep that station. One who can find, hire, and train a team of six men who would beard the very devil." Sumner paused, removed his bowler and ran his fingers through his hair. "For there it's the very devil you'll face."

Thomas had relit his pipe while Sumner spoke, and he blew another long stream of smoke toward the rafters. He rose from his seat on the barrel. "Kind words, gentlemen. Thank you for coming," he said formally and indicated Jacob, who still leaned against the post at the edge of earshot. "Jacob will see to your passage to wherever you need to go."

Sumner sighed heavily and looked to Congressman Yeates. The congressman was smiling slightly, and Kimball wrinkled his brow. Yeates stepped forward and offered his hand which Captain Hooper clasped and shook crisply.

Sumner started to turn away but was stopped by Yeates's low voice. "You know, Captain Hooper, your name came to us from an unusual place."

Thomas squinted at the Congressman. "That so?"

Yeates smile widened. "It is. The night of Mr. Kimball's confirmation, a certain Yankee you once knew very, very well brought up your name as the most competent man for the job along this coast. That Yankee was Admiral David Dixon Porter."

Thomas's eyes widened in recognition. "Well, Major Yeates, that *is* a surprise. I didn't think that Admiral Porter held me in very high esteem based on our...our past history."

Yeates chuckled. "Well, Mr. Hooper, it's a brave new world. Best to leave the past in the past. Wouldn't you agree?" Yeates turned to follow Kimball. "We'll be surveying the construction at the Cape and several other stations in the vicinity, Captain. Please feel free to stop by and see the stations for yourself."

Sumner followed Jacob toward the skiff. He hadn't bothered to shake the captain's hand. It was starting to drizzle as he walked down the pier. It was going to be a long, dreary ride back. Yeates caught up to him in a few quick strides, and smiled sideways. Sumner grimaced. He was in a foul mood.

"So much for that trip, Congressman," he sneered. It was as close to insubordinate as Kimball had ever been, and he quickly checked his tone.

Yeates barked a short hard laugh. "Think it was a waste of time, eh?"

Kimball's eyes narrowed. "Yes, I think so," he said in an edged voice, "I don't think he agreed."

Yeates continued to smile sidelong at Kimball, "Now let's have Jacob find us someplace to put our feet in front of a fire, put some brandy in our hand, and put some food in our bellies." He locked eyes with Sumner. "He agreed, Sumner, he just doesn't know it yet."

CHAPTER 10
July 1878
Ocracoke, NC

At the Hooper fish house, the afternoon sun cleared the fog and mist, and the rain stopped. Fishermen came and went throughout the day, and the salting and packing continued. Captain Hooper was lost in thought and sat on his upturned barrel, staring out across the sound. His pipe had gone out, but he sucked occasionally, drawing only air. G.W. came to his side and dropped down into the chair. He packed his own pipe from a tobacco pouch stuffed behind his belt and lit his pipe with a match struck on the floorboards between the two men. He sat back in his chair, and squinted at Thomas with his good eye.

"You'll feel better talking it out, Skipper," G.W. said around his pipe stem.

Thomas turned to G.W., reeling his eyes back from the hidden places in his own skull. He smiled wanly and pulled the long-dead pipe from his mouth. Glancing at the ashes, he grunted a hard laugh. G.W. offered his tobacco pouch, and Thomas filled the bowl, lighting it with a match that G.W. struck and offered.

Thomas looked at G.W. with a guilty half-smile. "Maybe so, G.W.," he said without conviction.

G.W. continued to squint at Thomas, and sat forward in his chair. "Skipper, I sailed under you and Cap'n James for nigh unto thirty years all told. You're all good men, but," he drew deeply on his pipe, "you're all good in different ways. You always been the best thinker among 'em. Do what you figure's right."

Thomas drew on his pipe and squinted back at the older man. G.W. always told it like it was; he'd been a top man on their ships for years and years. He had stood in as captain more than once for both him and his father before him. "Do you know what those men are asking of me?" Thomas asked.

G.W.'s face hadn't changed. "Yes sir. Overheard some. Got some rumors. Guessed the rest."

Thomas leaned forward and pulled his pipe from his mouth. "Whatya think, G.W.?"

G.W. sat back and scratched his thin beard. "I think you'll hold yer own council, Skipper," he smiled, "but, since ya asked, I'll give ya my opinion."

G.W. puffed his pipe and continued, "You spent the whole war helpin' others in need. Ya risked yer life, yer ship, and the lives of yer men a dozen times an' more. I seen you take on five Portuguese sailors with knuckle an' fist, so I know you ain't scared. I seen you refuse water, so yer men would have more, so I know you ain't common. I seen you handle boats from skiffs to five-hundred-ton barks. In short, I seen you become one of the bes' leaders of men that I've known or heard tell of." He drew on his pipe and paused before continuing. "And those men there, Kimball and Yeates, well, they seen it, too."

Thomas smiled, genuinely pleased at the words in spite of himself. "Thanks, G.W."

G.W. smiled back at his Captain and chided, "Now, Skip, don' let it go to yer head." He reached over and patted the younger man's knee.

Thomas stoked his pipe and glanced out over the Sound. "I'm not scared, G.W. I'm not worried about the duty, and I'm not worried about the work. I've seen most of it done, and done a good bit of it before." He looked G.W. squarely in his good eye. "I feel like I've done and given enough, G.W."

G.W. snorted in laughter and stared back at his Captain. "Captain Tom, some men were placed here to give, to help." He looked into his pipe; it had gone out. "You're a giver and a doer, Skipper; ain't no sense tryin' to change that now."

Thomas took a last pull on his pipe. He took it from the corner of his mouth and knocked it against the bare sole of his foot. The ashes and the last of the smoldering embers glowed red on his skin. He brushed them off without pain.

G.W. stood and stretched his aching back. It was time to call it a day. Thomas's gaze had shifted back to the waters of the Sound.

"Like I said, Skipper, hold yer own counsel," G.W. said. He turned from Thomas and took a frayed topcoat from a hook at the top of the stairs. Whistling, he went down the two steps and stepped off the pier, around the corner, and out of sight.

Deep in thought, Thomas didn't notice for several minutes that the man had left. He stretched and glanced around. The sun was setting, and the men had all gone for the night. He looked into the rafters at the two lamps. He wouldn't need a light tonight. He stood from his barrel seat and went to the wall hung with clean nets. With the ease of long practice he flipped a net over to one of the middle wooden timbers which held up the roof, and with a sailor's skill fashioned a quick hammock. He usually stayed at the fish house when he and the men were preparing for a voyage. Jacob wouldn't worry. His brow furrowed, and he wondered if Jacob had gotten his two visitors off toward their next destination. If Jacob had stayed on this side of the inlet he might see him yet tonight. So be it.

"I brought a basket, Tom," Della stepped from the gloom, "Momma thought you'd stay the night."

Thomas smiled and admired Della in the fading light. The last red glow of the sun caught in her wavy brown hair that fell nearly to her waist, and the green flecks in her eyes caught the same light. She wore a long skirt and faded shirt that could not conceal her lavish figure. The precocious girl had turned into a beautiful woman.

"Hey, D," Thomas said softly.

"Hey yourself, Thomas," Della smiled, her lips parting over even white teeth, "You all right?"

Thomas's grin broadened and he resumed his seat on the barrel. He gestured to G.W.'s vacated seat and waited for Della to join him. Della placed the picnic basket on the railing, gathered her skirt, and seated herself facing Thomas.

"Guess so, D. What did Rose tell you?' Thomas asked.

Della flashed another smile. "She told me that you were about to take the duty as the head surfman at Cape Hatteras."

Thomas chuckled. "She did, did she?"

Della continued to smile and reached over, gently caressing Thomas's cheek. "Well you are, aren't you?"

Thomas took her hand and patted her knee affectionately. "Hadn't decided."

Della threw her head back and laughed aloud. "Really!" she exclaimed her eyes flashing with mischief. "I find that hard to believe!"

Thomas's cheeks reddened beneath the tan. "Well, not for sure, anyway." He abruptly changed the subject. "And what about you, Della? The word is that you've turned away every single suitor on the Outer Banks, and some married ones, too," he teased.

"Is that what you've heard," she mocked.

"Yup," Thomas grinned again, "Heard some say you must not like men."

Della arched her back and stretched. Her shirt rode up, revealing a flat, tanned belly. "Oh Tom. I like men. I think you know that," she stared straight into his eyes, "or at least one man."

Thomas leaned back and lit his pipe. The light had faded and the two sat in the gloom of the fish house. "Della," he said in a low voice, "we've been through that. What kind of life would it be? I'm away at sea a good part of the time, or here in Hatteras, or..."

Della put a finger on Thomas's lips. "Shhh. I've heard it all before."

Thomas grinned in spite of himself. When he'd first gone to sea, Della was a little girl. Each time he'd returned she'd grown. Toward the end of the war, half his crew had dreamt of her. His grin lingered at the memory.

He took her hand from his lips. "I know, D, but..."

"Thomas, you went to sea, and I thought of nothing but you. You went to war, and I thought of nothing but you." The levity was gone from her voice; it had grown low and full of emotion. "I know that you're a sea captain. I know that you're white and that I'm not. God knows, I know that. But, I also know...." Her voice trailed off.

"I also know," some of the teasing tone had returned, "I also know that you're my best boy."

Thomas cleared his throat. Her lips were parted, her eyes half closed. The invitation was there. He shook his head and the moment passed.

Della's eyes sparkled and she rose from her seat. "Well then, at least let me feed you."

Thomas's pipe had gone out and he set it aside. "I'd like nothing better."

Della placed the basket in his lap. She bent over and kissed his head. "Well, I would, Tom. Like something better, that is." She turned, struck a match and lit a lamp, placing it carefully on the railing. The night sounds washed in from the sound like dinner music. She looked long and hard into Thomas's eyes, and he returned the stare. "But I've waited this long. A little longer can't hurt."

Thomas turned his eyes to the basket. "Thank you, Della. For supper, I mean."

"Tom. I'd wait forever." Without a backward glance, Della disappeared into the night.

Thomas ate slowly, with his hands: a fried chicken and a thick sandwich of venison and farmer's cheese. After eating, he took a woolen blanket from a shelf in the corner and turned to his hammock. The nights on the water could get quite chilly. He swung into the hammock and pulled the blanket up onto his legs. Lacing his fingers behind his head, Thomas stared at the ceiling. He fell asleep still staring into the rafters.

It was past midnight when Thomas snapped awake. Cold clammy sweat stood out on his forehead and chest, and his breath came in ragged gasps. He swung his feet over the hammock toward the sound, and was startled to see a man's silhouette against the water beyond in the half light of the night sky.

Jacob spoke from the darkness, "Didn't mean to startle ya, Tom."

Thomas could see the flash of Jacob's old yellow eyes and yellow smile. "'Sall right, Jacob. It wasn't you that woke me."

He saw Jacob spit into the water. "That so."

Thomas chuckled in the darkness.

Jacob stepped toward Thomas into the darker gloom of the fish house. "Got a heavy mind tonight, eh, Tom?"

Thomas whistled softly. "Sure do, my old friend. This surfman thing... you know about it?"

"Uh-huh, Tom. Maybe not the whole thing, but most of it anyway. I'd guess that those boys offered you the duty at Cape Hatteras," Jacob replied.

Thomas squinted at Jacob in the gloom. "Pretty good guess, Jacob, but I'm...I'm struggling with it," Thomas finished lamely.

It was Jacob's turn to chuckle. "Say, Tom... I ever tell you that story the Cap told me about a fisherman that specialized in big sharks down in the Indies?"

Thomas waited expectantly. "Don't think I know that one, Jacob," he said at last.

Jacob cleared his throat before continuing. "Well, that feller, he lost a child to a big shark when the child was little, and that man he lived fer many years without fishing fer sharks no more. One day, he went back to hunting sharks, an' the Cap said that he was the man on them big sharks from then on out."

Thomas studied his old friend. "That's what the Cap told you, huh." The corners of Thomas's mouth twitched with a slight smile. "Well, Jacob, what if the fisherman figured he'd killed enough sharks for one lifetime? What if the shark fisherman figured he ought to find a Mrs. Shark Fisherman and have some little shark fishermen?" He continued to study Jacob against the moonlight.

Jacob flashed a quick smile. Thomas could see the gleam of his teeth in the darkness. "Well, Cap'n Tom, a man can still hunt fer sharks an' have the other too. 'Specially if the shark fisherman's a young man." There was a long pause where neither man spoke. "I's sure that the shark fisherman's ol' friends would shore like to see some of dem lil' shark fishermen. Especially if he knew Mrs. Shark Fisherman pretty well," Jacob added, the amusement thick in his voice.

Thomas chuckled, and Jacob stepped close. He took Thomas by the shoulders and his eyes flashed. "I've done good things in my life, Tom, but best thing that I ever done was pullin' you out o' the sea." His tone had sobered and he spoke with choked emotion. "You done good things, too, but maybe now's the time for your best thing."

Without another word, Jacob released Thomas's shoulders, walked into the darkness and dragged a sleeping mat out onto the floor. He lay on the mat and rolled away from Captain Hooper. Thomas looked at the slight rise of the man's shoulders in the darkness.

Maybe it was.

CHAPTER II
August 1878
Hatteras, NC

The cry had risen at dawn up and down the wide sandy beach at the partially built Cape Hatteras station, and people had had congregated within the hour. Many were afoot, but some pulled carts, and an occasional horseman plodded through the heavy sand. Sumner Kimball and Jesse Yeates stood on a low rise and looked out across the throng at the stranded schooner beyond.

Yeates shaded his eyes against the morning sun. "Damnedest thing, Kimball. There wasn't even a storm," he commented around the cigar in the corner of his mouth.

Sumner nodded gravely, his eyes, too, fixed on the stranded vessel no more than one hundred yards off the beach. "It happens all too often, though, Congressman. Captains try to cut the corner here at the Cape, and the sandbars are forever shifting. Even experienced captains have been known to go aground in this stretch," Sumner replied, squinting into the the light.

Yeates frowned sourly. "I thought that's why we rebuilt the lighthouse in '70." He turned and studied the massive new lighthouse down the beach before turning back to Kimball. "Feels like we should be doin' something..."

Sumner nodded again. "You're right about the lighthouse, J.J., but some captains choose to tempt fate. As to doin' something, well, that's why we're here."

Yeates's frown deepened. "Well, we ain't helping that boat," he grumped and gnawed his cigar.

Sumner grimaced. "No, sir, we're not. But soon our actions will help them all." He continued to study the ship. "I hope that those men get ashore."

The ship foundered in the surf. The wreck must have happened some time during the night, but sailors still scurried about the deck. They hadn't swum for it yet. The locals were gathering along the beach; no-one had made an effort to swim or row to the ship.

Sumner turned inland and looked long and hard at the shadow of one of his nearly-completed Lifesaving Stations. He could picture the men of Cape Hatteras Station rolling their Beach Apparatus down out of the wide ramp that led onto the beach. They'd strain against the heavy cart. Coston flares would have been lit during the night when the wreck was first spotted. This morning, help would have been heralded by crisp signal flags in the morning breeze. Sumner sighed heavily.

It wouldn't happen today. Cape Hatteras Station wasn't finished. He stared down the beach that stretched into the distance, first south toward the recently completed Creeds Hill Station, and then north toward the Big Kinnakeet Station. This year, this coast would be teeming with lifesavers bent on their duties. But it wouldn't happen today. He removed his bowler and ran shaking fingers through his thinning hair.

Yeates seemed to read his thoughts. "Too bad it's not September, eh, Kimball?" he said, but there was no humor in his tone or eyes.

Kimball grimaced at the thought. One of the new provisions of the sweeping doctrine that had changed the Lifesaving Service last year was that the stations would be manned from September through April. September was a month away.

Yeates turned inland. "Enough of this, Sumner. Let's not worry about what could have been. Let's worry about what should be. Let's have a look at this new Cape Hatteras Station of yours."

With a final long look at the grounded ship, Sumner sighed and turned to follow Yeates. Time would tell the vessel's fate.

The two men trudged through the heavy sand toward the station, and Sumner glanced up at the lighthouse that towered above the beach. The Cape Hatteras lighthouse was huge, pointing a straight finger two hundred twenty feet into the morning sky. The black and white barber pole design glistened with sea spray and the night's dew. He looked from the behemoth to his squat station up the beach. One was warning sailors of a danger, the other was saving them from a disaster. He wondered absently which would be more effective.

The two men stepped up onto the wide porch of Cape Hatteras Station. Two local men were nailing heavy shingles into place on the roof above. Yeates nodded to the roofers and spoke quietly to Kimball, "It appears that you'll be complete here in a few weeks, Sumner. When do your equipment and provisions begin to arrive?"

Sumner tumbled the question around in his mind and said thoughtfully, "Based on what I'm seeing," he paused and continued, "around the third week of this month."

A man stepped out of the dim interior to meet the two on the porch.

"Congressman Yeates," Sumner said formally, "let me introduce John McGowan of Revenue Marine."

The man was short and sturdy. His thin linen shirt was already stuck to his chest and back with sweat from the morning's labors. He held out a flat thick hand to the congressman.

Yeates took the hand and smiled broadly at the man, "Mr. McGowan," he spoke with admiration. "So, you're the man that I need to thank for the construction of these beautiful new stations?"

Captain McGowan nodded soberly. "Yessir."

"Excellent." Yeates continued to smile. "Show me around."

Sumner stepped back from the pair as they disappeared into the building and leaned against the post bracing the porch roof. In the distance, he could make out the masts of the stranded ship. He carefully removed his bowler and wiped the sweat from the hat band. Construction was progressing well, but he still needed a keeper. There had been no word from Captain Hooper, and it had been more than a week.

The morning had given way to noontime, and the day had ticked toward dusk when a distant gunshot rang out. Sumner and Yeates had walked two-and-a-half miles to survey the sea shack that stood on the beach between the Durant and Cape Hatteras stations. The pair was on their way back toward the Cape when the heavy crack broke the evening stillness. They exchanged a glance and picked up their pace in the heavy sand. Not good.

They hurried past the Cape Hatteras Station and crested the slight rise where they'd stood early in the day overlooking the stranded vessel. Sumner groaned under his breath. Aboard the schooner a single man was gesturing wildly. The last of the light glinted off of the object in his hand. It could only be a rifle. Throughout the day the sailors had been abandoning the ship. Kimball grimaced; the captain had stayed despite the odds.

Sumner knew the reason for the shot. A small fleet of skiffs and scows circled the ship like hungry sharks. The gunshot made them stay honest and keep their distance, but that wouldn't last. He glanced down the beach. The throng that stood at the water's edge had grown since the morning hours, and he could make out the dancing lights of cooking fires just above the tide line. The people knew that it was but a matter of time. The captain on the vessel reloaded and snapped another quick shot at the circling boats. One must have strayed in too close.

Yeates removed a thick black cigar from his mouth and snorted with disgust. "Damn looting, if you ask me."

Another voice spoke from behind the two men. "No, Mr. Yeates," the voice chided softly. "That there is salvage."

Sumner turned toward the speaker, but Yeates's eyes were fixed on the sea in front of them as the scene continued to play out. "Good evening, Captain Hooper," he spoke without turning. "I'm glad you could make it."

Surprise was written across Sumner's face, and he held out a hand in the setting sun. He nodded in greeting, not trusting his voice.

Thomas Hooper shook the man's outstretched hand. "Evening, Mr. Kimball." He stared at the broad back of Congressman Yeates. "You too, Mr. Yeates."

Yeates grunted, his eyes fixed on the wrecked ship in the shallow waters beyond.

Thomas stepped up beside the two men. "Congressman," he began patiently, "the rules of the sea are clear. The people haven't boarded the ship. When the captain abandons the vessel, it becomes salvage. It's only a matter of time."

Yeates turned his head to Thomas and said grimly, "I know the rules, son. It's tragic nonetheless."

Thomas drew his pipe from the pouch on his belt, and Sumner studied him from the corners of his eyes. The shirtless, barefoot man with wild hair from the week before had been replaced by a sea captain. The change was uncanny. He was outfitted in a custom pair of loose black trousers, a black leather belt, and shoes of rich black leather. His silk shirt was open at the neck, but carefully tucked, and tailored to fit the lithe muscles of his shoulders and arms. A light waist-cut black suit coat completed the ensemble. His thick brown beard had been trimmed, and the hollows of his cheeks beneath the sideburns showed a fresh shave. The wild shoulder-length hair was combed and gathered in a tight ponytail beneath a brushed Captain's cap. The stormy blue-green eyes, though, were as intense as that first day.

Thomas lit the pipe and blew smoke into the evening sky. "Tragic it may be, Congressman Yeates, but tragedy, like beauty, may be in the eye of the beholder." He drew deeply on the pipe and continued in the same low voice. "Up and down the beach, people need timber for fish houses, for churches, for homes. In fact, I'd wager that every building from here to

Norfolk was built in some part from salvaged ship timbers and salvaged cargoes."

Yeates studied Thomas with a single raised eyebrow. "Well, Captain Hooper, you probably have me there."

Thomas smiled around the stem of his pipe at Yeates, and turned slightly to Kimball. "I believe that the Lifesaving Service and Revenue Marine have parameters set up for salvage, Mr. Kimball?" he asked innocently.

Sumner smoothed his moustache, sensing a trap. "We do," he said hesitantly. "The system until this past year was poor, as I'm sure you know. Under our new guidelines, keepers and district superintendents are in charge of categorizing and auctioning all salvage."

"That's what I'd heard," Thomas said quietly and breathed smoke from his nose. "But the stations aren't manned until September, and, well." He indicated the stranded vessel. "There you have it."

The three men turned their full attention to the surf. The Captain of the ship was in heated conversation with a boatman who had drifted in close. The men on shore couldn't hear the words, but the sense of defeat about the captain was a palpable thing. The captain clambered over the side and dropped into the skiff below. As the skiff pulled off from the ship, the first of the salvage crews pulled close with thrown grappling hooks.

Thomas snorted and knocked his pipe against his shoe. "Like I said, gentlemen, a matter of time." He gestured toward the building. "Let's have a seat, and see what kind of course Mr. Kimball's plotted for our Cape."

Thomas led the way back up the winding path amidst the salt grass off the beach. The men who had been working on the roof were gone, and there was no light from within the dark shadowed interior. INstead of stepping up onto the porch, Thomas walked around the building toward the road.

The comforting smell of sizzling bacon reached the men before they'd rounded the building, and Thomas grinned back at the other two with a knowing smile. Jacob was squatting next to a large campfire on the other side of the partially-constructed building. He was shirtless as usual, and quite busy pushing thick strips of bacon around a large skillet. A large flat-bedded wagon had been turned on its side and a large tarpaulin had been stretched from the wheels to two driftwood poles. The poles were held in place by ropes staked deeply into the soft sand. A single lamp was suspended under the tarp, and it washed a small table and set of chairs in yellow light. Sumner and Yeates were brought up short, and Sumner's mouth hung open in surprise.

Yeates broke the silence. "Well, I'll be damned, Mr. Hooper; you all work quickly, don't you?"

Thomas drew a seat from beneath the tarp. He flipped the wicker chair around backward and straddled it. He gestured for the other two men to take seats.

"Spoke briefly with Mr. McGowan and the men before they left for the day. Offered them to stay for supper, but they had to be on their way," Thomas replied to the unasked question and smiled at his guests. "Jacob's fixed us some supper, and he'll be joining us as well."

Yeates grinned broadly and dropped into one of the chairs. He drew a thick black cigar from his pocket and inspected it in the varying light from the fire and the lamp. Satisfied, he stuck it beneath his beard and clamped it in the corner of his mouth. Thomas packed his pipe bowl and lit it with a wood sliver from the fire. Sumner fidgeted; sometimes he wished he smoked. He pulled a chair next to Congressman Yeates.

Yeates began, smiling with his eyes, "Well, Captain, you had my esteemed colleague wondering. He was convinced that you wouldn't come."

Thomas smiled back, and toed a long piece of driftwood further into Jacob's fire.

"Your Mr. Kimball was just too persuasive, Congressman." Thomas turned to Sumner. "Well, Superintendent, you'd better give me the run down."

"Sir?" Sumner questioned, his eyebrows arched.

Thomas drew deeply on his pipe and rubbed the edge of his beard with the back of his hand. "I don't figure that you want me and six boys sittin' here around the campfire all winter, Mr. Kimball. Tell me about my new job."

Sumner's eyes brightened. "Well, Captain Hooper, I'd like you to run this station as the keeper. I've a manual which explains most of the ins and outs, shall I get it?" Sumner moved to rise, but was stayed by Thomas's half-raised hand.

Thomas locked eyes with Sumner. "In due time, Mr. Kimball. What are the broad strokes?"

Sumner sat back down and removed his bowler, running his fingers through his hair. "Well, sir," he began slowly, "you'll need to locate, hire and train a team of six men. You and your men will be responsible for monitoring the coastal waters with this as your central point. Your purview extends from halfway to the Creeds Hill Station," he pointed toward the south, "and halfway to Big Kinnakeet station up the beach. Where we sit is about the midpoint of a six-mile stretch." Sumner looked over at Thomas. Thomas was smoking and staring thoughtfully out toward the surf. Sumner knew he had the captain's attention.

He continued, his confidence growing. "There are surf shacks located both north and south at the midpoints to the next stations. Your men will need to walk a nightly patrol along the beach, with a weather eye toward the sea and shoals."

Yeates held his peace, staring at Thomas. He was impressed with Kimball; the description was concise and correct. Thomas glanced over at Sumner. "All right, Mr. Kimball, well-conceived. Say I've got a man walking his patrol, is he to meet a man at this surf shack from the other station?" he questioned.

Kimball nodded emphatically, "Yes, sir. We just adopted a new policy last season that worked very well. The men carry a

94

beach check, and swap with the man from the next station at the surf shack. That way each man can prove that he's walked his watch." Encouraged by a silent nod from Thomas, Sumner continued, "During the day, one man needs to be constantly vigilant at the station itself."

Thomas rolled the process around in his mind, "Say, we see a ship in peril, then what?"

Sumner shot Yeates a quick glance. "Well, then, Mr. Hooper, you'll be responsible for launching rescue efforts. Each station is equipped with a beach apparatus cart, and...hopefully, a Lyle gun. The system works by—"

Thomas interrupted, "Seen that kind of rescue up North, Mr. Kimball. We fire a stout cannon with a grapple into the ship's rigging. The crew aboard makes it fast to the mast, and we make it fast to the beach. Then it's a matter of pulling people back and forth with a running block." Thomas blew a stream of smoke toward the sky. "The problem is that it's limited in range, and making it fast in a hurricane will be a bit fierce, but I understand the process. What happens when the gun and line won't do the job?"

Sumner squinted at Thomas through the swirling pipe and campfire smoke. "Well, sir, then we row out and save them," he said calmly.

Thomas snorted a small laugh, "I thought that that was what you'd say. No less than I expected." He drew the pipe from his mouth and studied the slight glow from the bowl. He clamped it back between his teeth and continued around the stem. "As to the men of Cape Hatteras Station?" he questioned.

Sumner fumbled with the inside pocket of his suit coat. "Well, Captain Hooper, I've a list of local men that have applied at other stations or with the Service itself. Other keepers have relied on these lists to establish their crews." Sumner drew out a piece of folded paper and held it out to Captain Hooper in the light of the fire.

Thomas eyed the paper but made no move to take it. His eyes found Kimball's in the dim light. "No offense, Mr. Kimball, but you can keep your list."

Sumner arched his eyebrows. "Sir?"

Thomas pulled his pipe from the corner of his mouth. "The rest of the stations have existing crews, haven't they, Mr. Kimball?" Thomas continued without waiting for a reply. "I take it that your list is probably an indication of who's left. The men that didn't get picked up by other stations in the last year. Am I right?"

Sumner swallowed hard. "Probably a fair assumption, Mr. Hooper," he said softly.

Thomas stared at Kimball in the flickering light from the campfire. The seconds ticked by before he spoke again. "Mr. Kimball, I'm not interested in other men's discards. I'll need men who I know I can train, and, above all, who I know I can trust. It's the only way I'll have this station operable within the month." Thomas drew on his pipe and blew a stream of smoke skyward.

Sumner nodded slowly. This was going to be a hard man to push around.

Yeates spoke for the first time. "Captain, have you any men in mind?" he asked from around the stub of cigar.

Thomas smiled wryly into the fire. "Just one, Congressman, but I'll come up with the rest."

Jacob spoke from the table under the tarp where he'd begun setting out the evening meal. "Who's the one, Cap'n Tom?" he asked quietly.

Sumner looked from Jacob to Thomas, and finally to Yeates. Yeates arched his eyebrows at Sumner. Jacob was certainly fit enough, though it wasn't what either man would've expected. Thomas Hooper rarely did the expected; it was a fact that Yeates and Kimball were just learning.

Thomas studied Jacob in the wash of light from the lamp hanging just over his head. He saw the exchanged look between

Yeates and Kimball out of the corner of his eye. Jacob's face was inscrutable. Thomas knew that all three expected him to name Jacob. Time to change their minds.

"The Scotsman," Thomas said in a low voice, and surprised them all.

CHAPTER 12

August 1878

Cape Hatteras Station, NC

The following afternoon, Kimball found himself without his traveling companion of the past few weeks. In the morning, Congressman Yeates had said his goodbyes. His true duty, after all, lay in Washington. He hadn't sent for a wagon; he'd simply packed up his blanket roll and struck out on foot from the Cape Hatteras Station toward the village of Hatteras to the south. Before he left, he solemnly shook each man's hand and murmured a few kind words. When he reached Thomas, he drew the man in close and said only, "Clock's ticking, Cap'n Hooper." The two men had matched grip for grip, and then the congressman was gone.

Kimball had spent much of the day at the small table under the tarp reviewing charts and paperwork. He'd neglected his journals over the past week and painstakingly corrected this affront. As he worked, Hooper was never far away. He'd spent hours reviewing the manual which Kimball had provided, and Kimball was impressed with his careful study. He'd seen him writing copious notes in the margins.

The two men had little to say to each other. Each was busy with his own thoughts and his own work. Finally, in the late afternoon, it was Thomas Hooper who broke the day's silence.

"Mr. Kimball." Thomas had appeared beside the table, and Kimball dragged his eyes from the ledger. "I'll be headed down the beach this evening," he stated flatly. "You're welcome to join me if you'd like."

Sumner regarded his new keeper calmly. The voice had an air of command, and Sumner knew that he was going along. He looked sourly at the pages of his long script from the day; the paperwork never seemed to end.

Thomas grinned at the superintendent, reading his thoughts. "There'll be time enough to finish your paperwork on the morrow, Mr. Kimball. Tonight we've other business."

Jacob saddled the two broad-backed draft horses which had been tethered in the salt grass since he and Thomas had first arrived. The matched grays were well bred and stout, but more fit for pulling the flatbed wagon Hooper had brought than for the saddle. Kimball found his bowler hat and pulled it down low on his head. Better than walking, he thought.

Thomas was in the saddle first, and waited patiently for Kimball to mount. Thomas's mouth twitched wryly. The man may have done better had he and Jacob struck the tarp and righted the wagon. He wasn't comfortable astride a horse. The little Yankee didn't complain, though. Thomas scratched his short-cropped beard thoughtfully.

The two men walked their horses out onto the road behind the station, and Thomas led the way south. Kimball hurried alongside.

"So where's this evening's business leading us, Captain Hooper?" Sumner queried, smoothing his moustache unconsciously.

Thomas smiled sideways at the Superintendent. "South," he replied.

Sumner pressed his lips. He held his tongue. Obviously they were headed south. Thomas increased his horse to a canter on the hard packed road and the two men rode side by side without speaking.

They passed a few small houses, more than one man nodding solemnly to the pair as they passed. Sumner had no doubt that word had spread. Captain Hooper was the new keeper of Cape Hatteras Station. Everyone along the coast knew the man, if not by sight then at least by name. Kimball smiled to himself. But, then, most of the locals knew him by now, as well.

The pair passed Creeds Hill Station and Durant's Station. Kimball studied the two stations from the road as they passed. Both had been built two years prior; no light showed during the summer months. Kimball chewed the edge of his moustache. Based on his eyewitness account from yesterday, that would have to change sooner or later.

Thomas led the way across Bread and Coffee Ridge, then drew up. The village of Hatteras lay before them. Their vantage point atop the ridge was only a few feet above sea level, but they could make out the smattering of houses and buildings in the dim light. The first lamps of the evening glowed in some of the dwellings, but many remained dark.

Sumner cleared his throat and made as if to speak. Thomas only grinned at the superintendent and booted his horse down the slight rise. Kimball had no choice but to follow. Thomas drew up again only a few hundred yards ahead, in the shade of one of the few remaining live oaks, with Kimball at his side. He dismounted and staked out his mount beneath the tree. Kimball followed suit and waited expectantly.

Thomas grinned again, his teeth flashing in the darkness. "We'll walk from here, Mr. Kimball," Thomas spoke in a low voice.

"Are you ready to enlighten me, Mr. Hooper?" Sumner asked, an edge to his tone.

Thomas laughed softly. "Sorry, Mr. Kimball." He continued to smile into the darkness. "I've come to fetch a first mate, or as your book calls it...uh..." Thomas's mind reached for the term. "My Number One."

It was Kimball's turn to smile. The man was working yet; he'd begun to think that this was some crazy lark of the captain's. "Fair enough," he responded, "Why'd you bring me along?" he asked curiously.

Thomas looked at the man. His blue-green eyes seemed to flash in the darkness. "Mr. Kimball, I thought that you'd better see what I've got in store for Cape Hatteras Station before you announce my appointment," he said cryptically.

Kimball studied the man's outline. "I don't know what that means, Mr. Hooper," he said quietly. "Your men are yours, and yours alone. I expect the keepers to handle these matters."

Thomas reached out and touched the man's shoulder lightly. He leaned close, and the two men stared at each other in the fading light. "Don't worry, Mr. Kimball, I'll handle my men." He paused and glanced off the road at the cluster of lights from a few dwellings. "But, the man I'll seek might be a bit different from the men that you've come to expect from your keepers."

The two men stepped from the hard road, and Thomas led the way onto a wooden boardwalk that ran helter-skelter through the buildings ahead. The buildings themselves were broken down and shabby. Had the boardwalk not been there, the two men would've been knee deep in water and mud.

Thomas grinned over his shoulder at Sumner and spoke in a voice barely over a whisper, "Welcome, Mr. Kimball, to Sticky Bottom."

Sumner heard pigs grunting in the gloom somewhere to the left of the boardwalk. He squinted his eyes, but saw only black water and marsh grass. He wrinkled his nose against the stench of black mud and pig wallow.

Thomas led the way down the rickety boardwalk. He was obviously familiar with the place; he took the twists and turns of the slanted walkway without hesitation. In the gloom ahead, one building was larger than the rest. Its wide, low porch was railed, and several of the boardwalks converged on it from different directions. Thomas led them straight toward that building.

As the men drew nearer, voices and the tinkle of glasses could be heard from within. Kimball strained his ears; he could hear the notes of an out of key piano drifting on the night breeze.

The two were almost to the porch when the doors smashed open, spilling a large rectangle of light onto the porch and the boardwalk beyond. A single man reeled out of the tavern, hit the rail and flipped backward into the muck next to the boardwalk. He leapt to his feet in the marsh grass. Sticky Bottom's black water had soaked his shirt and trousers, and the mud squeezed up between his wide-spread toes. He shook the mud from his scraggly hair, putting a hand to his mouth. Blood seeped from a puffed lip, and there was a large split over his left eye. The man swayed drunkenly and started to pull himself back onto the boardwalk, cursing wildly under his breath.

Thomas stepped forward and took the man by the arm, helping him up onto the boards. "Evening, Seamus," Thomas said quietly.

The man glared up at Captain Hooper. His eyes were bloodshot with strong drink, and he fought to focus on the man pulling him to his feet. Recognition dawned in the reckless eyes. "Evening, Cap'n Hooper," the man growled in a thick Scots accent.

Thomas got the man standing on his feet by lifting him bodily onto the boardwalk, and Sumner smiled faintly. The man was little. His soaked shirt clung to his sunken chest and small arms. He might go one hundred thirty pounds soaking wet, Sumner though absently. His hair was long, tangled and red as the setting sun. Splotches of red and blond whiskers had tried to make themselves into a beard, but failed miserably.

"Bloody bastards," the man growled menacingly and took three staggered steps toward the door through which he'd just come.

Thomas hit him. Kimball gasped in surprise. Thomas's hand was a blur and the punch caught the red-haired man directly behind the ear. Seamus stumbled to his knees and dropped to his face, out cold.

Thomas flashed a quick smile at Kimball over the fallen man. "Well, Sumner, I don't guess any good could've come from him going back in. Give me a hand."

Sumner hurried forward from the relative safety of the shadows and glanced up at the closed door. The murmur of voices and tinkle of piano had started again. He stooped to help Thomas, and the man's head lolled sideways. Kimball caught the stink of a semi-digested meal and wine right in the face. He wrinkled his nose and swallowed hard, glancing at Thomas out of the corner of his eyes.

Thomas caught the look and winked at Sumner. "Mr. Kimball, I'd like to introduce Seamus Pennycuik." He paused and locked eyes with Kimball. "The Scotsman."

Sumner looked back at Hooper, his eyes questioning. Then, glancing down at the drunken man, he said, "You must be joking, Captain Hooper?"

Thomas grinned again. "'Fraid not." Without another word, Thomas dragged the unconscious man into a half-sitting position, and Kimball moved to help. The two men heaved the drunken man to his feet, and each looped a limp arm around his neck. The pair half carried, half dragged Seamus back the way they'd come through the maze of rickety boardwalks. Neither man had much to say; the little man was dead weight between them.

The unusual group found the horses without trouble. The moon had risen, and the ribbon of sandy road stretched in both directions. Thomas heaved Pennycuik onto the horse he'd ridden and mounted behind him. Sumner looked up, his eyes still burning with unasked questions. Thomas lifted a hand to ward off the questions.

"Mr. Hooper," Kimball began quietly, but there was a little steel of his own in his voice. "Is this a jest? Do you really think that this man," he patted the matted hair of Seamus, "is the right man to be your Number One at Cape Hatteras Station? Because, if you do, I think that you'd better..." Kimball let his voice trail off as he fought his anger. Thomas wasn't even looking at him, but staring off toward the ocean. The lilt of crickets and frogs had returned to the night, and it was several minutes before either man said a word.

Thomas broke the silence as he stared off into space, his hands fumbling absently at his belt for his pipe and tobacco. "Mr. Kimball," he said in a low voice, "Why do you hire local keepers for your Lifesaving Stations?"

The blaze in Kimball's eyes had began to abate. "Well," Kimball removed his bowler and ran his fingers through his hair. "Local men know the area and the local surf."

Thomas had gotten his pipe lit and turned his eyes down to Kimball. He squinted through the smoke. "Agreed," he spoke around the wooden stem of his pipe. "They also know the local men that'll serve under them."

Sumner nodded, looking up at the mounted man. He couldn't argue with that. Pennycuik started to snore quietly across the horse in front of Hooper.

Thomas looked back out at the horizon. The moon was half full and her reflection danced seductively on the sands and the waves beyond. He removed the pipe from his mouth. "Seamus Pennycuik served under me aboard the *Otter* during the war. He was a capable seaman, and probably would've been first mate had G.W. not served with me." Thomas paused and exhaled toward the stars above before continuing. "We'd been through the lines a half-dozen times with food for more than one port. Speed and stealth were our ally." He gestured to the moon. "As was the moon and the night. One such night, we came across the end of a naval battle off of the coast of South Carolina. There was a foundering ship; she'd taken too many blasts from the Union ironsides to stay afloat much longer... but we'd business at hand, and I ordered the helmsman to pass her by." He patted Seamus on the head. "But not Mr. Pennycuik. He threw a fit. What good were we if we didn't help, he pleaded of me." Thomas looked out at the sea, and Kimball could see him turn his head in the moonlight. "He was right, Mr. Kimball. What good are we if we can help, but choose not to? That's what brought me here."

"So what happened?" Sumner asked quietly.

"Well, there was no arguing with Mr. Pennycuik. We came about and spent the entire night saving her crew." Thomas looked at Kimball again and spoke in a voice barely above a whisper. "Now, Mr. Kimball, isn't that the kind of man that you'd want for your Lifesaving Service?"

It was Sumner's turn to grin, and Thomas saw his teeth beneath the moustache in the darkness. Sumner unhitched his horse from its ground stake, struggling into the saddle. "Well," Sumner asked in a quiet voice, "What are we waiting for?"

Thomas grinned back and turned his mount north, with Kimball following. Nothing. Nothing at all.

CHAPTER 13
August 1878
Cape Hatteras Station, NC

The door of the cookhouse at Cape Hatteras Station smashed open in the early morning light, and a disheveled Seamus Pennycuik burst from within. His red hair caught the morning sun. He was shirtless and had on only one shoe.

"Shanghaied!" Seamus shouted, cursing vehemently. "Bloody Shanghaied!"

The cookhouse was connected to the main station by a small wooden boardwalk, and Seamus staggered off the walk and landed hard on the sand below. Kimball was startled and glanced quickly at Thomas sitting in a chair on the other side of the fire. Thomas didn't look up. He turned his eyes to Jacob, who was squatting next to the fire frying four large eggs in a heavy skillet. Jacob didn't look up either, but Sumner noticed that he switched the skillet to his left hand and shifted his feet so that he faced the newcomer.

Seamus scratched the blotches of red beard on his cheeks and muttered curses and violent threats under his breath. He didn't move from where he'd fallen, but looked with hooded eyes around the small camp in front of the station.

Thomas was reading the newspaper. It was weeks old, but then again few newspapers made their way this far south on the beach. He sighed and turned the page. "Good mornin', Mr. Pennycuik," he said without looking up.

Seamus took his head in his hands and growled, "Wha's so bloody good about it, Cap'n?" He slowly got to his feet. His head was bruised from the night before, but the inside hurt much worse. "May I ask, Cap'n Hooper, where in the bloody hell are we?" he said, his voice thick with contempt.

Thomas folded the paper carefully and placed it in his lap. He took out his pipe and tobacco, packed the pipe, and lit it with a splint from the fire. He blew smoke into the air. Slowly, Thomas took in Seamus Pennycuik from his toes to the top of his head. Kimball smiled inwardly. Seamus straightened under the gaze.

"Mr. Pennycuik," he said quietly exhaling another round of pipe smoke, "where you are is at a crossroads." Thomas drew deeply on the pipe and continued, with smoke drifting out of his nose. "A crossroads in life. I've been given the command of the Cape Hatteras Lifesaving Station, Seamus, and I need you to be my first mate, or as Mr. Kimball from the Lifesaving Service," he indicated Sumner with a nod of his head, "calls it, my Number One. For that duty, you will be paid forty dollars per month, and will put your life at risk in the surf off Cape Hatteras every day between September and April. You may not live out the year." Thomas paused to let that statement sink in. "We will be responsible for hiring and training five additional men in the latest rescue operations. Our task will be saving every man, woman, and child aboard every ship that founders along our six mile stretch of shoreline. We will be operational by the end of August."

Seamus scratched his butt where he'd landed on it, and squinted in the morning light at Thomas. Suddenly, he broke into a devilish grin. "How could I say no to that fine offer, Cap'n?" he laughed. "'Specially the part where I'll be dead within the year."

Thomas smiled and continued to study Seamus. "Is that a yes, Seamus?" he asked innocently.

Seamus cackled with laughter. "Well, Cap," he looked longingly at Jacob's skillet, "hard to make that kind of decision on an empty belly. Could be that I'll need a mite of Jacob's fine breakfast first."

Jacob raised his yellowed eyes to Shamus. "Ye'll eat when the Cap'n says, Scotsman," Jacob growled in warning. He was well acquainted with the Scotsman and his antics.

Seamus grinned at Jacob, then turned and nodded affably to Kimball. Finally, he turned to Thomas. "Well, in that case, I'd guess I'll say yes to the offer, seeing as Jacob won't give up any breakfast 'til you say so, Cap'n." He extended a hand to Captain Hooper and, rising, Thomas shook it firmly.

Thomas gestured to the table where Jacob had set out salted mackerel, fresh pickles, fried eggs, and bacon. He returned Seamus's grin. "Let's have a bite to eat, then, boys."

Kimball eyed Seamus as the man fell to. He sat cross-legged in the sand, leaving the chairs for the other men. Thomas and Jacob chatted idly about the weather and construction of the station. Pennycuik butted into the conversation frequently around mouthfuls of food. He had an opinion on everything, and his opinions were always adamant and rarely correct. Sumner thought it best to steer clear of the little Scotsman; he'd be a tough one for the captain. Hooper could have him.

After their breakfast, Sumner thanked Jacob for yet another fine meal and sat back in his chair. He removed his bowler and raked out his thin hair, waiting to see what came next.

Thomas had lit his pipe and, exhaling, turned an eye to Seamus. "Get yourself cleaned up, Seamus. You stink," he said with a faint smile.

Seamus responded with a quick grin, hopped to his feet and kicked off his one remaining shoe. "Back in a flash, Cap. I think a quick dip'll clear me head." Without a backward glance, he headed down the path toward the beach. As he rounded the building he unhitched his trousers and kicked them into a pile at the corner of the building. Thomas grinned sideways as Sumner's face whitened. Seamus waved over his shoulder and headed across the sand stark naked.

Thomas reopened his paper and returned to his reading. Jacob took the dishes over to the rain barrel set next to the building and gathered Seamus's clothes up as well. Holding them at arm's length, he dropped them into the washbasin and went to work. Sumner was left to his own thoughts, and stared into the fire. This was an odd lot to be sure, but his new keeper certainly wasted no time. At this rate, he'd have the crew within the week.

Seamus returned after more than an hour. His flaming red hair had been raked out, and his clothes were still damp from Jacob's washing. At least he was dressed. He poured a cup of yaupon tea from Jacob's kettle, set on a flat rock next to the fire, and propped himself on the boardwalk between the cookhouse and the nearly completed station. He sipped the tea and winked at Sumner Kimball. Sumner's face reddened as he looked away.

Seamus turned his attention to Thomas. "Well, Cap, what now?" he asked.

Thomas folded his paper and studied the Scotsman again. He nodded with satisfaction. "We'll need five men, Seamus, to complete our crew. They need to be keen of sight and skilled in the surf. We've a month's time, give or take, until we need to be up and running. Any suggestions?"

Seamus studied the sand at his feet as Thomas spoke, and Kimball could almost see the gears turning in his little head. No one spoke for several minutes. At length, Seamus lifted his eyes to Thomas.

"Tha's a tough one, Cap," Seamus said in his thick brogue. "I don' know if the men I'll suggest would be fittin' for government work." He glanced at Kimball.

Thomas snorted, "Well, Seamus, Mr. Kimball let me take you. How strict could he be?"

Seamus cackled at the jibe. "Well said, Cap, well said." He scratched his uneven beard in thought. "Do you remember the Mahigan brothers? How 'bout them?"

Kimball watched the scene unfold. Obviously, Captain Hooper respected the man's opinion.

Thomas smiled around his pipe stem and nodded. "I remember them, Seamus. Good men, both of them." He looked through the pipe smoke at the Scotsman. "How will we find them, though?"

Seamus continued to scratch his splotchy beard. "Last I'd heard they were in fish camp up the Alligator."

Kimball smoothed his moustache apprehensively. "The Alligator River?" he questioned the two men.

Seamus nodded absently. "The same."

Thomas looked at the Scotsman coolly. "Ever been to their camp, Seamus?"

Seamus flashed a quick grin at Captain Hooper. "I have, Cap, but it's been awhile." He squinted with one eye at Thomas. "But I think I can find it."

Jacob snorted in disgust from the washbasin next to the rain barrel, and Thomas grinned broadly at Seamus. "Good, we'll push off in the morning." Thomas turned to Kimball. "You up for another boat ride, Mr. Kimball?"

Sumner looked at Captain Hooper and chewed the edge of his moustache thoughtfully. The work had continued to pile up while he'd been in North Carolina, and he'd yet to catch up. "Maybe one last ride, Captain Hooper. Then, I'll have to leave you men to your own devices." His work with the other stations could wait a bit longer.

CHAPTER 14
August 1878
The Alligator River, NC

Sumner wasn't comfortable. He hadn't been comfortable since they'd left Cape Hatteras Station the day before. He'd taken a seat in the bow of the skiff and had stared sullenly at Thomas and Seamus as they bantered in the stern. He glanced down at his suit. He'd worn it for days and days, and it was showing hard wear. His left cuff was unraveling, and the whole ensemble smelled of dried sweat. He needed a nice bath and a change of clothes.

Sumner turned his head forward and squinted through the morning sun's glare across the water at the edge of the swamp ahead. They'd camped last night on the Banks, in the shadow of Roanoke Island. This morning, Captain Hooper had rigged the small sail and they'd moved inland away from the surf. He grimaced. The swamp looked low and threatening. He'd never been up the Alligator River, but he knew from the charts that the swamp that lay between the sound and the Alligator was the roughest of rough going. The Alligator Swamp ended in the Great Dismal Swamp in Southern Virginia. He looked back at Seamus; he certainly hoped that the man knew where to find these brothers. A man could be lost forever in the twisted black-water labyrinth ahead.

Thomas turned the rudder over to Seamus, and, crouching low, moved to strike the small sail. As he unknotted it from the mast he winked at Sumner.

"How ya holding up, Mr. Kimball?" he asked quietly.

Sumner glanced past Kimball toward Seamus reclining in the stern, one arm draped lazily over the tiller arm. He turned his attention to Captain Hooper and said sourly, "I'm ready to get back to my work. I'm ready to head back to Washington, but, mostly, Mr. Hooper, I'm ready for a bath and ready to sleep on a mattress instead of your damp Carolina ground."

Seamus stifled a chuckle, and Thomas grinned at the superintendent. "Soon enough, Mr. Kimball, we'll pack you off north." He paused and continued to grin. "Soon enough."

Sumner removed his bowler and turned it in his hands. It had been jet black, but now looked dark gray. "Soon enough" couldn't be soon enough.

Thomas gathered the sail and Seamus lifted the tiller, then pulled the long push pole out of its cradle and nodded forward.

"Welcome to the Alligator Swamp, Mr. Kimball," he smiled, delighting in the man's discomfort.

Kimball turned. The massed roots and low trees were as threatening as ever. He swallowed hard as Seamus effortlessly guided the small skiff through the twisted passage. Thomas was unconcerned and worked over the sail. He folded it carefully and stashed it under the middle bench seat of the skiff. He looked up at Kimball and met his eyes.

"No worries, Mr. Kimball. Seamus has spent a good bit of time up this way." Thomas flashed another quick grin. "He'll find the way."

Thomas's confidence was not misplaced, and Sumner was genuinely impressed with the manner in which Seamus poled them through the narrow passages in the swamp. The sunlight was dampened and filtered, and dappled shadows danced on the water and the vegetation on both sides of the small skiff. Sumner could see that the black water below ran with a slight current, and Seamus made slight adjustments with the push pole to take full advantage of the running water.

Thomas spotted the clearing first. It was an open space in the trees ahead on slightly higher ground. "Seamus," he said quietly and pointed.

Seamus grunted in satisfaction and bumped the boat into the bank. It slid softly through the thick marsh grass, and stopped at the beginning of the black earth.

Seamus stowed the push pole and spoke quietly from the stern with a slight smile on his lips, "The Mahigans' fish camp, gentlemen."

Sumner squinted up the bank above the black water of the Alligator with trepidation. He'd visited fish camps up and down the coast. Usually they were active places, with a cluster of small shacks and a pier. This was unlike any that he'd been to. There was no loading shack leaning out over the water, no pier, just a dim opening in the trees with sunlight beyond. His frown deepened. Then he noticed that there were old and new marks from the bows of skiffs or canoes all along the dirt of the bank.

Thomas stepped past Sumner and was the first out of the skiff. He scrambled up the bank. Sumner raised an eyebrow. Hooper was dressed today as he'd been when they'd first met at the Hooper fish house. He wore faded pants rolled to just below the knee, and the thick porpoise-hide belt from which hung his heavy whalebone-hilted knife. As he stepped past, Sumner couldn't help but notice that the heavy thong that held the knife in place had been untied, and that when Hooper stopped his scrambling up the bank, he loosened the knife in its sheath.

Seamus caught his gaze as he stepped from the skiff and said in a soft voice, "Don't worry, Mr. Kimball, Cap'n Hooper just likes to be prepared."

Kimball hurried to catch the other two men as they crossed the bank into the bright sunlight of the clearing beyond. He paused and caught his breath at the top of the embankment. His eyes widened in astonishment. Seamus turned and stepped to his side.

Kimball turned his head to Seamus. "I'd thought Mahigan was a Gaelic name, Mr. Pennycuik."

Seamus grinned and winked. "Nah, Mr. Kimball. Can't have too many bloody lazy Irish or Scots down at your station. Mahigan's an Injun name."

The Mahigan fish camp was a wide clearing. A long shack of sticks with a rounded roof and smoke hole stood on one side of the clearing. Smoke curled from it, and a deer hide door stood open to the daylight. A stack of small barrels stood on one side of the clearing. A wide fire blazed in the center of the small clearing, and next to the fire squatted an ancient Indian woman. Her hair had long since faded from black to white, and was knotted in twin braids down her back. She wore a threadbare homespun dress. Her skin was baked leather, dark brown and seamed with wrinkles. She was smoking fish downwind of the fire on racks built from thick sticks bound with hide strips. She regarded the newcomers with cold gray eyes, and neither rose nor greeted them.

Seamus continued quietly, "Mahigan is the Algonquin word for wolf, Mr. Kimball. The Mahigan family wasn't as fond of the English settlers on this strip of sand as many of their Lumbee cousins. Oh, believe me, they're as American as you or I. Their ancestors shared English blood generations and generations ago, but the Mahigan family chose to remain, in many ways, Indian, while many of the Lumbee chose to become more, shall we say, white."

Sumner removed his bowler and swept his fingers through his hair. The Cape Hatteras station was full of surprises. The old woman continued to regard the men coolly, and spat into the dirt between her bare feet. Sumner and Seamus moved up next to Thomas. Thomas shifted his feet and glanced at Seamus.

"You Sheriff Brinkley's men?" the old woman crooned softly. Her face was expressionless, and her eyes were hard and flat.

Seamus glanced at Thomas and stepped forward hesitantly. "No, ma'am. I'm Seamus Pennycuik; we met a long time back. We're hunting Jon and Charlie. Are they about?"

The woman spat again, and the clot landed squarely on a black ant that was struggling with a bit of fish. She regarded the ant with satisfaction. "Know who you are, Pennycuik. My mind ain't gone, yet." She spoke without looking up from her trapped ant. "Who's the Yank?" She lifted her hard flat gaze and stared directly at Kimball.

Seamus swallowed. "He's Sumner Kimball, with the Lifesaving Service. Not the law, ma'am."

The old woman continued to stare at Kimball and shrugged her thin shoulders. "You say so."

Thomas stepped forward and patted Seamus lightly on the shoulder. He squatted next to the fire across from the old woman. She watched him silently. Thomas opened his pipe pouch and pinched a fingerful of tobacco into the bowl. He held the stuffed pipe out to the old woman. A hint of a smile flitted across her face. She shook her head slightly and pulled her own pipe from the slant pocket on her dress. She locked eyes with Thomas, and reaching over she pinched her own healthy portion of tobacco from Thomas's bag. She rocked back on her heels and lit her pipe with a small flaming stick, then drew deeply and handed the stick to Thomas. Thomas lit his own pipe, and the two regarded each other through the swirl of pipe smoke. Kimball shifted his feet impatiently, and Seamus threw him a hard look.

"Kwe-Kwe, kokomis," Thomas spoke quietly, and blew smoke from his nose.

Sumner questioned Seamus with his eyes, and Seamus whispered softly, "Algonquin, Mr. Kimball."

The old woman smiled at Captain Hooper, and blended her own stream of smoke with his. "You mus' be Cap'n Hooper."

Thomas eyes widened, and the woman chuckled around the stem of her pipe.

"You bees the only white man that I knowed still trolled around talkin' the old tongue." She said. "You all shows up with unusual comp'ny. Here to buy fish?" Her eyes had warmed since the initial glare.

Thomas smiled. Word spread fast on the Banks, but not that fast. "Yes, kokomis, I'm Thomas Hooper. I'm not here to buy fish. I work for the Lifesaving Service, now. I'd like to talk to the boys."

She smoked her pipe and nodded slowly after a long interval. "They's around, Cap'n," she said, waving her hand at the swamp that fell away from the hummock of high ground.

Thomas's brow wrinkled in consternation. "Any idea when they'll return, grandmother?"

She drew deeply on the pipe and shrugged. "Hard to tell, Cap'n."

Seamus grinned sideways at Kimball. Thomas continued to smoke silently; he'd turned his gaze to the strips of fish on the smoking rack.

"Do you think we'll be able to find them, grandmother?" he asked without looking back at her.

The old woman smiled for the first time. Her lips parted, revealing a broken row of uneven teeth. She squinted through the smoke at Thomas. "Cap, don't worry." She glanced at the two men that stood behind Thomas. "I reckon they'll find you." She giggled and patted Thomas on the knee.

Thomas returned her smile with one of his own, and rose to his feet. "Thank you, kokomis. In that case, we'll say goodbye and leave you to your work." He bowed slightly to the woman and turned to join his companions.

She still squatted in the dust, staring up at the captain. Pipe smoke wreathed her ancient head. "Good day, Cap'n Hooper, and good luck."

Seamus caught the old woman's eye and winked in her direction. She sighed heavily and shook her head. Seamus and Sumner turned toward the skiff, ahead of the captain. Thomas caught the two men in a few quick strides and the three scrambled back down the bank toward the skiff.

"I wonder how Congress will react to the hiring of Indians, with the troubles we've been having out west, Captain?" Sumner mused.

Thomas grunted and turned cool eyes to Sumner. "Tell them that we're hiring the best men for the job," he replied sternly. His voice brooked no argument, and Sumner worried at his moustache in silence.

Thomas spoke again as they reached the water's edge, his voice more gentle, "Mr. Kimball, the Mahigan family is Lumbee. The Lumbee have shared roots with English settlers of Roanoke Island for nearly 300 years. There are blond-haired, fair-skinned Lumbee or Croatoan Indians up and down this coast. I don't believe that your official report needs to specify that Charlie and Jon Mahigan are Indians. They're simply men."

Seamus waded out alongside the skiff and stood in the waist-deep water at the stern. "Aye, Mr. Kimball, and good men at that."

Sumner removed his bowler and carefully wiped the sweat from the band inside. He clamped the bowler back on his head and smiled faintly at Captain Hooper. "That bed and bath are sounding better all the time, Captain. I'm out of my depth here."

Seamus grinned at the Superintendent. "That's why you've us, Mr. Kimball. This is our depth." He nodded at Thomas, who stood on the shore at the bow, and chuckled. "I've never seen the water too deep for Cap'n Hooper."

Thomas glanced back toward the small clearing, holding his pipe between clenched teeth he spoke loudly, "Seamus, we sure need to speak with the Mahigan brothers, but it doesn't look like they're here."

The loud tone turned Sumner's head up the bank as well. He glanced furtively at Thomas. He was speaking for effect, but speaking to whom?

Seamus spoke from the stern. "Uh....Captain?" Thomas and Sumner's heads whipped back in his direction. His tone was high and tight.

Sumner's eyes widened in shock. A square built man with dirty blond hair stood dripping in the water over Seamus's right shoulder. His lips were parted in a wide grin, showing a perfect set of white teeth. But the dripping knife that he held under Seamus's chin wasn't smiling. Sumner gasped. The man's black eyes weren't smiling, either. The blade of the knife was pressed directly under Seamus chin, and, for once, the Scotsman's humor had evaporated.

"Ya prob'ly ought to take his head off, Jon." The voice came from directly behind him in the bow, and Sumner fell off the bench and spilled onto the deck of the skiff in surprise.

A thick-shouldered man, square built and shirtless like the other, leaned heavily on the bow. His jet-black, shoulder-length hair dripped with swamp water, and his green eyes glinted with hard humor.

The one called Jon grinned maliciously. His eyes sought Captain Hooper first, and then settled on Kimball. Jon's knife was still pressed upward just below Seamus's chin. "Shoulda done it when I had the chance, I guess, Charlie," Jon stated.

Seamus didn't look worried. Kimball thought this odd; he was petrified. "Not bloody likely, you Indian cur," Seamus sneered. Charlie burst out laughing and Thomas let out a low chuckle. Jon glanced down at the pressure between his legs. Seamus held an open straight razor against his manhood. Seamus continued, stifling a pretend yawn, but his blade didn't waiver. "Not if ya ever plan on having children, Mahigan."

Jon chuckled and took the blade away from Seamus's chin; Seamus grinned widely and closed the straight razor with a flick of his wrist. Charlie's eyes flicked between Thomas and Sumner, a faint smile on his lips.

"Sorry, boys, there's men back in here still waitin' fer the South to rise again," Charlie said, his faint smile lingering. "Cap'n Hooper." He nodded at Thomas and shifted his eyes to Sumner, who lay gasping for breath on the deck of the skiff. Charlie leaned forward and offered a hand to help the man up. "And you'll be Mr. Kimball." He shook the water from his hair.

Sumner took the offered hand, his eyes wide in astonishment. "Sir, how could you possibly have known that?"

Jon smirked from the stern, the corners of his jet-black eyes wrinkled in humor. "Croatoan magic, Mr. Kimball," he whispered.

Seamus roared in laughter, and both Thomas and Charlie grinned. "More like you overheard your grandmother." Seamus slapped Jon a stinging blow across the shoulder. "How've you been, old friend?"

Sumner's eyebrows knotted in consternation. Evidently these men knew each other well. Thomas stepped around Sumner and vaulted into the shallow water with a splash. He and the one called Charlie shared a firm forearm grip and greeting. These were the most perplexing of men.

Sumner resumed his seat in the skiff, but the others started up the bank toward the dying fire. Thomas glanced around and stayed the other men with a half-raised hand.

"My apologies, Mr. Kimball." Thomas canted his head toward the superintendent. "Rude of me." He indicated the two men. "Allow me to introduce Charlie and Jon Mahigan."

Sumner stepped from the skiff into the shallow water and shook hands with the two men in turn. He studied the men in the dappled light filtering through the trees above. Both men had the heavy shoulders and chests of men accustomed to hard labor. The two shared the same deep-set eyes and hooked nose, but their coloring was a deep contrast. Jon's shoulder-length, sandy-blond hair was pulled back in a loose knot at the base of his thick neck, and his eyes were as black as the swamp water that swirled around their feet. Charlie's hair brushed the tops of his broad shoulders like his brother's, but was jet black, and his eyes were the muddy green of the surf. Neither man had whiskers of any kind, and Sumner doubted that that they ever would. He scratched his unshaven jaws beneath his moustache without thinking. Indian blood had its advantages, it seemed.

The small group made their way back up the bank. The grandmother had disappeared. Charlie stoked the fire with small sticks, blowing it back to life. Sumner took a seat on a smooth log at the edge of the small circle, glancing upward at the faltering light. It was impossible to tell what time of day it was through the press of the thick canopy above. Thomas drew his pipe from its pouch and stoked it to life with a few quick puffs, and Jon studied his calloused bare feet. It was Charlie that broke the silence.

"What brings you to the Alligator to talk to us, Cap'n?" he asked. He lay on his stomach, his face only inches from the small fire. He spoke between slow even breaths blown into the nest of flames.

Thomas raised an eyebrow and gave a half nod to Seamus. The smoke from his pipe shrouded his face in the windless swamp. It was time for real business to begin.

Seamus had taken a seat on the ground at the right hand of Thomas and he scratched the splotches of red beard that covered his cheeks before replying. "Well, boys, we've come to offer you a job," Seamus stated quietly.

Charlie looked up from the flames and glanced at his brother out of the corner of his eye. Jon's eyes were riveted on the little Scotsman. "That so," Jon said flatly. There was no question in his voice.

Seamus leaned forward and held Jon in his gaze. "That's right, Jon. It pays forty dollars a month, and found."

Jon's eyebrows shot up, and he looked at his brother in open disbelief. Charlie sat up from the fire. The blaze had caught. He looked at his brother for a long hard moment before replying.

"Seamus," Charlie said, still staring at his brother. "Don' know what you've heard, but we're straight now."

Sumner removed his bowler, raking his fingers through his hair. His eyebrows knit together. Charlie's statement hung in the air like Thomas's smoke. It was a slow beat before Seamus began chuckling aloud. He waved his hand dismissively.

"No, no." Seamus continued chuckling. "Not like that, Charlie. This is honest work, working for the Lifesaving Service."

Sumner frowned at the conversation. Seamus had spoken of money, and the Mahigans evidently thought it to be too much money for honest work. His frown deepened as he rolled Charlie's statement around in his head. He noticed that, despite the fact that they thought it to be dishonest work, they hadn't immediately said no. Sumner turned a glare toward Thomas and found the captain looking at him with a slight smirk.

Thomas spoke for the first time. "Seamus is right, lads. I've agreed to keep the Cape Hatteras Station for the Lifesaving Service this winter. I'm in need of a few brave men that know the Banks and know the surf." Thomas paused for effect before continuing. "Seamus had your names at the top of his list."

The Mahigan brothers looked at Seamus as one, and Seamus threw them a wink. It was Jon that spoke for the pair.

"How will we get paid, Cap'n Hooper?" Jon asked.

Thomas smiled around the stem of his pipe. "Government chit. Federal dollars." His smile evaporated, and he held the men's eyes. "You've my word on that."

Jon and Charlie shared a long look, and the fire crackled in the stillness. Somewhere a loon called out in the swamp.

Charlie smiled and squinted at Keeper Hooper. "Well, Cap'n," he nodded to Seamus, "when do we start?"

CHAPTER 15
August 1878
The Beach at Cape Hatteras, NC

Sumner grinned into the water barrel next to Cape Hatteras Station. He was happy with what he saw. The thin stubble on his cheeks and chin had fallen to the razor, and his hair was neat and combed carefully. He placed the bowler on his head. It was time to return home, and his spirits were high.

Thomas had returned with him from their trip up the Alligator, but Seamus had stayed behind to help the Mahigan brothers get their affairs in order. On return to the station, they'd found that McGowan had completed his work and moved on. The workers had finished the steeply pitched roof in their absence and the outfitting of the interior, down to the wooden framed cots on the second floor for the men. Sumner studied the building carefully and could find no fault in McGowan's men's craftsmanship.

The completed building was twenty feet by forty feet. Its walls and roof were covered with hand-hewn shingles to keep the salt air and storms at bay. Sumner glanced in through the open front door, across the planked hard-wood floor to the wide backdoor that faced the sand and sea. He could envision that door being thrown open by the men of this station, the heavy surf cart being dragged from the first floor out that same wide door, down the ramp and onto the sand below. He pictured the men in their dusky blue uniforms straining against the beach cart on their way to saving lives in the Carolina surf. He smiled again. He was quite pleased.

Jacob had packed up as well, and Hooper was alone with Sumner for the first time. Keeper Hooper came around the corner of the station, and Sumner flashed him a rare grin.

Nothing could derail his capital mood this morning. He hadn't slept on the ground. He'd had the pleasure of a freshly-stropped razor, and Cape Hatteras Station was complete. He anticipated the arrival of the gear for the station within the week. He patted his belly thoughtfully. If only Jacob had still been at the station on their return to fix breakfast for the two men. He hailed the man who would be in charge of the work.

"We're getting there, Keeper Hooper."

Thomas stroked his beard thoughtfully. Sumner would head north today. His report would state that all was nearing readiness at the Cape; Thomas knew that his heavy work lay ahead. He smiled halfheartedly at Kimball, and turned his eyes to the sea in thought. In the distance, a heavy shot boomed out across the ocean, and a bright red flare lit the cloudless morning sky.

"Captain?" Sumner asked. "What, pray tell—"

Thomas patted the Superintendent on the arm. "Not to worry, Mr. Kimball," he said, reading the man's thoughts. "Not what you think." Without another word, Thomas vaulted the low railing that ran around the walkway of the station and strode down the winding path among the salt grass that led to the sea. He was whistling.

Thomas glanced back, lighting his pipe. "C'mon, Mr. Kimball. You're not due at the train station for hours yet. This you've got to see."

Sumner Kimball followed nervously and joined Thomas within a few strides. The two men took the sandy path toward the beach together.

"Sir?" Sumner began.

Thomas cocked an eyebrow at Sumner.

Sumner continued. "The Mahigans." He paused sought for careful words. "They didn't even ask what the job you'd offered entailed before they agreed."

Thomas grinned sideways. "Mr. Kimball, I've a feeling that they have a fairly good idea. But Seamus threw the money at them first. Men like the Mahigans haven't seen forty dollars a month in their lives. To them it's a fortune."

Sumner nodded solemnly. He'd thought as much. "Captain, the pay is high, but the risk is higher."

Thomas chuckled low in his throat. "Agreed, Mr. Kimball, agreed. Don't be concerned, though. There aren't many men that make a living on this barren stretch of sand that don't risk their lives on a daily basis. The nature of the beast, so to speak." The two men had reached the beach, and Thomas pointed past the crashing waves. "Case in point, Superintendent."

Sumner's eyes followed his outstretched finger. Four lapstrake dories bobbed in the surf beyond the breakers and sandbars. The more distant pair sat out nearly two hundred yards. Sumner could see several oarsmen and, even at that distance, could make out the line of a light net that stretched across the thousand feet of water between them. The net ran parallel with the beach. A man in the nearer of the two boats was standing and frantically waving a large red flag on a long pole. The second set of boats was closer in; Sumner could see the drag marks in the sand between a pair of heavy wagons and the surf, where the fourteen-foot boats had been launched. Two men squatted in the shade of the wagons, and the draft horses were picketed out in the salt grass beyond. The closer set of boats was deploying another net perpendicular to the first.

Sumner could hear snippets of the shouts and curses of the boatmen. He glanced at Thomas, who was now smoking calmly, his eyes squinted seaward.

Thomas removed his pipe from the corner of his mouth and spat in the sand. "Porpoise hunters, Mr. Kimball," he said by way of explanation.

Sumner shaded his eyes against the glare of the morning sun on the water.

Thomas continued, "Late in the season for 'em." He glanced sidelong at Sumner and grinned at the man's perplexed expression. "I've sailed the Atlantic Seaboard from Maine to

Florida, Mr. Kimball, but, as far as I know, there's only one active porpoise fishery, and this is it." He pointed at the boatman waving the flag. "The shot we heard and the flare were sent up by that flagman there. He'd spotted a waif."

Thomas turned his head to Sumner and cast him another sidelong grin. "A waif's a large group of porpoises, Mr. Kimball," he said, answering the unasked question. He pointed at the other outlying dory. "Those two boats stretch out a thin net to force the fish in toward the beach."

As they watched, the furthest out of the two nearer boats was rowing quickly, wheeling the net anchored on its counterpart in toward shore. Sumner could see the splashes of the frantic dolphins caught in the net's embrace.

Thomas knocked his ashes from his pipe against his weathered bare foot and continued, "Then those two boats in the near surf drive the waif in to the beach with the heavy net." He paused and winked at Sumner. "Then, the heavy work begins."

The two closest boats surfed the waves onto the beach with practiced skill. A cheer went up from the men on the outer boats as they gathered their net and began to follow. The surf at the breakers roiled with the dolphins below, as the crews from the two beached boats began hauling the heavy net.

Sumner looked toward the two wagons. The two men that had been lounging in the shade were on their feet. They were both stripped to the waist in the summer heat. A large knife flashed in the sunlight as it was tucked into a belt. The boatmen had hauled the net into the shallow water, and it writhed with porpoises. Big porpoises. Some of them would go six feet or more.

Three of the boatmen moved into the knee-deep surf and casually shoved thick fingers into the blowholes of three dolphins, then dragged them onto the beach. The dolphins' keening screams added punctuation to the shouts and laughs of the porpoise men. The two men from the wagons began the killing and skinning just above the surf line, and blood ran in rivers down the sand back into the ocean.

Sumner frowned and looked at Thomas, but it was Thomas who spoke. "Gruesome business, eh, Mr. Kimball?"

Sumner replied, his frown etching hard lines around his moustache, "You can say that again, Captain Hooper."

Thomas chuckled softly, relishing the man's discomfort. "Let me introduce you to the man that runs these oilers, Mr. Kimball." Thomas lifted his hand in greeting, and one of the boatmen returned the wave.

Sumner followed Thomas down the beach. The man who had waved stepped away from the crew and started toward Thomas and Sumner. The three met up at the high-tide line.

"Cap'n Hooper," the man said, extending a hand in greeting.

Thomas took the offered hand and the two shared a long firm grip. "How've you been, Ashton?" Thomas inquired pleasantly.

Ashton growled through a nest of whiskers. "The fishin's shit, Cap, but ain't no help to complain."

Sumner studied the fisherman. He wore a thin cotton shirt that was open at the neck, revealing a chest of thick white hair on his deeply tanned chest. He was narrow of waist, and his voice grated like white surf grated on sand. The man nodded in Kimball's direction, but there was no friendliness in his pale blue eyes. He wore a broad-brimmed straw hat; a few sprouts of white hair peeked from beneath the shady brim. His chin whiskers were long but evenly trimmed. Tobacco juice had stained the right edge of his beard, a slash of brown on a sea of white.

Thomas nodded his head and indicated Sumner. "Ashton, this is Mr. Kimball of the Lifesaving Service."

Kimball stepped forward and extended a hand of his own in greeting. "Good day, sir."

Ashton spat in the sand, and glanced at the man's outstretched hand. He didn't shake. "Goddamn Yankee," he rolled the wad of tobacco in his square jaws and spit a stream of brown juice into the sand between them. He turned cold eyes to Thomas. "You's trollin' with unusual friends, Cap," he stated flatly.

Sumner was taken aback and let his hand fall to his side. Thomas's green eyes snapped with quick humor at the Mainer's reaction. He turned his head to Ashton. "True enough, Ash, but you see, he's my boss, now."

Ashton had turned his back to Sumner, and now his eyes widened in shock. "Hell you say, Tom. These government bastards convinced you to run a station?" Ashton's eyes narrowed. "Which station, Tom?" he asked softly.

Thomas grinned at the older man, but it was Sumner that spoke from behind him. "The Cape Hatteras Station."

Ashton didn't turn to Sumner; he turned his head and spat another stream of juice onto the beach. "Didn't ask nothin' of you, Yankee." His eyes held Thomas. "Cape Station, Tom?"

Thomas continued to grin. "That's right, Ash."

Ashton spat again and muttered a curse under his breath. "I'll be forever damned."

Thomas look sobered and he met the older man's eyes. "Somebody had to do it, Ashton."

Ashton squinted. "Reckon that's right. G.W. running the boat and the business?"

Thomas nodded, "He is, Ash. Process the hides, and we'll ship like always."

Sumner cleared his throat. He didn't like being so obviously ignored. Ashton ignored the hint and kept his back squarely to the superintendent.

"Who's yer crew, Cap?" Ashton asked. He turned his head to the men working on the beach.

Thomas let his eyes follow Ashton's as the processing of porpoise continued on the beach below. "Got a few; Pennycuik's my Number One. He's north getting the Mahigan brothers."

Thomas glanced at the man out of the corner of his eye. "Still need a few though, Ash."

Ashton watched his men, and scratched his chin under his thick whiskers. "Take my man, Elijah, Tom. There ain't a stronger man in the surf along the beach."

Sumner frowned thoughtfully. The old man talked of "his man Elijah" like he owned him. Thomas caught the frown and the corners of his eyes wrinkled in silent humor.

Ashton took a step toward the men and whistled a loud sharp blast. One of the men looked up, and Ashton pointed toward the lone boat that held the back side of the net just past the breakers. He jerked a thumb in toward the beach. The man nodded, and waded into the surf. Sumner could hear him yelling to the boat, but couldn't make out the words.

Ashton nodded at Thomas, and Thomas smiled again at the older man. "Ash, I don't want to hurt your crew...but I sure appreciate it."

Ashton shot a brown stream of tobacco juice through broken teeth onto an unoffending ghost crab that was skittering past. The crab took the brown blast and lifted its claws defensively before scuttling into a nearby hole. "I'll need 'im back after the stormy season, Cap, but it'll be May afore we porpoise agin." He pointed to the dory that was riding the surf onto the beach. "Tha's 'im there, Cap. I'll tell 'im."

Sumner's eyes followed Ashton's outstretched arm. One dory had stayed at sea while the others had beached to help in the harvest. His thoughtful frown deepened. The other dories had a crew of four men. The boats, after all, had four oars, and each man tended one. The boat that slid effortlessly in toward the beach only had two men aboard. Sumner noticed the large red flag that he'd seen them waving earlier, sticking out past the gunwale of the small boat. The man that had been waving it tended a small tiller in the rear of the boat. The boat was equipped with an enormous single set of oars. At these oars rowed one of the largest men that Sumner had ever seen. The boat surfed the final waves and grounded on the beach.

Ashton nodded again to Thomas, and the two men started toward the beached boat. The flagman joined the men working, and the oarsman stepped from the dory onto the sand, where he stretched his back. Sumner followed at distance and studied the oarsman.

His skin was slick with sweat, jet black in the morning sunlight. Sweat beaded his bald head, and he windmilled his enormous arms to shake out any cramps. The man must have stood six-and-a-half feet tall, and gone well over three hundred pounds. Sumner gawked openly at the man's bulk. His arms were knotted with thick muscle, and his chest was broader than a wooden barrel. The heavy muscles of his shoulders ended in a thick, short neck. He was stripped to the waist, and his homespun pants ended well short of his bare feet.

"'Lijah," Ashton said flatly. "This here is Captain Hooper. I'm givin' ya to 'im 'til we porpoise again in the spring."

The immense black man known as Elijah kept his eyes cast down at the beach, and didn't look up. "Yes, suh," he growled. His voice was an abyss, deep and dark.

Ashton turned to Thomas and nodded. That was that. He started toward the men that were working down the beach, but Thomas stopped him with a light touch on the arm.

Thomas looked Elijah up and down. When he stood close to the man, he had to crane his neck to look up into his face. Elijah regarded him warily from beneath his heavy brow.

Thomas spoke softly. "Elijah, I'm Thomas Hooper, the keeper of the Cape Hatteras Lifesaving Station. I've work for you this winter if you're interested."

Ashton stared at Thomas with his cold blue eyes. "Cap, I already gave 'im to ya for the winter."

Thomas looked at Ashton. His usual humor was gone. Sumner cocked an inquisitive eyebrow.

Thomas spoke evenly. "I'll need to hear it from him, Ash."

Ashton rolled the tobacco in his jaw. There was a long moment of silence as the two men faced each other, but it was Elijah that spoke.

"S'all right with me, Mistah Hooper. I'll do as Mistah Ashton says. I'm a good nigger, suh," Elijah rumbled in his deep voice.

Thomas held Ashton with his eyes, but spoke to Elijah. "Don't need good niggers, son; I need good men."

Ashton's face grayed and he was frowning deeply at Thomas, but he held his peace.

Elijah lifted his head, cracking a kink in his neck by rolling his ponderous head around on his shoulders. He grinned over white teeth. "Well, suh, I be a good man, too."

Ashton snorted, and turned on his heel. Without a backward glance at Thomas, he strode across the beach toward his other men. Thomas watched him go and glanced at Sumner.

"Old habits die hard down here, Mr. Kimball." Thomas smiled at the superintendent.

"So I see," Sumner muttered. He felt a little ill.

Elijah spoke again, and Thomas turned his head up to the towering black man. "Ain't got nothin', suh. An' I just as soon not go on home with Mr. Ashton, now. Where's can I stay?"

Thomas extended his hand to the big man, and the two shook. Keeper Hooper was a big man, but his hand disappeared under the dinner-plate-sized hands of the black man.

"What's your whole name, Elijah?" Thomas stared up into the man's black eyes.

"Coal," the black man rumbled, "Elijah Coal. Elijah like the Good Book says, and Coal 'cause Mr. Ashton says that I's black as coal."

"Well, Elijah Coal," Keeper Hooper smiled, "Welcome to the crew of Cape Hatteras Station."

And then there were five.

CHAPTER 16
Late August 1878
Cape Hatteras Station, NC

Thomas felt the pull of morning on his dream, and the smell of freshly brewed yaupon tea forced his eyelids open. He lay still, taking in the morning sounds, locating the men by the noises from the open stairway that led to the lower level of Cape Hatteras Station.

The fresh tea could only mean that Elijah was at work on breakfast. The strong scent wafted in from the window thrown wide to the cookhouse below. The big man had joined them less than a week before, but he'd immediately taken over the cooking for the men. They'd had to push the table back from the cook stove so that he could bend down to tend it. Thomas had remonstrated with him at first, thinking that Elijah had adopted cooking because of his color. Elijah had set him straight. He'd learned to cook long ago, because there weren't many that could hold up to the task of preparing food for his giant appetite.

Thomas looked at the opposite set of windows facing the ocean. The sky was gray to the east. Daylight wasn't far away. He swung his legs over the side of the cot and stretched in the salty breeze that blew between the opposing windows. The breeze carried the swift thud and crack of the Mahigan brothers. On their arrival with Seamus, they'd taken on the arduous task of locating and splitting firewood for both the kitchen and the station. Tough work on a beach with no trees, but necessary.

He craned his ears, and could hear the soft lilt from Seamus as he tended the heavy draft horses in the stable across the sandy yard from the cookhouse. The service was to start providing horses this year up and down the coast. Thomas scratched his beard thoughtfully. Their horses must be with the rest of their undelivered gear. He'd sent a runner to Jacob on Ocracoke, who'd had a set brought for their needs.

Thomas slipped a loose cotton shirt over his head, and, tamping a pinch of tobacco into the bowl, lit his pipe with a match struck on the wooden floorboards. The men were still settling in. The season's official start was September 1, so they still had some time. He shook his head in consternation and blew a cloud of smoke toward the vaulted ceiling of the men's quarters. He still needed to fill two spots for his crew to be complete. He needed to start training the men that he did have immediately. The station's gear was incomplete; it had been arriving in fits and starts for the last week. He had his surfboat. It was a thing of beauty; the self-bailing variety that was rarely seen. Of course, he grinned to himself, he hadn't received any oars. He'd received his beach cart and much of the gear to complete the beach apparatus, but his Lyle gun seemed to be lost in transit. The Lyle gun was paramount to their lifesaving efforts, and if the manuals were truthful, could heave a line up to 600 yards. He doubted big Elijah could throw the line six hundred yards if they didn't get their gun. He shook his head.

Thomas glanced at his shoes at the foot of the bed and grinned inwardly. Rose would have his hide, even now, for not stamping into his heavy boots. But Rose was on Ocracoke. He made the decisions now. With a sigh, he rose from the cot and padded softly down the stairs to the work that had yet to be done.

The men were finishing the morning's chores when the supply wagon clattered into the wide yard between the buildings. Thomas slapped Elijah on the back and stood back from the axles of the beach cart they'd been greasing.

"Looks like we'll have a shot at this after all, Eli," Thomas exclaimed.

Elijah looked at the wagon apprehensively. They'd been waiting on the Lyle gun for the past week. Seamus had had the Mahigans place a fake mast, complete with rigging, in the sand between the station and the sea in preparation for the cannon's arrival. It looked like they'd have a chance to try the gun out after all.

Seamus and the Mahigans rounded the corner of the building, drawn to the long hail from the teamster aboard the wagon seat. The small crew exchanged glances, and Thomas stood back puffing his pipe. It was Seamus that spoke.

"All right, lads. Don't just stand there. Jon and Charlie, grab the crates with the kit," Seamus ordered. "Eli, have a go at lifting the cannon crate off the wagon."

The men jumped to the work at hand, and Thomas smiled around his pipe stem. The men had taken to Seamus's leadership like ducks to water. The little Scotsman was working out quite well. Elijah swung the heaviest crate from the wagon with little strain, and Thomas saw the Mahigans exchange a look as they struggled with the smaller crates. Thomas drew a hammer from inside the open door to the main building, where it had been leaning against the wall, and strode down the porch stairs to join his men. He handed the hammer to Eli, who nonchalantly smashed the lid from the wooden crate. The sides fell away under Eli's blows, and the squat cannon gleamed in the sunlight.

The Lyle gun wasn't large. It was squat and ugly, and looked more like a mortar then a true cannon. Seamus hopped from one foot to the other and winked at Thomas excitedly. The Mahigans glanced at each other.

Thomas saw the exchanged look and patted Jon on the shoulder. "You boys ever seen one of these?"

The Mahigans shook their heads as one.

"Gentlemen, let me introduce you to Cape Hatteras Station's most important crew member..." Thomas bowed with a flourish before continuing. "This cannon was designed by David Lyle, and can shoot a line nearly a third of a mile. So we can get a grapple out to a ship without even getting our feet wet." Thomas grinned in spite of himself. "Neat, huh?"

Seamus grinned through his patchy red beard. "Well, lads, let's drag her around and see what she's got. Eli..." He pointed at the gun, and turned to Thomas.

Thomas continued to smile. Nothing like a new toy to get the boys fired up, especially if the new toy involved gunpowder. Elijah swung the gun up and carried it around toward the sea. His bare feet left deep indentations in the soft sand from his bulk combined with the bulk of the gun cradled in his massive arms.

Seamus returned Thomas's grin. "C'mon, Cap. Let's have a go at the pole. We might need to use this bugger in a couple weeks."

Thomas followed Seamus to where the Mahigan brothers had brought the crate with the powder and instructions. They held out the paper instructions to Thomas; they couldn't read.

Taking the instructions from Charlie's outstretched hand, Thomas spoke around the stem of his pipe. "Easy now, boys. Let's handle this right."

Seamus looked up from crouching over the gun and spoke quietly. "Cap's right, lads. We've never done it, but let's figure this is a test."

The men looked from Thomas to Seamus, and then at each other. They'd never done any of this before. Seamus straightened and pulled his red hair back into a tight ponytail.

"Ship ashore!" Seamus screamed his face red with effort. "Let's move it, now, now, now! To the beach cart!" He turned and sprinted up the ramp and into the building. The men hesitated a moment, then raced to catch up with the screaming Scotsman.

Thomas stood off to the side, smoking thoughtfully. He could hear Seamus screaming at the top of his lungs, positioning the men around the beach cart. The heavy wheels turned in the building with a screech from their recent oiling, and the large cart rumbled down the ramp and into the sand. The sand grabbed the wheels for a moment, and Charlie Mahigan crashed his ribs into the backside of the cart at the hesitation. He groaned through teeth clenched in effort. Seamus and Jon were straining at the heavy sides of the cart, and Seamus continued a steady stream of orders and curses. The cart inched forward in the heavy sand, and might have stayed bogged down had it not been for the mighty strength of Elijah. The man picked up the tongue of the wagon, his feet churning the soft sand. The heavy muscles of his back and shoulders stood out in stark relief from the effort. The wagon moved forward. Charlie recovered and leaned into the rear of the wagon, and through the strength of four it rolled toward the cannon. Thomas studied the crashing surf and grimaced at the stiff crosswind. This would be interesting.

Seamus grabbed the box that was stuffed with line, carefully looped and wrapped around a series of pegs in an effort to avoid tangles: the faking box. He promptly overturned the box in his haste, and the carefully coiled line slopped out sideways onto the sand below. Jon Mahigan dropped the first powder charge into the sand and grabbed a second from the crate he'd just hauled from the front of the building. Charlie found the grapple shot buried in the same box, and spilled the contents of the crate onto the sand in an effort to disengage it from its packing place. Elijah stood back, hard lines of worry etching his face. He had no idea what to do next, and Seamus kicked him square in the behind as he sprinted by toward the cannon.

"Get the bloody gun in position, you big bastard," Seamus roared, his face matching his hair.

Elijah stepped forward and grabbed the cannon, accidentally butting Jon in the chest as he swung it up to carry it forward. Jon staggered back and tripped over the tongue of the beach cart, toppling into the heavy sand.

"Enough," Thomas roared into the stiff wind from the side, and the men stopped thrashing about immediately. Seamus was cursing in a half mutter, and Jon had found his feet. He bent over and rubbed his calf, sore from the cart tongue. Elijah blinked hard and squatted under the weight of the heavy gun. He hadn't set it down in the sand after the keeper's order.

Thomas studied the men in the hot sun, but no one had the courage to meet his eyes. The chuckle low in his throat turned into a guffaw. Seamus stopped cursing with a giggle of his own, and soon the five men of Cape Hatteras Station were rolling in the sand. Tears from laughter rolled down the cheeks of Big Elijah, as he dropped the cannon into the sand and rubbed his large backside where Seamus had given him a boot. After several minutes the laughter died down, and the men sobered.

Thomas relit his pipe with a match struck on the wooden ramp of the station and smiled broadly at the men. "Well, boys, I think that we might need a little practice," he snickered around the stem of his pipe. "Let's get this mess sorted out and give the gun a try, at least."

Seamus went to the faking box, and with Jon's help, began to sort out the tangled six hundred yards of line. The two worked diligently on rewrapping the line around the pegs in the faking box. Elijah joined Charlie in searching the sand for the dropped powder charge, and the two men made an effort at sorting out the wooden crate so that the grapple shot was on top, affording easy access.

"We ready, Seamus?" Thomas called. He studied the wind again blowing across the beach, and sized up the crew.

The four surfmen stood in a small semicircle around the rear of the gun, and Seamus answered the question. "As ready as we're like to get, Cap."

Thomas grinned sideways at the response. "I've got a dollar that says we aren't even close." He squinted at the mast that stood in the sand in the distance.

Charlie said, "I won't take that bet, Cap. The damned thing's pointed in the right direction, but none of us have ever shot anything like this." He gestured toward the squat Lyle gun.

Thomas continued to smile and, stepping forward, ignited the charge of powder. He stepped swiftly back and the men covered their ears. The cannon belched in a roar of gray smoke, and the grapple soared toward the mast. The line that had been carefully coiled on the pegs of the faking box sizzled off the beach, trailing the shot. Thomas studied the arc and nodded slightly. It looked good, but they missed by nearly fifty yards.

Seamus raised a bushy red eyebrow. "Well," Thomas remarked, "First shot. Wind really pulled on the extended line. Let's have another go."

The next shot missed by an even wider margin, and Seamus was cursing in earnest by the sixth shot. The Mahigans had retreated to the ramp, and Elijah continued to coil line time after time with the faking box. Hours passed, and Thomas's shirt bore heavy sweat stains around the armpits and back.

Finally, Thomas turned to the muttering Seamus. "Damnable thing, Seamus. We'd better get this figured out." He dug for tobacco and stuffed his pipe, squatting next to the little cannon.

Seamus's face was bright red, and he'd cursed so much that his throat was dry and his voice raspy. "We need a man who knows this kind of thing," he muttered, without meeting Thomas's eyes.

Thomas blew smoke and looked out past their makeshift mast across the open sea. "And fast, Seamus, we've got only weeks to go."

"Right you are, Cap." Seamus studied Thomas intently. "Might know a lad." He glanced at Elijah winding the line. "Don't know if he's the man fer us though, Cap."

Thomas returned the Scotsman's look and spoke around the stem of his pipe. "Why's that, Seamus? The money's damn strong."

Seamus shrugged. "We'll have a go in the morning, Cap." He paused and added cryptically, "Ain't the money, it's the company."

CHAPTER 17
Late August 1878
The Pamlico Sound, NC

Daylight found Seamus and Thomas moored just off a small snip of land jutting into the sound. Seamus had woken Thomas long before light, and the two had slipped out of the station before the other men had begun to stir. Thomas had asked no questions of the Scotsman. Captain McGuire had taught him long ago that the answers would come soon enough, and that patience was the key.

The sound was flat in the predawn light, and the shore crowded close to their bow. An enormous raft of ducks spun slowly on the water, no more than one hundred yards away. Down the shore some of the first Canada geese of the season hadn't begun their morning honking, but their slight murmuring said that they soon would.

Thomas whispered to Seamus, not wanting to break the morning's stillness. "All right, Seamus. You've sure piqued my curiosity." He breathed the words between short puffs on his pipe.

Seamus didn't answer, but screwed his eyes and gazed into the distance. Visibility was increasing by the minute. Then he pointed silently and grinned. Thomas saw his teeth pale against the shadows of his face and followed the direction of Seamus's finger to see... nothing. He glanced sidelong at Seamus and squinted into the semi- darkness.

Seamus breathed an answer to the unspoken question. "Sixty yards off the ducks, Cap, atween the ducks and the shore."

Thomas followed these directions and sought out anything in the general area. Then he saw it. A slight disturbance in the water. It was creeping slowly toward the ducks. It looked to be a piece of driftwood, but Seamus was grinning widely.

Flame leapt from the driftwood when it was twenty yards from the ducks, and the ducks exploded from the water in frantic flapping amidst terrified chatter. Dozens never moved again on their own, and more than one turned in slow, crippled circles. A man stood up in the water next to the driftwood, and Seamus gave him a long hello. The man lifted an arm in greeting and moved out among the dead ducks. Seamus grinned again at Thomas and stood, pushing the skiff toward the man.

Thomas exhaled a stream of smoke and returned Seamus's grin in the morning light. "Had me wondering there, Seamus. Market hunter, eh?"

Seamus chuckled and pushed the boat closer. "'S right, Cap. Said you needed someone that knowed cannons. Well, nobody around knows cannons like Sparrow Gray, Cap."

Thomas rubbed his whiskered chin with the back of his hand. His eyes flickered toward the man gathering his harvest. "Know the name, Seamus, but don't know the man."

Seamus pushed them forward. His eyes sought the sandbars hidden beneath the still surface. "You know the type, Cap. He's a Hatteras man, born and raised. Fought with our side during the war... Manly's Battery, First North Carolina Artillery. Took some shrapnel at Gettysburg, came home, been market hunting ducks ever since."

Thomas nodded. The tale was familiar. Similar stories were written up and down the coast in the South—and the North. Thomas stoked his pipe. At least the man had lived.

"How many'd he get, you figure?" Thomas asked, scanning the floating ducks.

Seamus smiled. "Quite a few, Cap. He's shooting a cannon gun of his own design. Got a barrel must be as big around as your arm. I think that his record's something like eighty-nine with a single shot."

Thomas whistled softly. That was a lot of ducks. "The driftwood, that was to keep him hidden from the flock, and I suppose the gun's mounted on it."

Seamus nodded. "Still warm enough for that, Cap. Another month or two and he'll switch to a sink box or something."

Seamus turned his attention to the wading man as they pushed close. "Whatcha say there, Sparrow?"

Sparrow Gray stood in the waist-deep water. A large burlap sack bulging with ducks floated behind him. He was a lean, hard man with a knotted, graying black beard. His hair was cut unevenly by unsteady hands, probably his own. His eyes were dark under a heavy brow. Thomas noticed that his left ear was a bunched mass of angry red scar. The man turned his good ear to Seamus.

"Huh?" Sparrow asked.

Seamus rolled his eyes and spoke more loudly. "Said hello, Sparrow, that's all."

The man glanced at the pair and nodded. He didn't say hello. He didn't verbally acknowledge the two at all. He went about gathering up his remaining kill. One mallard had a good bit of life left, and Sparrow grabbed the bird by the neck and flipped it in a short semi-circle, breaking its neck, and stuffed it in the bag. Sparrow spat derisively and waded over to their boat.

"Whatcha want, Pennycuik?" Sparrow demanded, his mouth set in a firm unyielding line.

"Well, Sparrow, like to have a talk with you," Seamus answered leaning on the push pole. "Me and Captain Hooper, that is."

Sparrow nodded gravely to Thomas, and turned his attention back to Seamus. "Throw my ducks aboard. I'll wade ashore and meet ya."

Seamus smiled crookedly and heaved the two burlap sacks aboard the small skiff. He nodded to Sparrow and pushed toward shore. Thomas raised an eyebrow at Seamus.

Seamus continued to smile. "Deaf as a post on the left side, Cap, but he knows guns and he knows cannons."

Thomas smiled to himself. The man seemed a likely candidate for their Cape crew. Kimball's last words echoed in Thomas head, and his grin broadened. "Keeper Hooper," he'd said, "so far you've hired a drunken Scotsman, a pair of Indian outlaws, and a nigger; I sure hope you know what you're doing." Thomas chuckled at the memory. At least this one was white.

The small skiff touched the bank, and the man named Sparrow waded after them in the shallow water. Seamus heaved the twin sacks of ducks out of the skiff and stacked the two bundles on the shoreline. The sun was beginning to come up, and Thomas and Seamus squatted in the shade of a twisted live oak on the sandy beach and waited on the waterman. Mr. Gray waded out of the water, drawing a piece of cloth from a sack next to the duck bags. Without a word to the two men he proceeded to towel the water from his feet, then pulled on his square-toed boots.

Seamus and Thomas exchanged a glance and waited in silence. The raft of geese down the shore had taken flight at the blast of the heavy gun. They honked loudly as they returned and splashed to a landing further down the shore.

Finally the man turned to Thomas and Seamus and questioned them with a slight frown, "Well?"

Seamus shot a look at Thomas and rose to his feet. Forging ahead he said, "Sparrow, I'd like to introduce..." His voice trailed off. The man's attention had become fixed on the gaggle of geese up the shoreline. He started to speak again, but Sparrow held up his hand for silence. After a moment he dropped his hand and turned his good ear to Seamus.

"Go, on," Sparrow said.

Seamus completed his thought as if there'd been no interruption, "Thomas Hooper with the Lifesaving Service." He indicated Thomas with a sweep of his hand.

Thomas rose with Seamus and extended his hand in greeting. Sparrow briefly gripped the extended hand and shrugged indifferently.

"So," Sparrow stated flatly.

Thomas grinned in spite of himself. Typical Outer Banker.

Sparrow met Thomas's eyes, and said, "Don' figure you bucks come out here to see me kill some ducks." He turned veiled eyes to Seamus. "What is it, Pennycuik?"

Seamus flicked his eyes to Thomas, and at the man's slight nod, continued, "I've been telling the cap'n here that you're the best man around with a small cannon, and, well," Seamus nudged the stuffed burlap sacks with his bare toe, "we're seeing some proof of that very fact this morning."

Sparrow squinted one eye at Seamus as if trying to divine his intent. He spoke guardedly, "You're right, Scotsman, I'm the best man, but 'why would that be of any matter to our good Captain Hooper here?"

Seamus grinned crookedly. "Well, Sparrow, we're in need of a man with just that talent."

Sparrow barked a hard laugh and spat through uneven teeth into the marsh grass. "That so?" His thick eyebrows furrowed together in a knot of black and gray.

Thomas spoke, "It is, Mr. Gray."

Sparrow broke his cold eyes from Seamus and turned them on Thomas. "Not interested, Cap. Lotsa men know cannons, lotsa men fought in the war, go find another pigeon." Without another word, he swept one of the sacks of duck from the beach up onto his back.

Thomas frowned, glancing at Seamus. Seamus winked at Thomas and scooped up the second sack of dead ducks. "Lead off, Sparrow," Seamus grunted under the heavy load. "By the way, what'll these ducks bring, Sparrow?" he asked innocently.

Sparrow glared at Seamus. "'Bout ten cents each, Pennycuik. Leave that un, I'll come back for it." He looked Pennycuik up and down with distaste before continuing, "Ain't the money, Pennycuik. It's the freedom. I hunt when I want and kill what I want. Better 'n takin' some gov'ment job with the damn Lifesaving Service." He bared his teeth in an unfriendly grin.

Thomas said, "Well, that may be, Mr. Gray. Wasn't too long ago I was telling myself the same thing."

Sparrow swung the bag off his thin shoulder and cocked his head to one side. Thomas smiled. At least the man was listening.

Thomas continued, "I felt I'd done my part during the war, and I wasn't all that excited by the prospect of becoming a government man."

Sparrow nodded slowly. Now the man was making sense. "So why do it, Cap'n?"

Thomas shook his head in reflection, "Can't really put it into words, Mr. Gray." He squinted in the man's own style back at him and changed the subject. "Seamus told me you fought up North during the war. I'd make a bet that you picked up that ear at Gettysburg?"

"Yep," Sparrow replied flatly.

"Well, Mr. Gray," Thomas asked, "Tell me about the march north."

Sparrow's eyes narrowed, but he shrugged. "Cain't see what that's got to do with anything."

"Just curious, is all. I spent most of the war at sea, but I've heard that the march up through Virginia and Maryland was brutal. Nobody below the Mason-Dixon line had been spared on Sherman's march toward Charleston, and I mean nobody; women raped and killed...children burned to death. A wicked, wholesale loss of life.... That's what I heard, at least."

Sparrow had been nodding throughout the keeper's speech. "True enough, Cap'n. War seems to breed wickedness in men. I saw...such things," Sparrow cleared his throat. "Suffice to say, Cap'n I still see those things in the quiet of the night."

"Me, too, Mr. Gray, me, too." Thomas replied quietly. "I'd guess that's the reason I took the job. I've seen enough death to last ten lifetimes, Sparrow. It feels pretty good to be focused on saving lives instead. When they came to me there wasn't anyone else, and I knew that I could do the job. I guess because I knew that I could, well..." Thomas paused. The gaggle of geese down the shore had moved closer, and the morning was still but for their murmuring. "Because I could..." He met Sparrow's eyes. "...I should."

Sparrow met Thomas eyes with a direct gaze of his own and nodded solemnly. "So I reckon that you're sayin' is that you ain't got nobody else, and that if I know that I can, I should, too, like you or Pennycuik there." Sparrow cracked a slight grin and took a last wistful look at the geese before turning his eyes back to Keeper Hooper. "Might feel pretty good saving lives instead of taking them, Cap'n."

Thomas Hooper smiled inwardly.

CHAPTER 18
Late August 1878
Cape Hatteras Station, NC

It was almost supper time the next day when Sparrow first laid eyes on Cape Hatteras Station. Seamus was shirtless and caulking the new surfboat. The Mahigan brothers were shaking out the station's full complement of nautical flags, which had just arrived. The flags were an important part of their duty to signal the ships that passed within sight of shore. Many a cautious captain had had the seaman atop the crow's nest translate the flags to determine sea conditions and predicted weather.

Thomas was deep in thought, bent over the brand-new telegraph key that had been installed earlier in the day. Thomas cursed softly as he reviewed the instructions, wishing that he'd had the foresight to hire a man who knew the key. Elijah was working over supper for the men, and the sharp smell of hams curing in the smokehouse wafted on the evening breeze.

Sparrow dropped his kit on the boardwalk and studied Thomas, hard at work in the dim interior. It was several minutes before Thomas noticed the man.

Thomas caught sight Sparrow out of the corner of his eye and smiled around the stem of his pipe. "Evening, Mr. Gray." He stood and stretched his back from leaning over the small desk. "Welcome to Cape Hatteras Station."

"Hmpf," Sparrow grunted in return. "Well, where's it at?"

Thomas's brows knitted in confusion. "Sir?" he questioned.

"This gun of yours, Keep. If y'all need me to shoot it, I'd better have a look." Sparrow dug his own pipe out from the pouch on his belt. Thomas caught a brief hint of humor in the man's hard dark eyes, but his lips were set in a firm line through his dark beard.

Sparrow continued, "We did say that if we could..." He paused in the dim light and lit his pipe with a match struck from a dirty thumbnail. "We would. So I'd better make sure that I can."

Thomas extended his hand and the two men shook. "All right then, Mr. Gray, right this way." Thomas led the way through the partially unpacked crates that littered the floor of the station's main level, down the ramp, and onto the sand. The squat gun's barrel caught the evening light and reflected it back into the sky.

"Have a look, Mr. Gray." Thomas pointed in the fading light toward the makeshift false mast along the beach in the distance. "There's our target."

Sparrow dropped into the sand on his knees next to the Lyle gun. His fingers caressed the short ugly barrel as he studied the intricacies of the cannon. Thomas raised his eyes from the man to the station. The Mahigans and Seamus had appeared at the top of the ramp. Seamus was busy wiping tar from his hands with a cloth. Their eyes giving away nothing, the Mahigans waited and watched in silence.

Mr. Gray's eyes swept the sands leading to the distant mast; he licked a finger and held it up to the wind. He was oblivious to the onlookers. His only concern was the gun. He muttered under his breath; the words were swept away on the evening breeze. Thomas caught Seamus's eye, and the Scotsman grinned broadly.

"This crate got the charges, Keep?" Sparrow asked without looking up at Thomas.

The question was perfunctory. His hands had already dug within and now they located the shot and the powder charge. Thomas flipped the faking box into the sand and extended the end of the carefully coiled line to Sparrow. Sparrow took the line, absently clipping it to the grapple shot. He pushed the gun gently this way and that, shifting it in the sand and seating it firmly. Thomas noticed that Jon Mahigan was whispering into Seamus's ear, and Thomas saw Seamus mouth the word "done".

Minutes ticked by, as Sparrow sighted the barrel from behind the squat cannon. The light was fading, but the mast and rigging stood in sharp contrast to the sand and the ocean beyond. Thomas studied the angle as Sparrow made minute adjustments. The man knew his business. Finally he struck a match and lit the fuse.

"Fire in the hole!" Sparrow barked. His hand flew to cover his good ear and he turned his face from the blast.

The shot caught Thomas off guard, and he was blinded by the flash and deafened by the roar of the gun. He blinked hard. Heavy purple spots danced across his vision. On the ramp to the station, Seamus let out a whoop, but Thomas couldn't tell if it was a whoop of triumph or dismay. He was too blinded by the flash.

Sparrow was studying Thomas from his squatted position in the sand behind the gun, and, for the first time, he was grinning. "Well, Keep, looks like you've hired yourself a cannon man."

Thomas strained his eyes, and at last he could see the shot line that Sparrow had fired buried deep in the rigging of their makeshift mast. A perfect shot.

Thomas grinned widely and turned to see the reaction of the other surfmen at the top of the ramp. Jon Mahigan was grudgingly digging a dollar from his belt, and Seamus was hopping from foot to foot with outstretched hand. Thomas bent down and patted Sparrow on the shoulder.

"I'd guess I have, Mr. Gray. Welcome to the crew." Thomas continued to smile in the dim light.

Sparrow's smile disappeared. He removed his greasy pipe and spat into the sand at their feet. "Now, what's for supper?" he demanded.

Thomas roared with laughter as he pulled Sparrow to his feet. "Ham, I think, Mr. Gray. Follow me."

Thomas strode up the ramp. Charlie had lit a lamp and the darkness fled from the light in the station. Seamus clapped Sparrow on the back. Hard. The cannoneer allowed another broken smile, and the five men trooped through the station across the boardwalk and into the cookhouse. As they came through the station, Jon and Charlie introduced themselves to the newest crew member.

Elijah had lit two lamps in the cookhouse itself, and the yellowish light illuminated a large ham and and earthen bowls overflowing with potatoes and greens set on the plank table that dominated the middle of the room. Two benches led down either side of the table. Elijah grinned broadly at the men as they entered the open door.

Thomas hesitated at the door as the men trooped in, laughing and talking loudly. He smiled warmly at the sight. His family was coming together.

The Mahigans and Seamus took one bench, and Thomas and Sparrow drew up the other. Elijah was cooking frying pan biscuits on the wood stove and hadn't joined the group.

Sparrow puffed his pipe and nodded toward Elijah. "Good nigger you've got there, Keep. Hard to find one worth a damn since the war," he said around his pipe stem, helping himself to a slab of ham.

No one responded to the comment. The Mahigans shared a sharp look, but held their tongues. Oblivious to the stir he'd created, Sparrow dished potatoes onto his plate. Thomas met Seamus's eyes in the yellow light, and the redhead arched an eyebrow in return. Thomas worked his jaw. He remembered the Scotsman's words from the night before: "Ain't the work...it's the company." Thomas noticed that Elijah was busy over the stove. His thick black neck was flushed to his ears.

Thomas turned a wary eye to Sparrow and said quietly, "Mr. Gray, Elijah isn't my nigger. He's a surfman, same as you or I."

Sparrow looked at Thomas startled. "Come again, Keep?" he said incredulously.

Thomas eyes clouded, and his tone held a fine edge. "You heard me, Mr. Gray."

Elijah turned from the stove and took his place at the table next to Thomas. He very busily studied his hands folded on top of the plank table, and he made no move to fill his own plate. Charlie reached across, took his plate, and overfilled it with ham and trimmings. He stared at Sparrow and slid the plate in front of Elijah.

Sparrow swore low under his breath. His eyes were dark and menacing under his heavy brow. "I don't keep truck with no niggers, Hooper," he snarled.

Thomas stared at Sparrow, and for minutes nobody moved or spoke. The only sound that broke the stillness was the sputter of grease in the fry pan around the biscuits. Sparrow pushed back from the table and rose from the bench. His eyes broke under the commanding stare of Keeper Hooper and he looked away.

"I hire men for their God-given talents regardless of the color of their skin, Gray," Thomas said evenly, his eyes sparking. "If you work at Cape Hatteras Station you'll work with a Negro, a Scotsman, two Lumbee, and a castaway."

Sparrow looked around, aghast at the prospect. There was no sympathy in this room. Five sets of eyes stared him down in the yellow light, and there was barely veiled contempt in more than one set of eyes.

"No, thank you," Sparrow growled, and he spat in distaste on the clean polished floor. Elijah's knuckles whitened, and the dark flush spread from his neck and ears to his ebony face. His expression was grim but he held his ground.

Elijah rose from his seat and picked up his plate. His deep baritone rattled the dishes. "Iz all right, Cap'n Hooper. I'll take my meal outside."

Jon shook his head adamantly. "Like hell, Eli. You're a surfman. You'll eat at the table."

Sparrow glared at Jon. Seamus's neck matched his hair, and his ears burned. He started to speak, his accent thickened with anger, but Thomas stopped him with a slight shake of the head. He'd risen to stand facing Sparrow.

"Stand fast, Elijah," Thomas purred. "If Mr. Gray has anything else to say, he'll address it to me." Thomas eyes crackled. "Isn't that right, Mr. Gray?"

Sparrow turned his glare on Thomas. "You some kind of nigger lover, Hooper?" he demanded.

Thomas retorted in the same even voice he'd used before, "I've told you my position, Mr. Gray."

Sparrow wavered in indecision. He'd made up his mind to come this far; but he was thinking he should just storm out of the building. No pay was worth this kind of backhanded insult. This station should meet the same fate that the Pea Island Station met the year before. That station had been kept by a bunch of niggers, even had a nigger keeper. The locals had burned it to the ground; he knew some of the men involved.

"Hooper, I'll be damned if I'll work aside the very niggers that I give my ear for a few years back. I fought that fight to keep his kind where they should be," Sparrow sputtered.

"So did I," Elijah rumbled. A vein stood out in sharp relief on his enormous bald head. His rumble grew to a roar, "So did I!" Elijah paused and fought for control. His hands flexed where he stood. "I fought with General Longstreet in the first corps up at Sharpsburg. I fought for our cause all through Maryland and Pennsylvania. I fought for the South, for my home, for my country. I fought as a slave. I fought as a free man. You says I didn't, and I'll fit you right now, Mr. Gray!"

Sparrow stared at Elijah. Thomas and Seamus exchanged a look, and Seamus flashed Thomas a quick grin. Thomas regarded the big man with new appreciation.

156

Turning to Sparrow, Thomas spoke. "Well, there you have it, Mr. Gray. His skin's black, but he bleeds Confederate gray. That good enough for you?"

Sparrow didn't answer. His eyes held Elijah's.

Elijah gestured toward the man's plate. The redness around his ears was abating. "Now, set down and eat, Mr. Gray. I didn't fix up this meal for nothin'."

Seamus broke the tension with a grin, and spoke around a mouthful of ham. "Now that's good thinking, Eli."

Thomas walked outside onto the boardwalk to calm down, and the other men fell on their food. After a long pause, Sparrow threw a leg back over the bench and joined the feast. Thomas stared into the night and lit his pipe. He'd said it to Sumner: Old habits die hard around here. He doubted that he'd seen the end of it...not by a long shot.

CHAPTER 19
Late August 1878
Cape Hatteras Station, NC

Dawn the next morning found the crew of Cape Hatteras Station gathered on the wide ramp that led to the ocean. Seamus had rallied the men before daylight. Though the season didn't officially open until September, it was time to get to get the men ready for the rescues ahead.

Thomas stood in the sand, smoking his pipe. The sun was brightening the horizon at his back. He studied his ramshackle crew and ticked off his notes in his head. The Mahigans had taken seats on the ramp next to Elijah, a show of solidarity after the night before, and Seamus had taken a standing position at Thomas's right hand. Sparrow squatted grim-faced on the opposite end of the ramp from the others. Thomas grinned to himself. This would be a challenge.

"Well, lads, now it truly begins," Seamus started in his thick Scottish burr. "Keeper Hooper's brought us together, and our mission is a single purpose. We will go out, regardless of the weather; we will go out and save those in peril..."

Thomas's eyes flicked from man to man. He and Seamus had discussed this morning's address at length last night. He and the Scotsman had scripted the words for this morning, and both had felt that Seamus should lead off. Should anything happen to Thomas in a rescue, the men would need to recognize Seamus as next in command. Thomas blew pipe smoke into the stiff morning breeze and let Seamus's words wash around him while awaiting his turn to speak.

"...So lads, we've all made a commitment to serve Thomas Hooper, a commitment to the Lifesaving Service, a commitment to those seamen off the Cape that are in harm's way, and a commitment to ourselves. Are we all ready to accept that commitment?" Seamus continued.

Thomas studied the men, and four heads nodded in agreement. Charlie's eyes turned toward Sparrow on the other side of the ramp, and Thomas followed the look.

Breaking in on Seamus, Thomas added, "And a commitment to each other, Mr. Pennycuik. Let's not forget that we are only as strong as the men around us. No single man could be charged with the task that we've at hand. It will take individual commitments, and the commitment of our group as a whole." Thomas paused as the morning sun crested the horizon. "That simple fact needs to be clear to all of us," Thomas ended. He scrutinized the crew, and his eyes sought Sparrow. The cannon man hadn't moved, but under Thomas's gaze he leaned forward, withdrew his pipe from from his mouth, and spat on the boards of the ramp. Well, it wasn't a standing ovation, but none had gotten up to leave.

Seamus turned to Thomas. "So be it. Cap'n?" he asked, turning the floor officially over to him.

"Gentlemen," Thomas began. His voice gathered strength and rolled on in command. "Our crew is gathered here by one simple fact. No one else would take this station. Other men thought it too risky to guard the Cape and the shoals beyond. We are stationed at the Devil's very beard. Our duty is to keep Davy Jones at bay, to help those that cannot help themselves, and to do it in the most wicked sea that our Eastern Seaboard can muster." Thomas indicated the ocean with a wave of his hand. "We're all men of the Outer Banks. Each one of us knows this sand and this sea. Each one of us has buried friends and family that were taken before their time by the very sea that we are here to fight. Each of us... myself included." Thomas had to pause for a moment.

"To fight, gentlemen. It will be a fight. When the winter storms thunder at our steps, our duty is not to put another log on the fire and ride it out in the comfort of our homes, but to face the beast and fight the surf. Here, where the currents collide. It is our duty to go out; not to come back."

Thomas studied the crew. The task was monumental, but there was little use in sugarcoating it. Thomas drew on his pipe, and the smoke from his lungs trickled out his nose as he continued. "To that end, we'll begin training at once. The season is days away. We'll schedule in the following manner: Monday will be for cleaning equipment, Tuesday will be dedicated to the surfboat and practice in both deployment and at sea, Wednesday we'll practice working with signal flags, Thursday's devoted to the beach apparatus and the breeches buoy, Friday we'll go over how to aid wounded seamen, Saturday you'll have time to work on your personal gear and around the station as required. Sunday will be our day of rest. Is that schedule clear?"

Jon Mahigan spoke from his squatted position next to his brother. "Keep, how will we handle the surfboat? It seems as if we're a man down. The boat'll require a man at the tiller and six oarsmen." He glanced at his brother for confirmation, and Charlie nodded, scratching his chin.

Thomas nodded. "It does, Jon. Until we've found another man, Elijah will handle the center position, rowing oars on either side." He grinned at Elijah. "We'll put that mountainous strength to use."

Seamus stepped forward changing the subject. "We'll deploy standard watches, lads; two six-hour watches during the day, and four watches each night. The day watches can be had from here at the station, keeping a weather eye on the sea. The night watches will require a foot patrol from the station itself, in either direction, to the surf shack. At the surf shack, you'll exchange beach tickets with the man from the next station, to ensure that everyone's walked their patrol." Seamus turned to Thomas.

Thomas picked up where Seamus had left off. "As Seamus says, gentlemen. Our duty will be to signal a stranded ship, by flare at night or flag by day, that help is on the way."

Sparrow spoke for the first time. "Keeper Hooper, how on earth do ya expect us to reach a ship durin' a hurricane?"

Thomas allowed himself a brief smile. "Well, if the ship's in close enough we're to shoot the line, and ferry men to the beach hand over hand. We've the best cannon man in the service, so I'm expecting us to fare well in-shore. If the ship can't be reached or is out of range, we take the boat."

"What if we can't get the boat through the surf?" Elijah asked plainly. The other men turned assessing eyes to Thomas. It was a good question.

"Well, boyos, that's why we train," stated Seamus flatly, meeting their gaze.

Jon and Charlie shared a look, and Sparrow spat onto the boardwalk. There was little confidence in such a prescription. They'd all seen the surf pound the shore along the Banks.

Thomas sighed, "True enough, Seamus." Thomas decided on another tack. "When I first went to sea, I used to ask Captain McGuire why we trained so hard. In my mind, the men knew their jobs. Do you know his response?"

Nobody answered.

"His response," Thomas continued, "was that the more we train, the less we bleed, gentlemen." Thomas shook his head. "I'll have none of your blood on my hands. So we train day or night, storm or sun, no matter what. Are there any other questions?"

There weren't. At least none that were asked just then.

Thomas turned to Seamus. "What day is it, Mr. Pennycuik?"

Seamus grinned broadly. "Tuesday, Cap."

Thomas turned back to the men. "Well then, gentlemen, let's have a go at the surfboat, shall we?"

Hours later, Thomas wished that they'd all stayed abed. The morning sun had given way to a light drizzle, and whitecaps had begun to pound the small boat as the breeze stiffened. He looked at the gray sky from his place at the tiller. Great weather to be out on the sea. They'd better get used to it.

The launching of the twenty-two foot boat had been disastrous. Seamus had been barking orders, but the men were only beginning to understand the little Scotsman's commands. His accent thickened as he angered. That only made things worse.

"I said hev' the bloody corker on the light side, damn ye!" he screamed at the men. His face flamed red, and his hair tangled in the wind.

Elijah had blinked at him. He'd no idea what a corker was, or where the light side lay. He'd thrown up his hands in frustration, and only the soft sand had saved Charlie's foot from serious injury when Elijah's side of the boat had smashed down onto it.

The combined stream of curses included Algonquin, English, and Gaelic during the haphazard launch. Thomas smiled to himself. At least the boys would be well versed in linguistics by winter.

Thomas snapped back to the present. He'd said little during the launch and even less as the rowing had commenced. Seamus had filled the gap left by his silence with an endless screech of obtuse cursing. Thomas was relatively certain that Davy Jones below was blushing at some of the more inventive diatribes.

The problem wasn't that the men weren't competent oarsman. Quite the contrary. They were each extraordinary oarsmen, but each was accustomed to rowing his own small skiff. They'd yet to row as a team.

As they continued to fight the current and started another lazy half circle just past the breakers, Thomas decided that it was time to interrupt. "Seamus, ease off," he stated quietly. Seamus trapped unspoken curses in his throat and swallowed hard. The men stopped their oars and looked to their keeper.

Thomas took command. "Elijah's pulling on both sides, boys. The stroke length and breadth is his call." Elijah raised his great bald head and looked at Thomas, a question in his eyes. Thomas met his eyes and smiled in the rain. "Call the stroke, Eli."

Elijah cleared his throat. "Yessir," he rumbled. "Pull when I say."

Elijah gauged the waves and current, "Pull," he said flatly. He timed the next strokes evenly with the first. "Pull."

The little surfboat instantly straightened, and Thomas's eyes smiled into the wind. His grip lightened on the tiller arm.

"Heavy port, now." Elijah continued his rhythm undaunted by the waves. He lofted his right paddle and pulled with the crew on his left. "Pull," he spoke again.

"From now on, Elijah has the call, gentlemen," Thomas said softly. He was surprised by the relief evident on Sparrow's face, and Thomas could feel his thoughts. Elijah Coal might be black as his namesake, but he sure knew how to handle a small boat.

Thomas let his grin spread to his lips and face. There might be hope for them yet.

CHAPTER 20
Late August 1878
Cape Hatteras Station, NC

The men loafed on the porch after supper that night. Things had gotten better on the sea, but the rain had gotten worse. Elijah's wet pants were hung in the cookhouse next to the stove to dry, and he waited beside them astride a bench. He'd donned his shirt; thankfully it was long enough to cover his behind and manhood. Seamus had made the others chuckle, indicating that it would take a mighty long shirt to cover the big man. It seemed that he was big all over.

The other men had all changed into their extra set of clothes, and the interior of the station was draped with trousers hung to dry. Sparrow was still aloof from the others, but Thomas had seen his face in the rain on the sea. Old habits die hard, but they do die. Eventually. It would take time.

It was Jon that saw the boy first against the steel curtain of rain that hid the landscape. He stood at the edge of the light cast from the lanterns on the porch.

"Cap?" Jon said nodding toward the figure huddled in the downpour.

Thomas eyes found him in the rain. "You there," he called. "C'mon in out of the rain."

The figure swayed and stepped toward the covered porch hesitantly.

"Over here, lad." Seamus had stepped to the ramp.

The boy came up the ramp and under the overhang. He stood dripping on the flat boards of the boardwalk. Thomas exhaled a plume of smoke. The boy was young. Hard to tell how old exactly; too big for a boy, but too smooth of face to be a man. The youth shivered in his sopping clothes, and his eyes were cast at his feet under the gaze of the surfmen.

Elijah appeared in the kitchen shack doorway and placed an old woolen blanket over the boy's thin shoulders. Without speaking, he retreated to the cookhouse and his drying pants.

The boy had a small satchel draped over one shoulder. His clothes were threadbare and badly in need of a good washing. His uneven brown hair hung damply down his forehead and into his eyes. Thomas noted his bare feet, and the wide spread of his toes. It was years since the boy had worn shoes, he'd guess. The boy hadn't looked up, but just stood there dripping.

"Bad night to be on the road." Thomas eyed the boy.

The boy nodded, and finally raised his head to the surfmen. "'Tis." His voice faltered and he cleared his throat before continuing, "Is this Cape Hatteras Station?"

Jon smiled at the lad kindly. He'd been wet before, too. "It is."

The boy nodded again and relief flooded his blue-gray eyes. He looked directly at Thomas. "Are you Captain Hooper?"

Thomas smiled, "I am." The boy's accent was different. He didn't have the lilt of the South, but he didn't have the sharper tongue of the North either.

Seamus pulled his long red hair back from his face. He spoke from where he sat cross-legged on the boardwalk. "What can we do for you, lad?"

The boy had eyes only for Thomas. "I've come because I'd heard that you were hiring men for Cape Hatteras Station," he said in a voice barely above a whisper.

Thomas studied the youth in the lamplight. "Where are you from, son?" he asked, evading the boy's statement.

"Virginia, sir," The boy answered. He straightened and wrung his hands together, visibly fighting the shivering.

Thomas's pipe had gone out. He carefully repacked the pipe and relit. He drew deeply before speaking again. The other surfmen held their peace, waiting on the keeper.

"Well, son, true enough we're short a man for the season," Thomas said cautiously.

"I'd like to apply for the position, sir," the boy said at once.

Thomas continued to study the boy. "What's your name, son?"

"Evan Thatcher, sir," the boy responded. Hope crept into his eyes. He was still too young to effectively hide his feelings.

"Well, Master Thatcher," Thomas spoke with some regret. He hated to dash the lad's hopes. "I'm afraid that the Lifesaving Service has rules, and one of those rules is that all surfmen need to be at least eighteen years of age. How old are you?"

Evan hesitated for a long moment before replying, and when he did he nearly choked on the lie. "Eighteen, sir."

Sparrow snorted and swore under his breath. Thomas sought the boy's eyes in the lamplight. The boy wouldn't meet his eyes and studied his own hands, which he had folded at his waist.

"Eighteen, huh," Thomas shook his head. The boy wasn't used to lying. "Well, Master Thatcher, I'm afraid I'd need someone to vouch for your age. Perhaps I could send a letter to your mother or father?" Thomas suggested. He pegged the boy for a runaway, but he was wrong.

"Won't do you no good, Captain. Father died at sea, and Mother took the fever last year." He lifted haunted eyes to Thomas. "They're both dead."

Seamus studied Thomas with one eyebrow lifted. Thomas's eyes were cloudy and inscrutable. The Mahigan brothers stood as one and went into the station to start folding the nearly dried clothes.

Thomas shook his head. "I'm sorry, my boy. I'd need someone to stand for your age before you're a surfman for Cape Hatteras Station." He stood. The hour was growing late, and the time at sea today had tired them all. "You're welcome to set your clothes out to dry by the fire in the cookhouse, and spend the night. I'd turn no one out in this weather." Thomas spoke loudly toward the cookhouse. "Elijah."

Elijah stepped to the doorway. His silhouette blocked the lamplight from within. "Sir?"

Thomas addressed the big man, "Could you see to it that Master Thatcher gets his clothes dry, and has a spot til morning by the fire?"

Elijah nodded, "Aye, sir." He turned to young Evan, "This way, Mr. Thatcher."

Without another word, Thomas turned and went upstairs to his warm blankets.

Dawn broke, but the continued rain kept the light at bay for longer than usual. The men were up and about their morning chores when Thomas woke. He glanced in surprise at Elijah's carefully made bed. It hadn't been slept in. Rubbing his chin thoughtfully, Thomas dressed hurriedly and made his way downstairs. At the foot of the stairs the Mahigans were arguing with Seamus over the placement of the nautical flags. Thomas grinned silently as he padded by. At least the men remembered that it was Wednesday.

Thomas went straight to the cookhouse, worried about Big Eli. It was unusual for the man to skip sleep. At the doorway Thomas stopped dead in his tracks and caught his breath. Elijah was working over slab bacon, slicing it neatly into the fry pan atop the cook stove, but it was the room that stopped him.

After the mud and sand from the day before, the cookhouse had been a wreck. Elijah kept it neat, but the cook shack that stood before him was immaculate. The wood of the floor had been scrubbed with careful hands, and the pots and pans shimmered with fresh luster on the wall beside Elijah. Someone had certainly been hard at work already this day. Thomas drew his pipe from his pouch and fingered it in the morning light.

"'Scuse me, Cap." The voice came from his back, and Thomas glanced over his shoulder. Evan Thatcher stood in the rain with an armload of wood. Thomas stepped aside and let the young man through. Evan carried it to the wood box next to the stove and carefully stacked it on the neat pile. He then straddled a bench and returned to a pot that he'd recently begun burnishing with a soft cloth. Thomas lit his pipe, and through the smoke saw Elijah smile at the boy and ruffle his hair. Thomas's eyes widened; the scene brought back too many memories.

He turned from the cookhouse and made his way back into the station. Seamus grinned around the Mahigan brothers. He nodded toward the shoes and boots along the wall inside the door. Thomas looked down and drew on his pipe thoughtfully. The shoes and boots stood in a neat row. The mud and sand had been whisked off, and they'd been polished. All of them.

Sparrow came up. "Look at that, Keep. The lad polished the Lyle gun, too. Don't see how he had time fer it all last night. He wuz done in when we see him."

Thomas glanced at Sparrow. The taciturn Outer Banker was scratching his belly thoughtfully. "That's a good boy... thinking of the gun in this dampness."

Thomas questioned the man with a grin.

Sparrow snorted, meeting Thomas eyes. "I didn't think of it, but he did." The man went back to unpacking crates and shelving the last of their items.

Elijah had Evan help serve the men during breakfast, and refused to meet Thomas's eyes. Thomas held his tongue. The rain would let up soon enough, and he'd set the boy on the road. The men didn't need any distractions with the season breathing down on them.

Thomas took his customary seat on the covered porch and lit his pipe after the meal. Young Evan had brought the dishwater, and he frowned at seeing Sparrow jump to help him. Elijah joined the captain on the porch.

"He's a good boy, Cap." Elijah spoke staring out at the rain.

Thomas rubbed a hand over his face and drew his pipe from his mouth. "I know, Eli. The rules are clear, though. How would we all feel, seeing a boy getting eaten by the sea?"

Elijah met Thomas's eyes for the first time that morning. "Don't figure we'd feel good seeing any of us getting eaten by the sea, Cap," he responded unblinking.

Thomas chuckled at the big man. "You've got me there, Eli." He replaced his pipe and puffed. "The answer's still no, Elijah."

Elijah stared at Thomas then dropped his eyes. "Very well, Cap, I'll let him know."

"Thank you, Eli," Thomas nodded. His eyes were cloudy, and he knocked the ashes from his pipe in disgust.

When the rain had ceased, Thomas watched Evan make the rounds. He shook hands with the Mahigan brothers in turn, and patted Seamus on the shoulder. He gripped forearms with Sparrow, and, at last, went to Elijah. The big man ruffled his hair fondly and glared at Thomas over the boy's head.

"Captain Hooper," Evan had reached him last. "Thank you for your hospitality. I appreciate the bed for the night," he said formally, extending his hand.

Thomas shook the hand, momentarily at a loss for words.

"Thanks again," the boy said and turned to the ramp.

Thomas found his voice. "Evan...good luck to you."

The boy answered with a wan smile and walked down the ramp onto the road. Thomas watched his back as the boy stepped around the largest puddles. Soon he was out of sight. He felt the men's eyes burning into his side and back. He didn't want to face their gaze.

Good luck to us all, he thought, and faced his men.

CHAPTER 21
Early September 1878
Cape Hatteras Station, NC

Thomas slapped Seamus on the back. "Well done, Seamus."

Sweat soaked the armpits and stained Seamus's shirt, and the shirts of the other surfmen. Seamus forced a grin.

"Took long enough," he grunted.

Thomas chuckled, wiping the sweat from his own brow. "But we did it." He glanced around at the surfmen and grinned broadly. "We just need to do it faster, boys."

Thursday had started before light, with Thomas waving a bright red coston flare on the beach while they'd all slept. He'd begun screaming "ship ashore" before 4 am, and the men had scrambled from their bunks.

This was their first deployment, and the men struggled in dawn's early light. The Mahigans had had trouble anchoring the shot line in the heavy sand on the cannon side. The anchor was imperative. It was the lifeline attaching the mast to the beach. They'd had difficulty attaching the hawser, and the rescue seat that pulleyed back and forth from the mast to beach had become tangled more than once. It was well over three hours before the crew had managed to pull the seat to the mast and back without a hitch.

Thomas squatted in the sand and lit his pipe for the first time that morning. "Well, men, I'd call that a success. We only get points for saving lives, though, not for effort... or for practice." He continued grinning at the men, and the truth of his statement took their minds off their tired backs. Sparrow was first to chuckle, and the Mahigans turned his direction in surprise.

"We gotta work on speed, boys. People may very well be dying when we deploy the beach apparatus." Thomas spoke around the stem of his pipe. "Stow the gear."

The men shared a smile. That wasn't too bad. Speed would come with time. Thomas watched the Mahigans uprooting the anchor from the beach and storing the heavy timbers aboard the wagon. Sparrow coiled the shot line into the faking box, and Elijah wrestled the heavy gun onto the cart. Seamus double-checked the work of the surfmen and smiled at Thomas.

Charlie patted his belly as he and Jon finished stowing the timbers aboard the wagon. "'Bout time for breakfast, eh, Keep?" he grinned at Thomas.

Thomas returned his smile, but the smile didn't reach his eyes. Charlie didn't notice. He went to help Sparrow finish coiling the line. Seamus retrieved the draft horses from their pickets in the salt grass just off the beach, and Thomas watched him hitch the animals. The cart squeaked plaintively as it rolled in the sand up the ramp and into the building. Thomas watched Seamus lead the horses down the ramp. The men stretched their backs in the morning sun.

Thomas finished his pipe and tucked it into the pouch at his waist. "Seamus," he said quietly, "Run it again."

Seamus raised his eyebrows. "Sir?" he questioned.

Thomas regarded him with cool eyes. "You heard me." Thomas raised his voice and gave the yell, "Ship ashore! Let's go, go, go!"

Elijah blinked at Hooper and the other men glanced around in confusion. Seamus's face reddened and he wheeled on the men, "You heard him, damn it! Let's move." He swung the horses back up the ramp and re-hitched the animals. The heavy cart rolled into the sand, and the process began again.

Thomas had walked about eighty yards down the beach and called for the men's attention. "Boys, not from there." The men had started to deploy the apparatus at the base of the ramp.

Thomas scraped a large X in the sand with his bare foot. "From here."

Sparrow swore softly. His careful range and wind calculations from the previous deployment weren't worth a damn over there. Seamus knew it, too, and cursed under his breath. He hitched the horses again, and dragged the cart toward Thomas.

The surfmen of Cape Hatteras ran the drill seven more times that first Thursday. Their speed increased every time. Charlie Mahigan threw up from exertion when digging his fifth placement for the timbers anchoring the shot line, and even Elijah's great strength was sapped by the sun and work. Thomas worked alongside the other men. They'd only hold up as long as he would. He knew that, and there was no give in him. He allowed Elijah to bring tea and biscuits during a break between the third and fourth deployment, but tolerated no other food or drink.

The men replaced the equipment in the setting sun. Sparrow and Jon went to bed without supper. Seamus joined Thomas on the porch where the man sat smoking in the waning light.

"Jesus, Cap, ya nearly killed us today," Seamus said softly. He would never allow the other men to hear him question the keeper.

Thomas blew smoke into the evening sky. "I know, Seamus, but we've got a long way to go and a short time to do it in. Remember, sweat more..."

Seamus interrupted irritably, "I know, bleed less. Believe me, Cap, I get it, but Jesus."

Thomas flashed him a smile. "Tired, eh, Scotsman?"

Seamus smiled grudgingly in return, "You bet your arse, Cap."

Thomas nodded, "Me too, my friend, me too." He fought to his feet. His pipe had gone cold. "Tomorrow's a new day, Seamus. It will get worse before it gets better."

Chapter 22
Early September 1878
Cape Hatteras Station, NC

"Every man ship oars and lean to port," Thomas commanded from the stern of the surfboat in a loud voice above the swish and roar of the breakers. "Eli, pull us about."

The men looked at each other in confusion. They were wet and tired. They could only see vaguely in the blackness of the dark night. Thomas saw the flashing whites of their eyes in the dim light of the waning moon and smiled grimly.

"You heard him, men," shouted Seamus and joined the keeper in leaning over the gunwale on the left side of the boat.

The other men followed suit, and Elijah swung them broadside to the waves. The first wave splashed a hundred gallons over the men, but the next answered the keeper's unspoken wish. The small surfboat rolled heavily. The water they'd taken from the first wave sloshed around them. Jon lost his grip on the gunwale and toppled backward into the surf below with a grunt and splash. The boat rolled ponderously over. In the final instant, Thomas caught Seamus's eyes and smiled. Then they were all in the water.

Thomas fought the rip to the surface and grabbed the capsized boat. Charlie was already there, coughing water. He heard Seamus roaring from the opposite side of the vessel.

"Sound off, damn ye," Seamus roared. "Sound off."

The men answered the call one by one, and Thomas grinned his relief through chattering teeth. The upturned boat rolled ponderously, pushed by the surf above and pulled by the rip below. Thomas could feel the current dragging at his dangling legs.

"Work together men", Thomas shouted over the waves.

"Steady," came the deep rumble of Elijah's voice from the water by the bow. The men began to kick their surfboat in past the breakers. The men of Hatteras Station and their boat crawled through the surf and sprawled on the broad beach in exhaustion.

"Cap, you've got to back it off," Seamus said quietly. He stood dripping wet in the dawn's early gray light.

Keeper Hooper hadn't lied. It had gotten worse. The training over the past several days had been fierce. Thomas had worked the men on the Lyle gun, on flags, and in the surfboat. He'd given the men little rest, and tempers were short.

This night he'd woken the men in the middle of the night with a red flare, and they'd practiced the surfboat launch in the murky light of beach midnight. Seamus stood beside him in all things, but he'd had enough. Every muscle of his small body ached from the drill of the night before. He shook the water from his hair and bounced on one foot, trying to release the water from his left ear.

Captain Hooper regarded the Scotsman from his squatted position on the beach. He led by example. Every muscle on his body screamed for relief. He smoked his pipe and squinted up at his Number One.

"The season's started, Seamus. We could go out today... tomorrow. Are we ready?" Thomas asked quietly. His eyes followed the men wrestling the surfboat in the gloom back onto the wagon down the beach.

Seamus ceased his hopping. His eyes followed the keeper's. He stuck his pinky in his left ear. Damn seawater. He answered Thomas in the same quiet voice. No sense letting the men hear the exchange. "Well, Cap, we're better than we were." His eyes turned back to the keeper. "Only time will tell."

Thomas chuckled softly and drew deeply on his pipe before responding. "True enough, Mr. Pennycuik." He pulled his eyes from the men and squinted back at Seamus. The surfboat was loaded. "Bring them up, Seamus."

Seamus saw to it that the boat was stowed properly in the station and gathered the men in a loose semicircle on the beach in front of Thomas. Thomas studied his men in the gray light of the breaking day. Sparrow shivered in the dawn and fought the chattering of his teeth. The other men looked no better, and there was no fondness in their eyes. The men were soaked and cold. The nights were growing cooler, and autumn had begun to drag at summer.

"Mr. Pennycuik says that you've had enough. That you're ready enough. Is he right?" Thomas studied the men, his face wreathed in smoke from his pipe.

The men didn't answer. They glared their response at the keeper, and Sparrow spat distastefully into the neat sand at the water's edge. They'd learned the last week that to answer the simple question might result in a new wave of drills. They'd all had enough. Thomas nodded slowly. So had he.

"Mr. Pennycuik's right, boys," Thomas smiled softly at the men. "You've the rest of today and tonight to yourselves. See family, find a woman, get drunk." Thomas's soft smile turned into a wide grin. "Cape Hatteras Station is open for business."

The Mahigans let out a whoop, and even Sparrow grinned. Elijah dropped heavily into the sand, and Seamus clapped Thomas on the shoulder. Thomas smiled back at the men amidst the rumble of happy voices, but his eyes showed his concern. He had a feeling that they all needed rest, but he also knew the habits of sailing men. Drink would come first.

They shipped out to a tavern that Sparrow knew, and Seamus was soon doing his best to quickly drink his weight in meal wine. Jon smiled at the Scotsman and glanced around the table. Thomas had stayed at the station, but the others were all there. Jon glanced at his brother. The two by unspoken agreement flanked Elijah. Men of color weren't welcome in most taverns. Based on the frowns and distasteful looks, this tavern was no exception.

Seamus raised his mug, grinning at his fellow surfmen. "Here's to the season, lads." He cackled drunkenly. "May we all live through it."

Sparrow had separated from the group, and Jon smiled to himself. It was one thing to be working with a nigger, but quite another to be socializing with one amidst men you might know. Sparrow leaned heavily on the wide planked bar that ran down one side of the tavern, deep in conversation with a man.

Two more men came in, and Jon knew they were in trouble. The two pushed through the door and stared, open-mouthed, at Elijah. One commented to the other, and spat a stream of tobacco juice onto the plank floor. Their eyes were mean and cold.

The scene wasn't lost on Elijah, and his dark eyes met Jon's in the smoky tavern. He pushed back from the table. "Don' want no trouble, boys. Probably time I leave."

Seamus glanced at the black man in surprise. He hadn't seen the looks cast in their direction, and if he had he would have paid them no mind. "Not so fast, big man," Seamus slurred slightly. "Have a drink."

Elijah shrugged, but shook his head slightly. "No thank you, Mr. Pennycuik," he said quietly, "I don' drink."

Seamus roared in laughter. "Me neither," he exclaimed and belched loudly on cue.

Jon smiled into his mug. He felt Charlie's eyes on him and raised his head. Charlie tilted his head slightly toward Sparrow across the room. The two newcomers knew Sparrow, and he shook both their hands at the bar.

"Maybe it's time we all leave," Charlie suggested.

Seamus snorted. "No way, lads," he shook his head adamantly.

Jon grinned at the Scotsman, but the smile didn't reach his eyes. "I believe my brother's right, Seamus."

Seamus grinned crookedly back at Jon. "Guess I'm outvoted, lads." He rose from his chair and stretched. The other men got to their feet as well. The Mahigans crowded close to Elijah on either side in a defensive maneuver.

Seamus was oblivious to the concern. He turned from his men and called out to Sparrow, "C'mon, Sparrow. The lads figure I've had enough. Time to head back."

Sparrow's face whitened above his thick beard, and his mouth pressed into a hard line. Without a word to his companions, he started toward the other surfmen. He'd made three strides before the men said something.

"What's this, Gray?" the larger of the two men growled to Sparrow's back.

Sparrow hunched as if struck, and his eyes met Seamus's. He didn't answer and kept walking. Seamus looked over his shoulder. The two men had stepped away from the bar. Seamus instantly sobered. His capital mood evaporated under their cold gaze. He glanced at Charlie out of the corner of his eye as the Indian stepped up beside him. Charlie's eyes were fixed on the two men as well.

"I asked you a question, Gray," the larger of the two men growled more loudly, and continued venomously, "You keepin' with niggers, now?" The conversation around the tavern stilled in the vacuum left by the man's words.

Sparrow paused. His eyes narrowed, but it was Charlie that spoke. "I'm keepin' with niggers, buck. You have something to say?"

Sparrow hadn't turned to face the two men. The whiteness around his eyes was being replaced with the flush of anger.

The large man sneered at Charlie. "Weren't talking to you, boy."

Charlie took a half step forward. "Well, I'm talking to you, mister," he said with quiet anger.

The large man's small fierce eyes narrowed and looked Charlie up and down in the smoky tavern. "Shut your mouth," he stated flatly. "This is a conversation that I'll be havin' with my old friend Sparrow." He nudged his buddy and grinned maliciously. "Not you, Injun."

Elijah took a long step backward toward the door. "Les' go, boys," he rumbled in a soft voice.

Seamus hadn't taken his eyes from the two men. His ears flamed and matched his hair. He took up his mug of meal wine and took a long draught, then he his mouth with the back of his hand. "Like hell," he purred. His accent was thick with drink and fury.

The smaller of the two men joined the fray. "Nigger that big ought be pickin' cotton down in Georgia at yer Uncle's place, eh, Sam?" he sneered to his companion.

Seamus swore softly under his breath and took a long step forward. Jon glanced toward the door. Three other local men were loafing nearby. They hadn't been there a few minutes ago.

"Leave 'em alone," a voice stated flatly. Elijah turned to the door on the opposite side of the room in surprise. The door led to the cookhouse beyond, and squarely in the doorway stood Evan Thatcher.

The man behind the bar turned a grim look to Evan. "Git back in the kitchen, dish boy."

Evan stood in the doorway and wiped his hands on a towel. He tossed the towel on the bar and looked at the man behind it. In a quiet voice he said, "No, sir."

The man called Sam glared at the dish boy. "Ya heard your boss, boy. You'd best shut your mouth." He turned cold eyes back to the surfmen and sneered. "Having a boy fight for ya?"

Evan started across the room to join the surfmen without taking his eyes off the men at the bar. The room was still as a church during collection time, and the room held its breath. As Evan walked past Sam, the man grabbed his thin arm. "Why you, you little..." he stammered.

Elijah stepped forward. "Keep your filthy hands off 'im, mister," he roared.

Sam blinked in astonishment. No black man had ever raised his voice to him before. Evan wrenched his arm free and hurried to the safety of the knotted surfmen. Sparrow's neck was purple and he joined the others in a few quick strides as well.

Sam was furious, "Why you damned nigger, I'll..."

A new voice cut the tense air like a whip. "That'll be all," the voice commanded from the front door. The men blocking that door turned their heads in surprise.

Keeper Hooper stood framed in the doorway, his back to the night outside. His eyes swept the room. "I thought that I'd join my men on their last night of free time. Imagine my surprise to find you boys haranguing my surfmen," Thomas's eyes sparked. "These same men that are charged with saving your lives. Show some respect." Thomas shouldered through the men at the door and they staggered out of his way.

Sam's lips curled in a snarl. "Stay out of this, Hooper," he growled menacingly.

Thomas's eyes held Sam in contempt. Calmly he struck a match to his pipe. He spoke around the stem. "Can't do that, Sam," he spoke quietly. His eyes bored into the other's and it was Sam who looked away. "These are my men."

Sam swore softly and half turned back to the bar. "This ain't over, Hooper."

Thomas blew smoke toward the ceiling and smiled without humor. "That's where you're wrong, Sam." He squinted through the haze of pipe smoke. "This ends right now."

Sam turned back to face the keeper. His fists were clenched and his knuckles were white.

"Eli," Thomas looked at the big Negro.

Elijah stepped forward, stripping off his shirt as he pressed through the knot of surfmen gathered around him. Thomas didn't look at his man, but held Sam's eyes. He saw the big man swallow hard. A shirtless Elijah often had that effect on men. Thomas's eyes took in the others around the tavern.

"You men hate him. Hate niggers. Now's your chance, one at a time or all at once," Thomas said, quietly addressing them all. Elijah stood in the center of the room. He was half a foot taller than the tallest man and twice as wide. Sam was big, but Elijah was bigger. Sam's eyes flicked to his companion, but the man looked away and wouldn't meet his eyes. Sam took a faltering step toward Elijah. He forced his feet to move against their better judgment.

A step sounded beside Elijah, and the big man glanced down. Sparrow Gray stripped his shirt and joined the black man in the center of the floor.

Sparrow taunted Sam, a grim look in his eyes, "C'mon, Sam. I've had a bellyful of you this night."

Sam's eyes narrowed and he stopped in his tracks.

Thomas chuckled into the still room. "That's what I thought." His voice was thick with contempt. "Gentlemen."

Without a backward glance Thomas started toward the door. The men in the room studied the ceiling and the floor. No one met another's eyes. They'd been called and none had answered.

The surfmen backed toward the door following their keeper. Thomas flicked his eyes toward Evan. The boy chewed his lip in indecision, and he took a faltering step toward the retreating surfmen.

"Where ya think you're headed, boy?" The man behind the bar demanded. "Get your arse back to the dishes."

Evan met Thomas's eyes with a bleak expression. He continued to bite his lip, and his eyes welled with unshed tears. Seamus took a long look at the keeper and back at the boy. His eyes narrowed to the man at the bar, "'Fraid he can't do that, mister."

The barman looked at Seamus coldly. "Yeah, Scotsman?" he said thickly. "Why's that?"

Thomas smiled at the barman from the doorway. He looked at his men and turned to go. His voice trailed after him. "He's already got a job. He's a surfman of Cape Hatteras Station."

The crew of Cape Hatteras Station was complete.

CHAPTER 23

Late September 1878
Cape Hatteras Station, NC

"Sparrow, why do you hate Eli?" Evan asked. It was Evan's watch, and the older man had decided to join him on his patrol to the surf shack down the beach. Sparrow glanced at the boy beside him in the darkness. His pipe glowed, lighting up his hollow cheeks and graying beard.

Sparrow drew his pipe from his mouth and spat into the sand. "Why ya say I hate Eli?" he asked.

The two shuffled through the sand in silence as Evan considered. The two-and-a-half mile walk to the surf shack was a long one. He'd lit a lantern, but Sparrow had told him to put it out. The man was right. He could see out across the water much better with his eyes adjusted to the darkness. He'd also been walking in the heavy sand. Sparrow had steered him to walk right at the surf line. There the sand was much firmer, and the walking much easier. Evan huddled into his woolen blue coat. The nights were growing cooler and the days shorter.

Evan turned the wool collar of the coat up around his face. The wool was new. The blue uniforms had arrived just a week before, and Evan had never had such a nice coat. Keeper Hooper had them made by a local seamstress under contract with the Lifesaving Service. The men had taken their turns being fitted, and the suits were exceptional. He breathed deeply of the fresh wool.

"Is it because he's black?" Evan asked.

Sparrow burrowed in his blue woolen coat as well and glanced over at the boy. His pipe jutted from between his tight lips. He puffed the pipe again, and the smoke floated inland on the night breeze. "Evan, I spent an awful long time fighting for the Confederacy. You was just a youngster back during the war. When I was a boy, niggers had a place. The war changed all that." He flashed a crooked grin at the younger man. "Not exactly that I hate *him*, jus' hate the change."

Evan glanced at Sparrow. He was surprised. It was hard for the Banker to put such feelings into words. The two trudged on in silence. Evan's eyes swept the sea. He carried a sack with a lantern and two red coston flares slung over his shoulder. He touched his pocket, and felt the outline of the beach ticket within.

"I never met a black man before Elijah," Evan said wistfully.

Sparrow glanced again at the boy in surprise. "Never?"

Evan shook his head. "Nope," he responded.

Sparrow relit his pipe. It had gone out. He was incredulous. "How could that be, Evan? You'se from Virginia, right?"

Evan nodded, but held his peace.

Sparrow continued, "Well, they've got niggers in Virginia, don't they?"

Evan smiled at the perplexed expression of the older man. "Sure, Sparrow. It's just that I never met any or knew any, that's all," he answered.

Sparrow turned the statement over in his mind, remembering his own youth. He remembered growing up, and he remembered his time in the war. He shuddered at the memories of Gettysburg. That had been the beginning of the end for the South. Even they had known it at the time. "Well, Evan, truth be told, don' know if I ever *knew* any either."

Evan's eyes widened. "Really, Spare?" he questioned.

Sparrow didn't answer. He was alive with his own thoughts at the realization.

Evan continued hesitantly, his eyes searching Sparrow's face, "My father always said you should reserve opinion 'bout people 'til you get to know 'em."

Sparrow pursed his lips, and his beard twitched with the hint of a smile. "My ol' man tol' me the same thing."

Evan tilted his head in question. "Then why wouldn't ya?"

Sparrow chuckled dryly, pulling the pipe from his mouth. The boy had a point. Why would he? The two continued to walk toward the surf shack. At length Sparrow shrugged off the self-doubt, putting the question under lock and key in the back of his mind. He patted the boy on the shoulder and pointed to surf shack ahead.

"Let's git out of the wind for a minute. Maybe the boy from Kinnakeet's already here." Sparrow led the way in.

The man from Kinnakeet wasn't there yet. Evan lit the lamp that he'd carried in his sack, hanging it on a peg set in the wall. Wind swirled around the interior of the shack. The two men crouched against the back wall and looked to the sea.

"Don't figure the man's comin', Evan." Sparrow spoke flatly breaking the silence. The only sound for almost an hour had been the sea wind whistling around the eaves of the sturdy little building. Evan's eyelids had been growing heavier by the minute, and he tried to shake the sleep from his foggy head.

"Guess not, Spare. Guess we'd better be headed back," Evan replied groggily.

Sparrow's eyes were hard as he leaned in and snuffed the lamp. This wasn't the first time. Hooper'd hear about this at breakfast. He rose to his feet, and with Evan in tow, started back up the beach in silence.

"It ain't the first time, Keep," Sparrow said around a mouthful of bacon the next morning. The hot tea felt good on his chilled hands.

Jon Mahigan had the morning watch, and was the only surfman not gathered around the table in the cookhouse. Evan had reported the infraction to the keeper on their return to the station. Thomas had accepted the information grimly and joined the men for breakfast. His report this week would note the variance. Thomas looked at Seamus; the Scotsman was shaking his head.

"They didn't show two night watches o' mine last week either, Cap," Seamus voiced his displeasure.

Thomas scratched his whiskers and glanced around at the men. The system was designed around the checks. The idea was that the men exchanged tickets at the surf shacks in either direction to confirm that they'd walked their watch. The system wouldn't work if one crew didn't show up.

"Why don't you use the telegraph to reach out to Keeper Smyth, Cap? Might be that he doesn't even know it's happening," Seamus suggested, after a swallow of brutal yaupon tea. He winced at the bitter taste.

Thomas felt for his pipe, but it was still upstairs next to his cot. He looked in consternation through the wall toward the telegraph key, his lips thinning in disgust. He had a hard time on the key and they all knew it. Nodding slowly he said, "I think I'd better handle this one in person, boys. I'll head to Kinnakeet this morning." He glanced at Seamus. "Saddle the horse for me, Seamus."

Seamus nodded in the lamplight. The men finished their breakfast and trickled out into the dawn.

CHAPTER 24
October 1878
Big Kinnakeet Station, NC

Thomas Hooper rode into the yard of Big Kinnakeet station under the bright autumn sun. The humidity of summer was gone, but the glare that accompanied the fall was fierce. His eyes swept the haphazard buildings. Big Kinnakeet was older than Cape Hatteras and set further from the beachhead. He glanced to the south. He couldn't see his own station, five miles in the distance, but the Cape Hatteras lighthouse jutted into the sky beyond his station, giving him some sense of distance. The black and white tower stood in sharp relief against the blue sky.

A heavyset man sat on a splintered rocking chair on the porch of the station, and a mangy black and gray dog lolled in the shade at his feet. Thomas studied the man. His head was tilted forward in sleep. The man's dirty gray beard rested in a tangle on his chest, and his uniform jacket underneath was soiled and spotty. Thomas glanced around. No one else seemed to be about.

"Helloooo," Thomas hailed the man on the porch without dismounting.

The man's eyes snapped open, and he blinked at Thomas in the bright sunlight. Thomas waited, both hands in plain sight on his saddle horn.

The man on the porch studied Thomas coolly, his eyes sharpening at the blue Lifesaving Service uniform and the gold Keeper's bars. He hoisted his large backside from the rocker. He then hitched his pants up over his ample belly and scratched his large rear end.

"What you need?" the man asked sternly. His face was like boiled leather, and two murky blue eyes peered at Thomas without friendliness.

"Is Keeper Smyth about?" Thomas asked with a smile and added, "I'm Thomas Hooper with Cape Hatteras Station."

The man didn't answer right away. He paused and put a large wad of tobacco into his mouth from an inside pocket of his jacket. He chewed it into the corner of his jaw and spat a stream of juice into the yard. "I'm Keeper Smyth. Figured you might be Hooper." Smyth reached behind himself and drew the rocker back to his rear. Sitting down, he spat again. "Light and set, Mr. Hooper."

Thomas swung down from the saddle. In doing so he took note of the station. The buildings were in general disarray. The front door leading from the porch had a broken hinge and canted sideways. He glanced at the shed that served as a stable. Judging by the odor, it hadn't been mucked in some time. Frowning, Thomas joined Keeper Smyth on the porch.

Smyth waved a hand dismissively. "Welcome to Big Kinnakeet Station." He spat a stream of brown juice onto the porch where it joined a puddle of similar spit on top of stains from spits before.

Thomas fought his frown and kept the smile stayed on his lips; his eyes were thoughtful. "Thank you, Keeper Smyth." Thomas's eyes continued to assess the dismal station. "Are your men out training?"

Smyth studied Thomas through narrow eyes and sneered derisively. "Two of 'em's home. The others are about somewheres." He puffed out his chest. "See Hooper, my men have been with the service for two years, don't need much training. Just waitin' on a shipwreck."

Thomas lit his pipe and leaned against the corner post holding up the porch roof. He didn't respond. The way that the man had stressed *two years* nagged at the corners of his mind.

"That so," Thomas said flatly, sarcasm thick in his voice.

Smyth returned Thomas's cool look with one of his own. "That's right, Captain."

"We got good, God-fearing *white* men here at Kinnakeet, Hooper," a voice spoke from the dim interior of the station. Thomas raised an eyebrow at the voice, and his eyes scanned the gloom, hunting the speaker.

Smyth grinned broadly at the jibe. His teeth were stained with tobacco and many were missing. He gestured toward the doorway. "Keeper, I'll have you meet my Number One, Jack Johnson."

Jack Johnson leaned nonchalantly in the broken doorway. He was a broad, squat man. His shirt was badly in need of laundering, and Thomas noted the slick, greasy collar that stood open part way. His homespun pants were held up with a length of line that was knotted under his soft belly. Smoke from a shag tobacco cigar wreathed his greasy, graying hair.

Thomas's eyes snapped at the comment. "What's that, Mr. Johnson?" he asked evenly.

Jack blew a few wisps of tobacco from his lips. "Just saying, that's all."

Thomas's frown etched hard lines into his cheeks. "Just saying what, Mr. Johnson?" Thomas knuckles whitened under the pressure of his clenched fists.

Keeper Smyth snorted a rough laugh. "Easy Hooper, we're on the same side."

Thomas eyes flicked back to the keeper before returning to Johnson. "Keeper Smyth, I believe that it was Mr. Johnson that spoke. He'll answer for his words," Thomas stated flatly.

Johnson met Thomas's eyes with a baleful stare. "Just that I'd hate to see another station git burned out cause of niggers," he muttered.

The rumor was that Pea Island Station had been burned three years before by locals upset with the appointment of the service's first black keeper. Sparrow had mentioned the fact. Thomas grinned maliciously at Johnson through a curtain of pipe smoke. "You needn't worry yourself, Mr. Johnson. No man will burn my station," he said quietly. Abruptly Thomas changed the subject, "Seems that some of your men aren't walking their watch, gentlemen." His voice dragged over the word "gentlemen" like the surf tumbling over rocks. "They haven't appeared at the waypoint."

Smyth spat his tobacco juice onto the porch and nodded toward Johnson formally. "Make a note in the log, would ya Jack?"

Johnson shared the joke and didn't move from the doorway. "Sure thing, Keeper Smyth." He patted his pants and shirt. "Soon's I find something to write it down with."

Smyth grinned broadly at his Number One. "Say, Jack, you cain't write can ya?"

Johnson rolled the cigar into the corner of his mouth. "Damn, nearly forgot, Keep." He smirked at Thomas. "Guess I won't be writing it down in the log after all."

Smyth chuckled and turned his narrow gaze back to Hooper. "Well, I reckon that's handled, Keeper. Anything else you want to tell us how to do?"

Thomas bit his tongue and slowly unclenched his fists. "Good day, gentlemen," he said as he stepped off the porch and into the sand below.

Smyth's voice punched him in the back as he mounted his horse. "Don't forget, Hooper, we been doing this job for years. I was appointed to this station while you was sailing for a living." Smyth paused before continuing. "The men of Kinnakeet have saved our share of men."

Thomas swung his horse back to face the two men. His voice was crisp with anger. "That may be, gentlemen," Thomas said through gritted teeth, "but I'm not worried about the ones you've saved... I'm worried about the ones you've lost."

Thomas dug his heels into the horse and cantered from the yard before the two could banter a reply his way. He continued to frown. His ride had only proven one thing.

He'd find no help at Big Kinnakeet Station.

CHAPTER 25
Early November 1878
Cape Hatteras Station, NC

"Out of the boat, boys," Thomas smiled from the tiller.

The Mahigans glanced sideways and exchanged a look. Even Seamus cocked a red eyebrow at the keeper from his place at the oar in the bow next to Evan.

"Wha's that, Keep?" Elijah blinked in confusion. "Sound like you said to git outa the boat."

Thomas grinned and glanced out over the pitching waves. The summer that lingered long in the south had given way to fall, and though no storms had come, the water was unsettled and dark gray. The gray sky met the sea in the distance and the beach was a dim, dirty, distant line. Thomas took a final draw on his pipe and knocked the ashes loose against the gunwale before returning it to the pouch on his belt. He met Elijah's eyes and let his eyes roam over the men at the oars in the small surfboat.

"I did," Thomas continued to smile. The wind was chilled and strong out on the water. It tousled his long hair as he surveyed the men.

The men stared back at the keeper, and Seamus sighed heavily before snapping to delivering the keeper's orders. "You heard the keeper," Seamus grunted. His heart wasn't in the order, but at least he was trying. Seamus grabbed the gunwale and vaulted into the cold water, boots, coat, and all.

He sputtered to the surface and grabbed one of Elijah's oars. He drew a deep breath. The cold fought to clamp his lungs, and it was a moment before he could get up to typical Pennycuik yelling level.

"Now, lads," Seamus chattered from the water, "Damn it, you heard him. Now!"

Evan splashed in next to Seamus, and Elijah tumbled in with a mighty splash. The Mahigans looked at the keeper as one, but wilted under Thomas's stare. Then they too were in the drink. The men jostled for position alongside the bobbing boat. Their hands gripped the outstretched oars and gunwales. Thomas leaned over and looked at each man in turn before speaking.

Thomas spoke in a quiet voice, his words drifting on the stiff sea breeze. "Is it cold, gentlemen?' he asked gently.

Seamus gritted his teeth to stop the chattering. "Bloody right, Cap."

Evan's lips were white. Thomas smiled. It would be a while before they turned blue. "It's only the beginning of November, men. You might well be in this very sea in January. It will be a damn sight colder then."

Elijah cleared his throat. "All right, Mistah Hooper, can we's get back in the boat, now?"

Thomas turned his eyes to the big man, "No, Elijah, you can't. When we're called upon to save men in the sea, the water will be cold, and it's my charge to be certain that we're ready for it."

The men continued to scissor kick below the surface and hold on to the boat. Thomas turned, squatting to the heavy sea bag at his feet. He drew open the drawstring and peered inside. With a nod, he looked back to the men.

Thomas addressed Jon, who was holding on for dear life while stifling a yawn, "Bored, Mr. Mahigan?"

Jon straightened in the water under the keeper's gaze. "No sir."

Thomas squatted back in the boat and lit his pipe. It took two matches to get it going in the stiff breeze. "There's a doctor up north that calls this hypothermia, boys. It's when the body gets too cold. One of the first signs is yawning." He grinned at the men. "After shivering and chattering teeth, of course," he said around the pipe stem.

Charlie muttered, "Don't care what it's called, Keep, but it ain't much fun, that's for certain."

Elijah coughed a deep laugh. Sparrow remained silent, and his mouth was set in a grim line. He nodded curtly at Charlie's statement. Thomas studied the taciturn Banker. His lips beneath the beard hadn't colored like everyone else's, and his teeth weren't beating a rough tattoo like Evan's. Interesting. It stood to reason, though; the man had more exposure to this type of thing than the others.

The men's heavy coats were cumbersome in the water, and he could see the woolen uniform pulling at young Evan's legs. Thomas set his jaw firmly, not liking what he was to do next. "Let go the boat and oars, gentlemen," he said calmly.

Fear washed over more than one set of eyes, but the men let go. They treaded water next to the boat. Evan was the first to sputter. He'd gotten a faceful from a wave swell, and he gasped for breath. His eyes darted to the boat, and he was close to panic. Sparrow swam a few strokes awkwardly to his side. He pulled Evan's head to the surface and continued to tread water with his other arm. He glared at Thomas, spitting heavily into the sea. Seamus had gone nearly limp. Only his mouth and nose rode on the top, his long red hair fanning out below the surface as his head tilted back.

Thomas squinted at the men and spoke loudly. Their ears were clogged with water. "These'll help you float."

Thomas tossed the heavy sea bag over the side and it splashed amidst the men. Seamus kicked toward the sea bag as it bobbed on the waves. He drew the drawstring and pulled a vest from the large bag. The vest was ringed with cork, and Seamus guffawed through chattering teeth as he struggled to get the cork vest on over his sodden coat.

He grinned crookedly at the keeper, "That'll help, Cap." He pushed a vest through the water toward Sparrow. "Get that on the boy."

The men struggled and pulled at the cork life vests, and Thomas grinned to himself. Each man helped the other. At length the men bobbed on the waves, a scattering of brown cork and blue wool. Relief showed in Charlie's eyes. They might freeze, but at least they wouldn't drown.

Thomas whistled tunelessly around the pipe stem and seated himself in Elijah's center seat. Without another word, he pulled for shore. It took the men a minute to realize that they were being left. They were busy with their new cork vests, elated by the fact that they weren't drinking water. Jon noticed the keeper pulling away first.

"What in the name...?" Jon's eyebrows were raised, partially hidden beneath his wet hair.

Thomas smiled to the men as he leaned into the oars. "Work together, boys. I'll see you on the beach."

Evan was close to panic again, and Elijah stared at the retreating boat dumbfounded. Sparrow was cursing under his breath, and Charlie shook a raised fist at the retreating surfboat.

"Well, lads, it's on us," Seamus said through clenched teeth. "Looks like we've got a swim to make." He looked at Evan. "Steady, boy."

Sparrow's cursing trailed off and he glared at Seamus. "I'll help him, Pennycuik," he snarled.

"So will I." Elijah rumbled as he kicked to Evan's other side, meeting Sparrow's eyes over the bobbing head of the boy.

Sparrow stared long and hard at Elijah. The swells pushed Jon into his back. Sparrow grunted and the moment was broken. He glanced at Elijah and nodded. With that, the surfmen struck out for the beach and the keeper who waited on the shore.

CHAPTER 26
November 1878
Cape Hatteras Station, NC

Thomas blinked the sleep from his eyes, squinting up from his cot at Evan's flushed face lit by the small lantern. "What?" Thomas demanded.

Evan hurriedly jerked his hand from the keeper's shoulder. "I said, there's a ship aground off Big Kinnakeet, Mr. Hooper," he said breathlessly. In his excitement his words ran together and it took Thomas a second to sort them out. He'd been fast asleep.

With a start, Thomas jerked upright in bed. He heard the snoring of the other surfmen scattered on their cots. He blinked at the dim light again. "Calm down, Evan. Has Kinnakeet lit a flare?" It was Evan's watch, and the young man seemed to have a handle on what was happening.

"Aye, sir," Evan nodded emphatically.

Thomas kicked into his boots, his mind under full sail. "Can you see the ship, Evan?"

Evan's cheeks huffed in and out as he drew deep, ragged breaths. "Aye, sir. I saw it from down the beach. It must be a half-mile up beach of the station. It sent up a flare, that's what drew my eyes. Ran back here as fast as I could."

Thomas pulled his shirt over his head. "Well done, Evan. What time is it?"

Evan's breathing was steadying. "Must be just after five, Keep."

Thomas stole a quick look at the window. Dawn was a ways off. He could just make out a hint of light over the sea. "All right." Thomas stood. "All right, Evan, wake the others. Muster in the cookhouse in ten minutes."

Thomas took the steps onto the lower level two at a time and went directly to the telegraph key. It was silent. He grimaced at the device grimly in the darkness. Big Kinnakeet wasn't raising the alarm, nor were they calling for help. His eyes turned to the ceiling in silent prayer. Hopefully, Keeper Smyth and Jack Johnson were alert and up to the challenge. Thomas stuffed and lit his pipe, lighting the lantern next to the telegraph key with the same match. He drew the stool under him and opened the telegraph booklet. Studying the booklet, he pecked out an inquiry to Big Kinnakeet Station.

"B. Kinnakeet." Stop. "Do you require assistance." Stop. "Cape Hatteras." Stop.

The key didn't chatter a reply, and Thomas stared at it in the yellow glow from the lantern. He heard jumbled voices from the sleeping quarters above and heavy boots on the stairs. The men ghosted past en route to the cook shack. Only Seamus stopped for a word with the keeper.

"What's the word, Cap?" Seamus asked quietly.

Thomas spun on the stool away from the key. "Nothing yet, Seamus. Get 'Lijah to stir up some breakfast, we've got a good hour 'til sunrise. Make sure they're all fed. It might be a while 'fore we get to eat again."

Seamus scratched his scraggly red beard and nodded to the keeper. "Aye aye, Cap."

Thomas swung back to the silent telegraph key. He studied the user guide and tried again.

"B. Kinnakeet." Stop. "I say again." Stop. "Do you require assistance." Stop. "Cape Hatteras." Stop.

The minutes ticked by, and Thomas studied the telegraph key. There was no response. Seamus appeared out of the gloom. He held a blue chip mug of steaming tea in one hand and a plate of eggs in the other. He laid the keeper's breakfast alongside the key, and Thomas accepted the mug of tea thankfully. He raised an eyebrow to Seamus, then shook his head at the silent key. Seamus swore under his breath.

Thomas took a sip before speaking. "Seamus, have Charlie mount up and dash up to the station. They're not answering their key."

Seamus nodded and turned to the open door and the cook shack beyond.

Thomas caught Seamus's eye as he turned away. "Tell him be quick, Seamus."

Seamus continued nodding and left the room. Thomas looked at the plate of eggs. His stomach was tight and knotted. No eggs for him this morning. He settled for tobacco instead and relit his pipe. With his tea in hand, Thomas crossed the room and flung open the large seaward doors to the breaking day. A cold shiver stung the back of his neck in the cool morning breeze as it blew into the building. The opposite door slammed shut as the suction of the large doors opening swung it closed. Thomas sipped his tea, clenching his pipe in his free hand, and stared out across the salt grass and beach to the water's edge. The predawn light left the beach indistinct, and he turned his eyes northward. It wasn't light enough to see anything yet. Thomas walked down the broad ramp into the sand, skirted the building and stepped up onto the boardwalk at the cook shack. They'd wait for Charlie to return before they deployed.

It was approaching two hours when Charlie cantered back into the yard of Cape Hatteras Station. The morning had broken, but the sky was low and gray. There'd be no sun today. One look at Charlie's face as he kicked loose of the stirrups and slid off the horse told Thomas the story, and he frowned.

"Well?" Seamus asked for them all.

Charlie twisted the reins around the pole holding up the porch of the station before turning to answer Seamus. His mouth was set in a grim line as he spoke. "Said they don't need no help." Charlie turned his head and looked at the keeper.

"Told me to let you know they figured we was out *training*." Charlie shrugged, his eyes flitting between the keeper and the men.

Thomas rubbed his whiskers with the back of his hand, his pipe pinched between his thumb and forefinger. Elijah flung the contents of his mug into the yard in disgust and turned back to the cook shack, and Seamus swore.

"What do you mean?" Evan asked incredulously. "They don't want help?"

Charlie nodded to Evan. "That's right, Ev."

Thomas straightened from where he'd been leaning against the building. "Where did they stand when you were there, Charlie?" Thomas questioned.

Charlie drew his wind-loosened hair back into a tight knot at the back of his head, staring at the keeper. "They was just deploying, Keep. The boat's only about two hundred yards off the beach. Looks like they'll hook her with the beach rig."

Thomas nodded. "Charlie, hook up the supply wagon." He turned to Jon. "Give him a hand, Jon."

Jon glanced from his brother to Thomas. "The beach apparatus, Keep?" he questioned.

Thomas smiled. "No, Jon, the men of Kinnakeet appear to have this one. Just the springboard. We're taking a ride." Thomas turned to Seamus. "On second thought, have the beach cart rolled out just in case. Have 'em ready in five, Mr. Pennycuik. We're taking a ride."

Seamus grinned broadly at the keeper, "Aye aye, Cap!"

The surfmen of Cape Hatteras station bounced over the dunes in the springboard wagon. As they crested the last of the dunes, Seamus stood and shaded his eyes into the rising sun. The ship seemed to be hard aground no more than two hundred yards from the beach, and the Scotsman could plainly see a dozen crew on deck.

Thomas glanced at Seamus while the rest of the men jostled for position in the wagon for a look at the foundering ship. "Well, Seamus. She looks to be aground."

Seamus nodded without taking his eyes from the wreck. "Believe she is, Cap. No danger to the men aboard. Water's pretty calm out past the breakers and weather's decent."

"Nevertheless, them boys from Kinakeet are taking their time, eh, Keep?" Sparrow grunted from his perch on the side rail of the wagon.

Thomas shrugged in response.

A little while later, the men were scattered around and on the wagon, which was drawn up in the lee of a dune overlooking the wreck site. Below, the crew from Big Kinnakeet had finally gotten their beach apparatus cart in position on the beach. Thomas flipped open the cover on his gold pocket-watch and glanced down at the time. It had taken Keeper Smyth nearly three hours to deploy the cart down the beach. Thomas shook his head in disgust. Good thing the waters were calm today. If the sea had been rough, they'd be running thin on survivors aboard the wreck.

Sparrow took his pipe from his mouth and spat into the sand of the dune. He studied the sky and the sea and jutted his chin from the collar of his coat, feeling the wind on his face. He squinted toward the floundering ship. "Easy shot," he muttered to no one in particular and spat again.

Thomas drew deeply on his own pipe and kept his eyes fixed on the wreck. "We'll see," he said quietly.

Charlie leaned over from the seat of the wagon and slapped Elijah on the back. "Damn, Eli, takes two of them to move their gun."

Elijah rubbed his shoulder and grinned sideways at Charlie. Two of the Kinnakeet men were struggling with the squat gun in the thick sand, wrestling it into position. Sharp orders floated on the wind, but they couldn't make out the words.

Evan stepped up beside Thomas, glancing at the keeper out of the corners of his eyes. "Will they get them off, Keeper Hooper?" he asked hesitantly.

Thomas continued to draw on his pipe. He spoke around the stem. "Should, Ev."

They saw the flash of the Lyle gun before they heard the heavy report. Thomas strained his eyes to try to make out the shot line sizzling off the beach, but he had to be content with picturing it in his mind.

Sparrow muttered from behind him, "Missed."

Thomas scratched his chin thoughtfully. Two of the surfmen were hauling the line back in hand over hand. They'd missed indeed. By fifty yards.

"Want Sparrow to go down and give her a go, Cap?" Seamus asked.

The men of Kinnakeet finally hooked the rigging with the third shot, and after a poorly organized struggle got the chair up and running from the ship to the beach. Thomas watched as they pulled the first man to shore above the waves. The first of the salvage boats had begun circling the wreck, and he watched as one separated from the others and ground into the beach below the wreck site. A man vaulted onto the sand and lifted a hand to Keeper Smyth. Separating himself from the rescue operation, Keeper Smyth met the man on the beach like an old friend. Thomas rubbed his jaw. The two talked for several minutes, and Thomas's eyes narrowed as the man passed a pouch to Keeper Smyth.

"Well I'll be damned," Seamus rose from his seat. He, too, was watching the little scene play out between the keeper and the boatman. He looked at Thomas in consternation. "Is that what I think it is, Cap?"

Thomas mouth was set in a hard line broken only by the pipe stem at the corner. He didn't look at Seamus; his eyes were fixed on the Kinnakeet Keeper. It was the charge of the Lifesaving Service to inventory the wreck, return what they could to the rightful owner, and set the rest for public auction. It was certainly not in the purview of the service to accept an apparent payoff from a salvage crew. Mr. Kimball had worked hard to remove such men from his new Lifesaving Service. Thomas looked out across the surf and the blue-green sea beyond. It seemed old habits really did die hard.

"Let's go, boys. I've seen enough." Thomas strode to the wagon without a backward glance.

Keeper Smyth was not only inept, but crooked as well.

CHAPTER 27
Mid November 1878
Cape Hatteras Station, NC

"Cap'n, the telegraph's chirping," Seamus shouted across the yard.

Eli and the Mahigan brothers were winding line onto a spare faking box in the yard while Thomas looked on. Thomas hurried toward the station. The faking box forgotten, the others trailed behind.

"What's it say, Cap'n?" Elijah rumbled.

Thomas lifted his eyes from the telegraph. After glancing at Eli, he pinned eyes on Pennycuik. "Get the apparatus ready, Seamus. We've got a ship ashore to the south. Where's Sparrow on patrol?"

"That direction for sure, Cap'n," Seamus answered before turning toward the men. "Eli, load the Lyle gun. C'mon, gents, quick work now."

Thomas helped push the beach cart down the long ramp into the sand while Charlie brought the horses around. Sparrow had appeared at the head of the beach trail and was frantically waving a flare. Thomas lifted a hand, and the little Banker scurried back across the dunes to the south.

When the cart caught up to Sparrow he was breathing heavily and had stripped off his overcoat.

"Where, Sparrow?' Thomas shouted from the seat of the cart.

Sparrow pointed out to sea.

At about one hundred sixty yards, a large frigate was snagged tight in the sand. All sail had been stripped by the crew, and the surf broke against her side in a mist of salt spray.

Thomas turned toward Sparrow. "Spare?"

Sparrow squinted against the sun and lifted a hand to shield his eyes. Quickly, he licked a finger and held it in the air, testing the wind. "All right boys, let's get her going."

With a grunt, Elijah lifted the ugly little cannon from the back of the wagon, and the Mahigans wrestled the faking box full of line into place.

"Where's the card?!" Seamus roared.

Evan dove into the cart, searching for the wooden card that had directions for the sailors. His head was still pushed down among the gear when the first shot roared toward the stricken ship.

Thomas stood on the cart, ignoring the rummaging of Evan, and lifted his spyglass toward the ship's rigging. The shot had landed squarely in the rigging, and the sailors aboard scurried to make the line fast to the mast. He snapped the glass shut and glanced at the sky. It was a clear, cool day. The ship had sought better speed and run aground in the shifting sand bars.

"Damn fool," Thomas muttered to himself.

Evan shouted in triumph and handed off the card with directions to Seamus, who snatched it from his hand with a baleful glare.

Thomas returned his eye to the spyglass. Her name was *Endeavour*. It was printed in black letters outlined with white on her bow. She bore no figurehead, only a solitary bowsprit. Her main mast flew the stars and stripes. She was quartering toward the shore, and Captain Hooper couldn't make out her port of call on the stern. His spyglass fell upon the captain of the vessel. The two regarded each other thoughtfully across one hundred sixty yards of surf through identical spyglasses. The ship's captain raised a hand in salute. Thomas returned the wave.

The Mahigan brothers had finished burying the anchor while Evan and Eli hauled the beach apparatus chair from the cart. In short order, the surfmen of Cape Hatteras were pulling the chair across the tops of the waves toward the stranded vessel.

Thomas flipped open his pocket-watch and grinned. It had been less than an hour since they'd reached the beach. The first of the sailors had climbed into the beach chair, and at Pennycuik's order the surfmen began hauling him toward shore.

It was the better part of two hours before the captain hit the sand. The sailors had helped the surfmen haul their brothers through the waves, and Evan had broken out some hard bread and water from the cart. Two sailors rested against its wheels and ate what was offered. Jon handed out fresh woolen blankets, and the sailors wrapped themselves in their warmth against the late autumn chill.

"Thank you, Keeper," the captain offered his hand to Thomas, "Well done."

Thomas shook the offered hand. "Our pleasure, Captain. I'm sorry for your loss."

The captain's face was gray, his lips pressed tightly together. "Not as sorry as I."

Thomas regarded the captain gravely. "We'll send a boat and inventory what's aboard, Captain. At least the vultures haven't arrived yet." As he spoke, Thomas glanced in both directions out to the open sea.

"You'll do what you can, Keeper, uh...?"

Thomas nodded. "Hooper, Captain. Keeper Thomas Hooper, Cape Hatteras Station."

The Captain nodded crisply. "Just so, Keeper Hooper. I'd like to provision and reboard with your men, just in case." The Captain turned his eyes to his ship. "I'll stay aboard and keep the vultures at bay should they come."

Thomas's heart went out to the captain. "Of course, Captain. The ship's in little danger as she sits, as long as the weather holds."

Turning to Pennycuik, he said, "Seamus, send a man to Hatteras and fetch back Will Marshall and his sons. Let them know we've cargo to bring ashore, and that I need a few honest ferrymen. Have the Mahigans and Eli ready a surfboat to land on the ship, and send Evan with a logbook to keep a full accounting. The Captain will attend them. See that his crew is taken back to the station and set them a proper meal."

Seamus nodded, "Aye, Cap'n."

Thomas lit his pipe and blew a contented smoke ring as Seamus dispatched the orders. Cape Hatteras Station was a success.

CHAPTER 28
Late November 1878
Cockburn Town, Turks Caicos

The square rigged, four hundred eighty-seven ton barquentine, *Fearless*, basked in the late afternoon sun alongside Government Wharf in Cockburn Town, on Grand Turk Island in the British West Indies. The *Fearless*'s heavy sails were furled tight, and the warm, salty breeze whispered around the rigging. A score of dock men wrestled heavy barrels amidships and stowed them below decks.

"Trying to get off afore Thanksgiving, Captain Logan?" rasped a uniformed man. His thick accent spoke of years on the wharves of a faraway London. The man was razor thin. His pinched, clean-shaven face bobbed on a narrow neck, and his uniform spoke of Turk's allegiance with Her Majesty.

"I am," growled Captain Logan. He didn't turn to the thin official, but continued to concentrate on the loading of his ship.

Captain Nathaniel Logan was in a foul humor, and the last thing he wanted to do was share idle banter with the Englishman. Logan was a man of fierce visage, and his crew knew him to be of fiercer temperament. His short-cropped gray beard framed a leather-hard face that was seamed from years of squinting across the sea. A short homemade pipe jutted over the grim line of his square-cut jaw.

"Well, sir, the weather seems clear enough?" the Englishman continued. It was more of a question than a statement.

Logan drew the pipe from his mouth and spat onto the pier. He raised an eyebrow at the Englishman, "Does it." It was more of a statement than a question.

"Ah," the Englishman stammered, "Appears so."

Logan continued to burn holes into the Englishman with his eyes. "Mr. Douglass. The weather's never clear between Turks and Baltimore in late November." He stuck the pipe back into his mouth and rolled it to its customary corner before continuing. "Hard to tell what the bitch will have in store for us."

Mr. Douglass retreated a half step. "Ah, yes, then...well, I'll have your departure paperwork and tax papers prepared for the shipper no later than tomorrow morning."

Logan nodded crisply and turned his eyes back to his ship. Despite his complaints, he was being forced by Willis Shipping to make the run this late in the season. The demand for salt in Baltimore and Washington was great, and the shipper considered it to be worth the risk of late-season weather. Logan removed his pipe from the corner of his mouth and scowled in distaste.

Mr. Douglass had turned to go, but Captain Logan turned back to the Englishman. "Mr. Douglass, do you have any communication with Nassau or Kingston?"

Mr. Douglass shook his head; his eyebrows knit in concern. "Not officially, Captain. However, we do have two ships due within the next few days that may bring word." He glanced at the men loading salt. "I assume that you're looking for a weather report out of your Signal Corps."

Logan nodded and shrugged. He'd expected no better, but it hadn't hurt to ask. The Transatlantic telegraph cable had been run twenty years ago, and the capitals of both the Bahamas and Jamaica had access to the eight-hour weather report published by the US Signal Corps. Logan spat again. Not Turks and Caicos. Damned Brits.

Mr. Douglass had begun to prattle about the efficiency of transatlantic telegraph lines, but Captain Logan cut him short. "That will be all, Mr. Douglass."

Mr. Douglass opened and closed his mouth, and his face reddened at the impolite response. Without another word, he turned on his heel and started toward his office at the end of the wharf. He straightened his uniform coat. So impolite, so, so… Yankee.

Captain Logan strode purposefully down the gangplank and, with a curt nod to the crewmen loading the barrels of salt, went directly to his cabin. The captain's cabin aboard the *Fearless* was broad and expansive, as befitted a ship of her size. Squarely in the center of the cabin was a small oaken table, its legs firmly bolted through the deck to keep it in place against the pitch and roll of the open sea. Logan bent over the table and the large chart of the Eastern Seaboard that was spread across it. He placed the stub of a middle finger on Turks and traced his way to the coast of Florida. His other hand idly tapped a worn set of brass calipers on the edge of the yellowed chart. His perpetual frown deepened as he traced their way north along the coast to Baltimore.

The weather aside, he'd lost some crew and was short for the run North. The *Fearless* could keep a dozen able bodied seamen busy, and he'd be making this run with only seven hands, the first mate, and himself.

"Skipper?" a voice spoke from the open doorway.

Logan glanced up, his frosty blue eyes hooded against his concern. "Yes, Jubbs?"

The man in the doorway was square built and solid. His broad chest was bare and matted with curly black hair. Backlit by the bright tropical sun, his skin was the hue of polished oak. "We've loaded," the man said quietly. His heavy eyebrows arched as he stood awaiting orders.

Logan's jaw clenched unconsciously and he nodded to the first mate of the *Fearless*. "Very well, Jubbs." The captain turned his eyes back to the chart.

Jubbs took a long step into the room out of the sun. His dark eyes fixed on the captain's finger as it traced the coast. "Along the coast, eh, Skip?"

Logan raised an eyebrow at Jubbs and met his eyes. The first mate's dark eyes did little to reveal his thoughts. "That's right."

Jubbs continued to lock eyes with the captain, and he arched his own eyebrow. A hint of a smile wrinkled the corners of Logan's eyes. Jubbs had been first mate aboard the *Fearless* for three years, and in that time he'd never questioned a single decision made by Captain Logan. Logan puffed his pipe. Seconds ticked by on the large brass wall clock, and the voices of the crewmen drifted on the warm sea breeze through the open door.

Jubbs broke eye contact with the captain and glanced down at the chart. He turned to go.

Captain Logan cleared his throat, and Jubbs turned his head to the captain. "We're going to be home in Gloucester for Christmas this year, Jubbs," he said flatly. The tone of his voice brooked no argument.

Jubbs rubbed sweat from his brow and ran his calloused fingers through his stiff black hair. He nodded slowly at the captain's statement, and turned his eyes to the chart beneath the captain's hand. "You say so, Skip."

"We'll grab the Florida current and the Gulf Stream," Logan's finger retraced the coast of Florida up to Cape Hatteras, "and let the northern current ride us up the coast. We'll pick days up based on that five knots of current, Jubbs."

Jubbs nodded. He reached over and tapped Cape Hatteras. "Just so, Skip; you know better than me, but the Cape's the devil's teeth this time of year. The southern and northern currents meet, and if there's any weather..." His voice trailed off.

Logan sighed as he watched Jubbs tap North Carolina's finger that jutted into the sea. "Agreed." His eyes sought Jubbs's in the dim light of the cabin. "I've made promises, Jubbs."

Jubbs nodded again, but didn't meet the captain's eyes. Logan had promised the shippers and the merchants of Baltimore. The die was cast. Jubbs shrugged off his concerns.

Logan was still staring at the chart, but his thoughts were in Massachusetts. His promises had nothing to do with the shippers and merchants. His thoughts were with three little boys, two little girls and a wife that he loved. His mind's eye saw a Christmas table and a warm fire, not barrels of mined salt.

Logan straightened from the table and relit his pipe. Enough worrying. He was the captain. "Tomorrow's Thanksgiving, Jubbs." Logan's voice had reassumed the mantle of command. "Have the men back aboard the boat by sunrise Friday."

Jubbs glanced at the captain in surprise. He'd assumed that they'd be off at once. "I'd hate for the brothels of Cockburn Town to be unattended on a holiday," Logan grinned wryly in dry New England humor.

Jubbs nodded briskly and turned to the door. He paused with his hand on the knob, glancing back at Captain Logan. "Let's hope the weather holds, eh, Skip."

Logan continued to smile, but the smile didn't reach his eyes as he nodded to the first mate.

Both men already knew.

It wouldn't.

CHAPTER 29
Late November 1878
Cape Hatteras Station

The first glow of morning was just beginning to brighten the Eastern horizon over the Atlantic when the wagon rumbled into the sandy yard at Cape Hatteras Station. Thomas and Seamus were nursing brimming cups of yaupon tea in the cookhouse, and Charlie Mahigan had just gotten back from his patrol. The three men exchanged a glance at the sound of the wagon, and Thomas rose and opened the cookhouse door. The rectangle of lantern light fell across the yard, and Thomas's face broke into a wide grin. A large buckboard had swung into the yard.

"Couldn't have you boys starve on the holiday, Tom." Jacob swung from the seat and held up a hand to help Rose down to the sand.

Thomas strode quickly to the older black man and wrapped him in a quick hug. "Welcome, my old friends." Emotion was thick in his voice. Seamus came to the open door and whooped into the cold morning.

Rose pushed her husband out of the way. "Tarnation, Jacob, he don't wanna see you," she said in half-anger. Her eyes were wet with tears.

Thomas swept his foster mother off her feet and swung her in a broad circle. "Rose, the love of my life, how I've missed you!"

"It ain't me either, Tom," Rose smiled at the hug, and Della sprang lightly down from the back of the buckboard.

She wore a heavy cloak open at the throat, and kissed Thomas lightly on the cheek. "Hello, Tom."

Thomas hugged her, and the Mahigan brothers exchanged a knowing look in the doorway to the station.

"Momma said that you've probably starved without us to cook your meals," she teased.

Rose interposed herself between the two. "Now, we'll have that kitchen house, Mr. Tom. Git them men outta there," she commanded, smiling.

Jacob was standing off to the side, his weathered face split by his tremendous grin. "Now, Rose, I figured you'd be all about a roomful o' men. They's a little young for ya, though."

Rose spun on Jacob, "You old devil." She glared at Thomas. "Really, Mr. Tom, this is what you've lef' me with." She shook a finger at Jacob scoldingly. "Now, get your worthless self unloadin', you old devil. Della and I've a dinner to set out."

Seamus was hopping from one foot to the other. His thick accent had turned his words unintelligible. He swung onto the back of the buckboard and began rifling through the baskets and sacks. The crew of Hatteras Station was trickling into the yard. Taking a large bite of a green apple, Seamus began barking orders at the men and the unloading began.

Rose left the unloading to them, gave Thomas a quick peck on the cheek, and brushed past Elijah into the cookhouse. Elijah shrugged and swallowed hard, trying not to stare at Della.

"Surprised, Cap'n?" Jacob asked quietly, with a wide grin.

Thomas grinned back at his lifelong friend. "I'll say, Jacob," he said warmly. He threw an arm around the older man's shoulders. "Let me show you around." As he led Jacob into the station, Thomas cast a glance at Seamus and met his eyes. "Today's training is cancelled, Mr. Pennycuik."

Sparrow was carrying a bushel of apples up the step and into the cookhouse. "Well, reckon that makes me happy," he grinned over his shoulder at Seamus. It was Thursday, and Thursday's training involved the Lyle gun and extra work for him.

Seamus smiled back at Sparrow, then turned to Evan. "Still need to stand watch, Ev. You're on this morning."

Evan's smile evaporated. He'd forgotten. Sparrow paused on the step and studied Evan in the morning light. He held the young man's eyes for a brief second. "'S all right, Seamus, I'll stand his watch. Let him enjoy the holiday."

Seamus nodded to Sparrow, still grinning. "Fair enough."

Elijah had returned to the wagon and was headed toward the cookhouse with a sack of potatoes slung over his shoulder. He'd heard the conversation in passing. "Hold on now," he rumbled, "I'll come spell ya so you can eat, Sparrow."

Sparrow's thick beard parted to reveal a broken-toothed grin. "Ya better get me afore you eat it all, Eli," he joked.

Eli grinned back at the taciturn little man and pushed past him up the step to the cookhouse. "Don' count on it."

The two men disappeared into the cookhouse, still haggling. Jacob glanced at Thomas out of the corners of his eyes. Things must be coming along fairly well at Cape Hatteras Station.

"Ev, I'd like you to meet my oldest friend," Thomas called the young man over. "This is Jacob."

Evan walked over and extended his hand. "Good to meet you, sir."

Jacob shook the outstretched hand, his eyes twinkling. "You too, my boy," Jacob grinned sideways at Thomas. "Reminds me of someone, Cap."

Thomas busied himself lighting his pipe and the corners of his eyes wrinkled at Jacob's comment. He looked up, blowing smoke into the morning sky. "That so, Jacob?"

Evan frowned in confusion at the exchange. "Who's that, Mr. Jacob?"

Jacob continued to smile at Keeper Hooper. Thomas rolled the pipe into the corner of his mouth. "Me, Ev," Thomas said quietly. "He means me."

Evan's eyes went wide at the compliment, and he glanced hurriedly at Jacob. "No sir, Mr. Jacob. I jus'...I just..." he spluttered.

Jacob threw an arm over the boy's shoulder. "Easy now, boy." His eyes continued to twinkle. "If you don't want to be like Cap'n Tom, I understand..."

Evan's face went white at the comment. "Oh, no!" He shook his head quickly and threw his hands in the air. "No, it's not that, I..." His voice trailed off in embarrassment.

Thomas barked a laugh and smoke trickled from his nose. "He's just hassling you, son." He wagged a forefinger in mock reproach at Jacob. "Be good, Jacob."

"Ah, he can take it." Jacob ruffled Evan's hair. "Now show me this station of yours, Evan; I can't abide hearing your keeper brag his lies if he walks me around."

Evan had let out his breath and his color was returning. The two men, young and old, walked into the station house, leaving Thomas to his thoughts.

Thomas stepped onto the boardwalk and peeked in the open kitchen door. He smiled inwardly at the sight. Rose had rapidly put the men to work. Elijah stood peeling potatoes into a large wooden bowl. His broad hands worked clumsily with the small potatoes. Sparrow had drifted back toward the cookhouse, drawn from his post overlooking the sea by the activity, and he heckled Eli good-naturedly through the window, which was cracked to allow some of the stove heat to escape despite the day's chill. Seamus stood next to the stove, and by the deep blush in Della's cheeks was regaling the woman with off-color jokes and stories. Jon and Charlie were both covered in good white flour from biscuit dough. A powdery handprint showed clearly, square in the middle of Jon's back. Thomas pulled his eyes from the scene within and to watch Evan trying to show Jacob how the hawser connected on the beach apparatus. Jacob caught the look and grinned at Thomas, his hand rested lightly on the boy's shoulder.

Thomas glanced at the sky in silent happy prayer. His family was together for the holiday. The sun above was trying to break through the low November sky. And the weather was holding. A brief shadow crossed Thomas's eyes at the thought.

At least for now.

CHAPTER 30
Early December 1878
Cape Hatteras Station, NC

Distant thunder woke Thomas out of sleep with a start, and he heard the first lashing rain as it peppered the roof of the station. He blinked and shook his head, trying to clear away the cobwebs of deep sleep and an unremembered dream. The room was cool, and the fire lay untended in the hearth down to gray ashes and hot coals. Thomas swung his feet over the edge of the bed, hurried to the fireplace and placed two pine knots on the fire. He shivered in the gloom and swiftly shrugged into his shirt. The wind outside whined around the eaves of the station, and a flash of distant lightning lit the interior of the room.

Thomas snatched his wool coat from the hook at the edge of the bed and made for the kitchen building. As he crossed the porch between station and kitchen, another bolt of lightning lit up the damp sand of the yard. A light burned in the kitchen, and he squeezed through the door into the safety of the room beyond.

Charlie Mahigan looked up from a game of solitaire laid out on the wide plank table, and Seamus snored in the rocking chair in the corner. His head was at an odd angle and he gurgled uncomfortably in his sleep. The room was warm, and the cook stove glowed hotly in the yellow light of the single lantern. Charlie regarded the keeper, his eyes pools of darkness and his Indian features accentuated by the shadows.

Thomas nodded to Charlie and cupped his hands to the glow of the stove. "Trouble sleeping, Charlie?" he asked quietly so as not to wake the snoring Scotsman.

Charlie nodded in return. He made as if to speak but closed his mouth and turned his eyes again to the cards.

Thomas took a cup from the shelf and helped himself to the kettle of steaming tea on the stove. He took a slow sip before turning his eyes again to Charlie. Charlie's attention to the game had faded and he was staring at the black window.

"What is it, Charlie?" Thomas asked gently.

"Couldn't say, Keep," he said softly. "Couldn't sleep tonight."

Thomas regarded him soberly. Charlie's unrest gave him a queasy feeling in the pit of his stomach.

Thomas's eyes followed the Indian's to the window, and each man was left to his own thoughts. Seamus groaned in his sleep.

The kitchen door bounded open and smashed the wall with a thud. Evan shouldered into the room. His black wool coat was soaked from the rain, the collar turned up to shield his face from the wind. He took quick stock of the room and looked relieved to find Keeper Hooper already there.

"Ship ashore, Keep! Just south, maybe two miles down," Evan said breathlessly, the words tumbling out.

Seamus, who'd awoken at the crash of the door, appeared at Thomas's elbow and handed the youngster a brimming cup of tea.

"How far out, Ev?" Thomas asked quietly.

Evan took a quick gulp and wiped his mouth with the back of his hand. "She's out there, Keep. Could barely see her flare in the rain. Maybe a thousand yards or so."

Thomas nodded and turned to Seamus. "Be light in a couple of hours, Seamus. We'll need the boat. I'd like to get there before it's full dawn."

Evan interrupted. "Something else, Keep. The wind's solid from the east, and growing."

Thomas and Seamus nodded solemnly. An east wind was bad. It bounded across the sea, driving the rain and waves before it. By the time it reached the beach, the surf would be as fierce as any they'd seen.

Thomas laid a hand on Evan's shoulder. "Don't worry, Ev. I need you to go back and keep an eye on her 'til we get there." He turned his attention to Charlie, but the Indian was already struggling into his coat and boots. The two exchanged a brief look.

"I'll go along, Keep," Charlie said abruptly.

Charlie clasped Evan's shoulder, and Evan took another quick gulp of tea. The pair shoved through the wind and into the fading rain beyond.

"Cap?" Seamus asked.

Thomas lit his pipe. "Better start getting the men ready, Seamus. I think we're in for one hell of a day."

Seamus straightened. "Aye aye, Cap."

Thomas blew smoke toward the rafters as Seamus left the kitchen, wondering to what the Scotsman was agreeing.

"God bloody damn it!" Seamus roared over the howling wind. "Get this bloody boat into position."

Thomas strained under the weight of the surfboat alongside his men and cast a dubious look out across the crashing waves. The wind was due east and whipped the foam from the crests of three lines of enormous breakers. The rain had petered out, but the racing gray clouds above were pregnant with the promise of another deluge before the day's work was done.

Evan groaned at Thomas's side as he leaned his back into the bulky little boat. "Keep, she's way out there, huh?"

"Keep your mind on the work at hand," Sparrow growled at the boy from the other side.

Evan shot a quick sidelong grin at Sparrow. "Trying to, Spare, just thinking it's a long way is all."

Thomas looked at the Evan from the corner of his eyes. Evan looked like a drowned rat. They all did. To a man, their cheeks were flushed with cold and their heavy woolens were sodden from rain and sea spray. Thomas flexed his fingers and knew that theirs felt the same: numb and chilled to the bone.

"C'mon, boys," Thomas smiled and spat with the wind onto the sand, "I know she's tough, but we're tougher. Let's not give Seamus anything else to yell about." He tightened his grip. "Heave!"

The surfboat inched down the beach as the sand drank the retreating waves. Once her bow floated the men clambered unceremoniously aboard.

"Stroke," Eli shouted, his massive chest swelling under the wool coat, the buttons nearly popping from the strain.

Seamus held his position at the small tiller. "Faster, lads!" he commanded urgently.

The first wave threatened to crest and plunge the group into the swirling torrent. The men pulled as one and the small craft slipped over the first wave, and the second. Thomas grinned in spite of the effort. The days and weeks of practice with the surfboat had paid off, and paid well.

Evan elbowed the keeper roughly and said with a broad smile, "Almost through the worst, eh, Keep?"

Thomas smiled back, but when he saw the expression on Seamus's face he whipped his head around to see the third and final wave crest.

"Lean forward!" Seamus screamed. "Hold on."

The surfboat rode up the wave. Her bow pointed at the sky and the men leaned forward.

"Pull, Eli!" Thomas's roar joined the commands of Seamus.

The froth of the wave's crest hit the boat amidships, and for a moment Thomas thought all was lost. But the nose slammed forward and down. The men of Cape Hatteras Station landed in a heap, a tangle of arms and legs, but the surfboat was afloat past the breakers. A small wave swept over her gunwale as the boat spun sideways.

"To oars, damn you," Seamus pulled himself back into position with the tiller handle. "We'll get washed in."

The men disentangled quickly and returned to their oars.

"Cap'n!" Seamus gasped.

Thomas spun at the tone. The Scotsman's face was rigid and stark white.

"Evan...where's Evan?" Seamus continued.

Thomas stared at the boy's missing place. His oar was gone, and a red smear of blood was quickly washing away under the sea water on the white gunwale.

"To shore, men!" Thomas howled, his eyes searching the water, and Seamus lunged to his feet to cast about in all directions.

"Ev....?" Charlie Mahigan said in a low tone, his voice strained with grief.

Thomas's eyes followed the Indian's outstretched oar like a long wooden finger. The bulky shape of a cork lifejacket was just visible as a cresting breaker swept toward the beach.

Thomas fixed the point. "Pull, men—pull!" he commanded. "We've got to reach Evan!"

The surfboat bashed through the waves, and Thomas vaulted over the side before she touched the sand, splashing into the waist-deep water. He felt the pull of the current, but he grabbed the life vest before it could be sucked out. He wrenched the vest over. The boy would need air.

Thomas raised his head to the sky and howled in rage and disbelief. In the distant village of Hatteras a dog howled in return. The cork life vest was empty.

CHAPTER 31
December 1878
Off the Coast of South Carolina

"She's a big one, Cap," Jubbs said, as he slid down the rigging onto the deck of the *Fearless* next to Captain Logan.

Captain Logan chewed the edge of his moustache in thought but didn't answer Jubbs. His gaze was directed to the southeast and the dark horizon. The sky was dark gray in the distance, almost black. Intermittent flashes of lightning lit the storm clouds. The distance was still too great to discern the individual streaks, but the towering black and gray cloud mass lit the sea below at irregular intervals. Logan glanced up at the American flag on the mainmast. It snapped in the wind.

"What you think, Cap?" Jubbs asked, raising his voice against the building wind.

The wrinkles around Logan's eyes were seamed in concern. Without a word, he turned and ascended the ladder to the quarterdeck. Jubbs hurried to follow him.

"I'll take the helm," Logan called to the seaman at the wheel. The seaman hurriedly backed off in relief and nearly bowled Jubbs over as he scurried for the ladder and the relative safety of the deck below.

Logan braced the heavy wheel with his leg and lit his pipe. He had to cup it and shield it with a shoulder. He tapped the heavy brass compass. The needle was fixed like an arrow away from the storm. He pulled his eyes from the compass and turned squarely to the building gale.

"I think we're going to get wet, Jubbs," Logan said, quietly regarding the first mate in the odd orange-ish light.

Jubbs laughed softly without humor. "Reckon you're right there, Cap."

"We'll make a try at outrunning her..." Logan's voice trailed off as he plowed the bow of the *Fearless* through a long trough. The sea was running straight away from the wind. The heavy ship dug her bow into another large swell and slowed perceptibly as the wind pushed her up and over. "Full sail, Jubbs, throw up everything we've got."

"Aye, Cap," Jubbs nodded and swung down the ladder. His voice thundered with command to the crewmen below. "Full sheets, boys."

The crew of the *Fearless* leapt into action, and Captain Logan felt the heavy boat surge under the strain of the added sail. He nodded grimly and braced the large wheel with both hands. Logan blew smoke into the wind, glancing over his shoulder at their froth-flecked wake. The horizon beyond flashed in the distance. He nodded again, and the distant lightning reflected the piled up gray clouds in his frosty blue eyes. The heavy clouds stretched as far as he could see to port and starboard.

Maybe they'd make it. Maybe.

CHAPTER 32
December 1878
Cape Hatteras Station

The faces at Cape Hatteras Station were long and solemn in the crisp winter sunlight. The surfmen stood in a semicircle around a smooth stone marker, and Jacob stood with them. The wind whispered in the scrub bushes that were scattered around the wide yard, and the faint clink of pots and pans came from the kitchen shack where Rose and Della prepared lunch.

The men wore their long woolen coats, their caps pulled tight and collars turned up. Thomas, at the center of the loose semicircle, blew his breath into the wind, where it clouded and joined the breaths of the others in the winter cold. His tortured eyes turned again to the chiseled inscription on the rock. *Evan Thatcher. Surfman. Dead so that others may live. 1878*. There was no year of birth, because the men of Cape Hatteras Station didn't know. There was no grave, and no interment. Evan's body was lost to the sea.

Elijah was the first to break the silence. His deep, quiet voice sounded loud in the thin air. "*Amazing grace, how sweet the sound, that saved a wretch like me...*" Eli's voice lifted in song.

The other men joined in. "*I once was lost, but now am found. Was blind but now I see.*"

The voices trailed off, and Sparrow sniffled loudly behind the upturned collar of his coat. Thomas cleared his throat and swallowed audibly.

"We've gathered to give Evan Thatcher into Your hands, dear Lord," Thomas said. His voice was raw with emotion. "Please take our friend into your arms, Lord. His time with us is done."

"Amen," stammered Elijah, and he hung Evan's summer uniform jacket over the rock.

Thomas swallowed again and looked to Seamus for help.

"*Beannachd Dia dhuit*," rolled Seamus in Gaelic, his eyes wet with tears. "Blessings of God be with you."

The other men nodded. Jon opened his mouth as if to speak, caught Charlie's eye, and pressed his lips tightly together. Jon held two fingers to his left eye and gestured deliberately toward the polished memorial stone. Charlie followed suit.

Sparrow lit his pipe and spat into the sand. "He was the best of us."

Elijah caught the smaller man's eye and nodded his assent. "Amen."

Thomas drew out his own pipe and pushed tobacco into the bowl. Carefully, he struck a wooden match on the button of his uniform coat and puffed the pipe to life. He nodded to Jacob. "Boys, Jacob and Rose have brought us supper. We've duties to attend to."

Seamus drew in a long, slow breath. "Aye, Keep. Spare, you've got the watch."

Eli coughed and touched Sparrow on the arm. He spoke to Seamus. "I've got Sparrow's watch, boss. Give him a few minutes."

The rest of the men turned and started for the kitchen. The usual chatter and banter was gone, replaced only with silence. Thomas clenched his fists against the cold and continued standing over the memorial.

He was still standing there when Della spoke quietly. "Come inside, Thomas."

Thomas glanced at the woman and drew on his pipe. The tracks of tears traced his cheeks, but his eyes were dry. "It's my fault, D. He was only a boy." There was no anger in his voice, only sadness.

Della looked down at the marker before raising her eyes to Thomas. "It wasn't your fault, Tom. It wasn't anyone's fault. He knew the dangers. You all do." Her words hung in the chill air.

"Do we, D? Really, do we?" he asked plaintively. "Evan was just a boy. How could—"

Della interrupted him with a raised hand and a shake of her head that set her long hair swaying. "No, Thomas. Don't do that to yourself. He was a man. I've heard you say that the definition of a man is the willingness to accept responsibility for his actions. In fact, I heard Captain McGuire say the same when we were both too young to matter."

She took Thomas's hand and brushed it lightly with her lips. Her eyes met his. "Evan was a man. He accepted his responsibility on that day, and you accepted yours too, Thomas. You all did when you stopped searching for Evan and rescued the men aboard that ship." She cleared her throat to steady her trembling voice. "You are the surfmen of Cape Hatteras Station. Evan was a surfman of Cape Hatteras Station too."

Thomas drew deeply on his pipe and exhaled the smoke through his nose. "That he was, D, that he was."

CHAPTER 33
Mid December 1878
Cape Hatteras Station, North Carolina

Thomas leaned against the broad door jamb at the top of the ramp overlooking the sea, a steaming mug of yaupon tea in his hand. The sun wasn't breaking over the distant horizon this morning. The sky was low and ugly and the early morning light had a red-orange tinge that Keeper Hooper didn't like.

Up ahead on the beach proper, Charlie Mahigan had the morning watch. Thomas eyed the distant figure. He was a bit closer to the station than usual and was pacing back and forth on the edge of the salt grass. As the days had grown colder, the men had taken to pacing back and forth on the day watches. It was better than sitting still.

Thomas flipped the dregs of his tea into the sand below and thoughtfully stuffed his wooden pipe. He struck a match on the doorjamb, cupping it against the wind, and blew the first draw of smoke into the stiff breeze. He strode down the ramp and made his way along the winding sandy trail toward Charlie.

Charlie was beating his arms, flapping them against the cold. "Morning, Keep!" He smiled from behind the upturned collar of his own coat. He and his brother had been inseparable since Evan's death, and Thomas was surprised not to find them together.

"Morning, Charlie." Thomas nodded. "Anything new?" He dropped into step beside the pacing Indian.

Charlie shook his head. "Not really. Sand, sun, sky," Charlie snorted. "Tide's up awful high this morning though, Keep."

Thomas saw this was indeed so. The tide was way up the beach, and tendrils of frothy water had found their way as far as the salt grass. The breakers were a little above average, but it was the swell of water that he didn't like. The swells were long and large.

Thomas nodded to Charlie. "Right then. Keep a sharp eye this morning. I don't like the way she looks." His eyes flicked back out over the water.

"Aye aye, Keep," Charlie nodded in return and added, "Always do."

Thomas smiled wanly and turned back to the station.

"Morning, Cap." Seamus stood in the dim interior. He'd just shrugged into his heavy coat and stamped his feet into his boots.

Thomas brushed past him without answering and strode toward the telegraph in the corner. Seamus raised his eyebrows in surprise at the keeper's brusque manner and followed him to the telegraph key.

Thomas stared at the silent key, then turned and looked up at Seamus. "Seamus, has the key gone off at all?"

Seamus rubbed the red stubble on his jaw. "Not in weeks, Cap. Lines might be down, or something."

Thomas shook his head, lost in thought. "When's our last weather report from the Signal Corps?"

Seamus shrugged and pointed to the logbook. "Ain't had one since Evan," Seamus swallowed, "since Evan died, Cap."

Thomas stared at the logbook on the desk and spoke without looking at Seamus. "Try to hail anyone. Let's see how far away it's broken." Thomas had trained Seamus as best he could since Evan had died, but the Scotsman was a poor telegraph replacement.

Thomas met Seamus's eyes in the dim light. "Set the flags for a heavy storm, Seamus. I can feel it."

Seamus glanced out the broad open door at the surf before heading up the stairs. "Aye, Cap."

Thomas nodded absently at Seamus before turning back to the station door. He'd only seen a sky this red-orange, and such a heavy swell, one other time in his life. That storm had taken his parents.

CHAPTER 34

Mid December 1878
Diamond Shoals, North Carolina

"Sheet in the mainsails!" Captain Logan shouted over the wind.

He glanced at the sky as the *Fearless* dropped into another steep trough. He'd been wrong, thinking to outrun the gale. The ship had made a valiant attempt, but the first sheets of heavy rain had caught her over an hour ago. With the rain had come the wind. It howled in rage at the ship and had already tattered the foresail and the jib.

Jubbs staggered up the ladder and stuck his head over the quarterdeck. "Cap'n..." Jubbs voice was lost to the wind.

The *Fearless* shoved into an upswell. Captain Logan's eyes narrowed as the bowsprit disappeared and thousands of gallons of water swept across the deck. The black water took one of the crewmen behind the knees as he struggled to reef the mainsail lines tighter. The man slid across the deck and was brought up short against the aft bulkhead. He rose and staggered back to his station. The blood that streamed from the gash across his forehead mingled with rain and salt water, staining his white tunic pink before it blanched white again under the torrent.

Jubbs fought to hold himself on the ladder, and his knuckles whitened under the strain. "Cap'n," he screamed against the wind. "We can't hold her! Heaving to ain't enough."

Logan glared at the first mate before raising his eyes to his ship. The tattered foresail flapped wetly in the wind. The bow pulpit had splintered and a large section was missing. He could feel her straining through his boots, and knew the creaks and groans would only grow louder. After he glanced at the telltales on the mainmast and the flag above, Logan whipped his eyes to the compass. Their heading was northwest. The wind was coming around. Logan swore. Only hurricane winds swirled like this.

Jubbs stared at the captain. The sky to his back was black and veiled with torrential rain. The lightning had caught up to the ship, and the jagged streaks made a stark silhouette of the captain struggling with the wheel. Thunder roared its presence and the sea churned, kneeing the *Fearless*'s unprotected belly.

"Jubbs!" the captain howled over the deadly symphony of the storm. "Set her..." The wind whipped his words out across the sea and Logan struggled with the wheel. "Set her to lay ahull. If you can't furl the sails, cut 'em loose."

Jubbs nodded and repeated the command to be certain that he'd heard it correctly. "Lay ahull, Cap? Strike the sails and try to ride her out?"

Logan nodded grimly.

"This a bad one, Cap. I, uh... I'm not sure..." Jubbs trailed off before finishing his thought.

Captain Logan narrowed his eyes at the first mate. "That's the order, Mr. Jubbs. Are we clear?"

"Aye, Cap. Preparing to lay ahull." Jubbs nodded and staggered off into the storm.

With the sails furled or cut free the *Fearless* swung sharply crosswise to the heavy swells. Despite not having sails, the wind pushed her masts and gunwales angrily, and the boat listed hard over. Logan swung from the quarterdeck and staggered into the relative safety of the cabin below. The cabin was a wreck. Logan's charts and trinkets littered the floor; most lay along the wall as the sea shoved the boat onto its side.

Jubbs was rummaging through the charts and glanced up at the captain framed in the doorway. He held up a rolled chart and nodded to his captain. Logan squatted next to the man, bracing his shoulder against the cabin wall.

"It's in God's hands, now, Jubbs," Captain Logan said through clenched teeth.

"Aye," Jubbs agreed as he unrolled the chart on the floor between them. Logan reached out and held down one side.

Jubbs looked at the captain, tapping the chart with a dripping hand. Logan studied the paper and nodded at length. The first mate's assessment was probably right, based on their run to this point and the current swells.

Jubbs continued to tap Diamond Shoals, and the *Fearless* began to come apart.

CHAPTER 35
December 1878
Cape Hatteras Station

The rain raked Cape Hatteras Station, beating the windows and batten siding before tearing across the lonely sands beyond. Having risen from a howl to a shriek, the wind screamed angrily at the sand and kicked water up the beach to swirl beneath the very floorboards of the station itself. The gray and black storm clouds that swirled above like Mother Nature's skirt-hem had long since blocked out the late afternoon sun.

"Seamus, have you removed the plugs?" Thomas turned to the Scotsman.

Seamus squatted against the wall. He was half-asleep, his head lolled forward, but at the question he raised his head, blinking in the yellow glow from the single lantern.

"We done it, Keep," Charlie and Jon answered the keeper as one.

Charlie pointed to three large wooden plugs that had been taken from the floor of Hatteras Station. The builder, McGowan, had designed the plug system to allow rising water up through the floor in an effort to keep the station from floating out to sea. He jerked a thumb toward the back right corner of the building, "Couldn't get that one out, Keep; moisture's got it swelled tight."

Thomas stared at the plugs on the floor, but his thoughts were on the angry sea beyond the walls. He patted his pipe pouch at his waist. At not feeling the familiar comfort, he rapidly patted the pockets of his uniform coat. Jon took two quick strides to the telegraph desk and returned with the keeper's pipe. He held it out to Thomas, but Thomas didn't notice and continued to search his pockets.

"Sir?" Jon asked quietly, holding the pipe before Thomas's eyes.

Thomas's gaze snapped back in focus and he winked at Jon, taking his pipe from the outstretched hand. "Thanks, Jon." Thomas turned his head back to Charlie and smiled sheepishly. "Sorry, Charlie, must have dozed off." He glanced again at the wooden plugs. "Three ought to do it. We wouldn't want the station house to float away."

The wind and rain rattled the windows through the thick wooden shutters. Seamus stood and stretched, walking over to Eli and Sparrow. The two were deep in a game of dominoes on an upturned wooden crate.

"Looks like you're gettin' beat," Seamus grinned at Sparrow.

The tough little Banker didn't even glance up. His focus was on the game, albeit through a cloud of pipe smoke that he was steadily exhaling like a steam engine through his nose. Elijah grinned up at Seamus, a flash of white against his dark skin in the dim lamp light. The two had developed an unusual bond after Evan's death.

Thomas rose and ran his hand lightly down the gunwale of the surfboat that rested in its wooden cradle. "Well, boys," he began.

Thomas waited until all eyes turned his way. Elijah reached across the domino game and nudged Sparrow, pointing toward Keeper Hooper.

Thomas cleared his throat and let his eyes gather the men before resting last on Seamus. "Who has first watch?' he asked, his voice barely audible against the noise of the storm.

It was Jon Mahigan that spoke. "That'd be me, Keep," he said, his eyes revealing nothing, shadowed by his brow in the yellowish light.

"Very well," Thomas nodded.

Charlie studied a hole in the toe of his sock before reaching over and pulling his heavy boots across the floor. Jon looked at him, a question in his eyes.

"I guess I'd better come along and make sure you don't get lost, little brother," Charlie answered the unasked question.

Seamus grinned at Thomas. "Good idea, Charlie. In fact, let's double up tonight for all watches, lads."

The others nodded agreement. Thomas lit his pipe, and the domino game started up again.

Seamus pulled a wooden crate around to face Thomas. "Cap'n, what do ya think?"

Thomas studied the swirl of pipe smoke against the ceiling. At length he said, "I think it's going to be damned hard to see out there, Seamus." He paused removed his pipe, rubbed his jaw with the back of his hand and squinted at the Scotsman, "Let's put on a good supper tonight, Seamus. Work with Eli; we might need it."

"Aye, Cap'n, we might indeed," Seamus nodded and toed Eli in the rear end with his boot. "C'mon, Eli. Help me with supper."

The man rubbed his rump in mock hurt and started for the cookhouse, leaving Thomas to his thoughts and Sparrow to play dominoes by himself. The storm outside thundered on.

Dinner came and went. The men of Cape Hatteras Station ate quietly; competing with the roar of the rain and wind was pointless. The men stared at the walls of the station, trying to divine the storm without; and Thomas stared at the men, trying to divine the storm within.

Seamus cleared the dishes and trooped back to the cookhouse. They'd brought dinner into the main level of the station. The roof of the cookhouse was leaking badly, and there was more room to dodge the drips in the station itself.

"'Nother game, Eli?" Sparrow queried as he lit his pipe.

Elijah had risen from his seat on the floor, and he reached up, adjusting the lamp wick. "Not tonight, Spare, I've got next watch with Seamus. I's gonna try an' get some sleep."

Sparrow nodded. His mouth drew a grim line through his gray beard where the pipe stem disappeared. He'd thought as much. The man might have the wrong color skin, but he did have sense. Sparrow pulled the pipe from his mouth before speaking. "My pappy always used to say that you oughta sleep when you've got time." He stuffed the pipe back in his mouth and finished around the stem, "Never know what lies ahead, an' all that."

Thomas watched the exchange from his seat on an upturned crate. He, too, rose and stretched, then followed Elijah up the stairs. Sparrow's pappy was right. He glanced back at Sparrow. The man had hunkered himself deeply into his woolen coat and was staring blankly at the heavy wooden doors facing the beach. He'd sleep here and be ready.

"Cap...Cap'n," Seamus's voice was low and insistent. Thomas felt the hand on his shoulder and his eyes snapped open in his bunk. The wind and rain had subsided from a roar to a dull drumming on the eaves and roof above, and Seamus didn't need to yell to be heard. Thomas blinked hard in the darkness. All he could make out was Seamus's profile in the gloom. The Scotsman hadn't struck a light. The rattling snores of the other sleeping men continued unabated.

Seamus leaned close, and Thomas could see the whites of the man's eyes. "Ship ashore, Cap'n," Seamus breathed.

Thomas nodded and sat up on his bunk. He held a finger to Seamus's lips. "Give me the rundown downstairs," he whispered hoarsely. Seamus disappeared into the gloom and Thomas swung his legs over the edge of the bed. Pulling on his pants, he followed Seamus down the narrow staircase to the dimly lit main floor of the station.

Elijah was just closing the front door. His sleeves dripped, and his black cap was soaked through. Three cups of steaming yaupon tea were clutched close to his body in relative protection from the blowing rain. He held one out to Thomas, flashing the keeper a quick grin.

Thomas took a quick sip of the brew and sucked his breath through his teeth. It was scalding hot and wicked strong. "Let's have it then, boys."

Seamus narrowed his eyes at the keeper, cupping the steaming brew in both his hands to allow the warmth to creep into his half-frozen fingers. "Still too dark to see the ship, Cap. She's bloody far out, fetched up on one of the outer bars. We did see thar' flare though. Kinnakeet answered with a flare of their own."

Thomas's own eyes narrowed at the mention of the other station. "She's fetched up in their waters, then."

Elijah spoke for the first time. "Tha's why we woke ya, Keep."

Seamus explained, "She's right at the edge 'atween them an' us, Cap."

Thomas flicked his eyes between the two men. The concern on their faces matched his own. "Eli, light our own flare." He turned a silent prayer toward the rafters before continuing. "It's time to go to work."

CHAPTER 36
December 1878
Diamond Shoals, just offshore of Cape Hatteras

"Two flares, Skip!" Jubbs stuck his head into the captain's cabin. His curly black hair was matted from long soaking in the torrential rain, and his dark eyes flashed under the shadow of his heavy brow.

Captain Logan studied the first mate from his hunched position over the chart on the up-tilted deck. Behind Jubbs, Logan could make out the ruin of the shattered mizzenmast, tangled in the rigging of the mainmast, in the predawn light.

"Very well, Jubbs. Have the men continue bailing out the hold. We'll have to stay afloat 'til they get here," Logan answered quietly, and squatted back against the wall. His eyes were sunken with exhaustion. He could feel the dying *Fearless* groaning beneath his feet. They'd come hard aground almost two hours ago. At sea, the *Fearless* had bobbed and weaved around the worst of the blows. She'd been devastated, but her bottom had held. Now snagged by the shoals below, the sea could mount her and beat her without mercy. It was only a matter of time until she gave way. The salt water had already begun to send searching fingers in around the failing beams. Captain Logan sighed heavily. Only a matter of time. He raised his head toward the sky above as he'd done so many times in the hours past, and beseeched the Lord to keep her together just a little longer.

"Skip, coming on light. Might want to have a look," Jubbs stuck his head in the door again.

Captain Logan nodded to the first mate, rising to his feet. He straightened his jacket and absently stared at the long rip along the forearm. He'd have to get Margaret to sew that one up before he could wear it again, he thought, as he staggered across the slant toward the open door.

Logan paused in the doorway. His eyes were drawn to the far eastern horizon and the dawn. The sun would be late today, held at bay by the gray sky trailing in the wake of the storm. The waves crashed into the exposed side of the *Fearless* and gurgled over her decks. Logan rubbed a shaking hand over the stubble on his neck, straining his eyes toward the west.

The Carolina shoreline was just a thin line of deeper shadow on the white-flecked sea. It wouldn't be light enough to make out the sand for an hour or so. Logan pulled the collar of his coat more tightly to keep the cold rain from running down the back of his neck.

The *Fearless* shifted and splintered, and Logan rubbed the shattered deck railing, stroking it, quieting it like he would a child or favorite pet. He glanced skyward again and lifted his thoughts in silent prayer. Only an hour or so.

CHAPTER 37
December 1878
Cape Hatteras Station

"An hour or so." Seamus squinted out toward the eastern horizon.

The large beach doors on Cape Hatteras Station were thrown open to the weather, and the men stared fixedly out at the open sea from the top of the ramp.

Sparrow's pipe wagged in agreement with Seamus. "What's the word?" he called over the wind that whipped into the open doorway.

Jon beat the rain from his sopping woolen cap hat against his thigh. His cheeks were still flushed from his jog down the beach. "She's layed to pretty far out, Spare. Don't believe we'll get to use your gun today," he said.

Thomas lit his pipe and turned his head to Seamus. "Break out the surfboat."

Eli and Sparrow exchanged a glance. The men could hear the roar of the surf on the wind. Taking the boat into the waves was a chilling thought indeed. The memory of Evan and their last foray in the surfboat was heavy on all their minds.

Thomas blew smoke from his nose and the wind whirled it into a wreath around his head. "The Kinnakeet men started out yet, Jon?"

Jon replaced his on his head before responding. "Don't think so, Keep. I left Charlie out on that hammock to keep an eye on the ship." Jon squinted at the keeper. "And the Kinnakeet men."

Thomas nodded. "Right, then." Stepping out onto the ramp, Thomas drew a heavy breath. "All hands, men. Let's go to work."

Seamus smiled warily at the keeper. "Aye aye, Captain. To the surfboat, lads. Let's have at it."

Charlie Mahigan watched them come with eyes slitted against the rain and his chin burrowed under the upturned collar of his uniform coat. From the high hammock, his view out across the sea was a good one, and he'd seen the foundering ship come hard aground. The driving rain made the stranded ship disappear at irregular intervals. He was forced to keep a watchful eye to make sure that he didn't lose it in the storm, and he hitched himself up higher on the hammock of grass and scrub-covered sand.

"Lay it out for me, Charlie," the voice spoke close to his ear. Charlie jumped and looked over his shoulder. He'd been so intent on watching the ship and the men of Kinnakeet Station struggling down the beach that he hadn't heard his keeper approach.

"She's come to rest on one of the outer bars, Keep." Charlie's finger pointed across the waves, then swung through an arc towards the north. "Kinnakeet's coming up the beach."

Thomas's eyes followed and he frowned at the sight of the scattered men of Kinnakeet Station. He could see the squat form of what had to be Keeper Smyth gesturing wildly astride the surfboat on the wagon, but the keeper's words were drowned by the roar of the sea and the distance. Thomas turned his attention seaward, squinting against the rain.

"She looks to be around six, seven hundred yards out, eh, Charlie?" Thomas spoke loudly to be heard against the storm.

Charlie nodded, "Seems about right, Keep. Too far for the gun."

Thomas's jaw was set in a firm line around his pipe and he chewed the stem thoughtfully. The breakers towered over the sand in two distinct lines. The closer line crested at well over ten feet in height before growing white fangs and chewing into the beach. Heavy foam flecked the crests like spittle of the beast. The further set of swells was greater than the first, out over the closest bar. The swirl and eddies created between the two gave shape to the monster beneath the blanket of black water. The day that Evan had died it hadn't been any better, but it hadn't been worse either.

"Aye," Thomas whispered into the wind as he watched the surf.

"Where they putting in, Cap?" Seamus asked as he struggled up the mound of sand to Thomas and Charlie.

Thomas cupped his pipe against the wind and drew heavily before nodding toward the Kinnakeet men on the beach beyond the hammock. The other Hatteras men staggered up the sand dune.

Elijah followed in Seamus's footsteps, and he rested bent over, with his huge hands on his thighs. His breath fogged heavily in the cold air. He had worked as hard as the heavy draft horse bringing their beach cart and boat from the station.

Elijah was studying the surf and the breakers. Suddenly, he stood and pointed. "There, Keep!" he shouted. "It be better there! See, where the rip breaks, the sea ain't as bad!"

Thomas sighted along Elijah's outstretched finger. There was a fold in the pounding surf. The wave action was still fierce, but without the towering swells that plagued most of the beach. Thomas nodded and smiled at Elijah. Such eddies came and went; it took a very knowing eye to discern the slight break.

Thomas turned to Seamus. "Have Jon keep an eye on that break, and Charlie stay with the wagon. You other men, with me." Without a backward glance, Thomas slid down the dune and struggled against the storm toward the men of Kinnakeet Station.

"I said to untie that side, you worthless son of a whore!" Jack Johnson screamed at one of his men.

"I heard ya the first time. I cain't get it loose," the man retorted through clenched teeth.

Swearing mightily, Johnson shoved the man aside and swept a knife through the line holding the surfboat on the wagon. With a crash, the boat lurched awkwardly onto the beach. The force of the fall sheared the tiller arm with a crack of broken timber.

"Goddamnit!" bellowed Keeper Smyth. He grimaced; the stub of tiller would just barely be enough to steer the boat. He glared at his Number One and spat forcibly onto the sand.

"Well, what do we got here?" One of the Kinnakeet men elbowed Johnson lightly in the ribs and nodded toward the four approaching Hatteras men.

Johnson turned and leered at the men coming up the beach. He glanced sideways at Keeper Smyth and nodded in satisfaction at the keeper's grim expression; Smyth had seen them coming as well. Johnson held his peace. Let Smyth tell these bastards where they could get off.

Thomas lifted a hand in greeting to the Kinnakeet men. "'Lo, Keeper Smyth, how can we help?" he shouted as they drew close enough.

Smyth blanched at the offer and his jaw set in a hard line under his gray beard. "We got this, Hooper. Don't need no help." He looked from the Hatteras men to the dunes beyond. "'Sides, seems like you're a man short."

Thomas bit his tongue on an angry retort. "My man saw a decent break down the beach sixty yards or so. Be a good place to launch your boat, Keeper. That's where we'll be putting in." Thomas fought to keep the dislike from his tone and face, but knew he only half succeeded.

Smyth sneered at Hooper and spat a stream of tobacco juice within an inch of his boot. "We're launching here, Hooper. Don't really care what your man might think he might 'ave seen."

Seamus's eyebrow shot up in surprise at the keeper's response. The man hadn't called them liars, but it was close.

"Surf's not as good here. That rip's just down the beach." Eli stated flatly, pointing toward the break in the waves down the beach.

Johnson immediately stepped forward between his Keeper and the Hatteras men. "Nobody asked you nothing, nigger. Shut yer goddamn mouth!"

Eli took a half step backward from the violence of the verbal attack. Johnson clenched his fists and took another angry step forward. His small eyes sparking with rage, he'd made as if to step even closer.

That's when Sparrow hit him. It was a fierce shove from hard hands and Johnson staggered backward. His foot caught the tongue of the surfboat wagon, tripping him and toppling him onto the wet sand beyond.

Johnson landed in an awkward heap. With a curse, he was off the ground and launched himself at Sparrow with a flying tackle that rolled both men into the swirling water on the beach. In a blink, the beach was a roil of fighting men. As soon as Johnson charged Sparrow, Seamus had promptly sunk an elbow into the stomach of the closest Kinnakeet man.

Thomas locked eyes with Smyth and shook his head. There was enough to do today, but Smyth only glared back.

"*Enough!*" Thomas's voice boomed above the din. His voice carried the tone of command, and the men, both Hatteras and Kinnakeet, paused in the rain. "We've the sea to fight, damn it, not one another. That's enough!"

The men broke apart. Johnson spat blood in the sand, and Sparrow wiggled a loose tooth with two fingers. Seamus and Jon backed away toward Hooper.

The blue-green of Thomas's eyes was a storm of its own, but his voice was firm and even. "Hatteras, with me." He turned and started back down the beach toward their own surfboat. His anger was a palpable thing as he fought for control. The men felt it and hung back. Seamus grinned sideways at

Sparrow, and they followed the keeper back to their own stretch of beach.

CHAPTER 38

December 1878
The Beach at Cape Hatteras

"Think they'll make it, Cap?" Seamus questioned over the howl of the wind.

The men of Hatteras Station had worked their surfboat free of the wagon and it lay above the tideline. Eli stood in the waves; the angry surf tore at his legs as he read the wave break. The others stood back, watching the Kinnakeet men wrestle their boat into the heavy surf. Thomas shrugged uncertainly in response, while keeping his gaze fixed on the struggle with the sea and sand. His lips pressed together in a grim line; his thoughts were of Evan's empty life vest.

Sparrow's eyes were livid and he held a handkerchief to his split lip. "Hope the bastards drown," he mumbled, venom in his tone.

Thomas's eyes flicked to the fierce little man. Just the anger talking. "Let's hope not, Mr. Gray. There are enough lives in the balance this day." His eyes took in the other Hatteras men. "And we all know what that feels like," he added quietly.

Sparrow muttered, put his handkerchief back in his pocket, spitting bloodily onto the wet sand at their feet.

"Shove off, there!" Johnson howled over the wind.

The men of Kinnakeet struggled against the waves. Icy water dragged at their legs, alternately as deep as their ankles and their thighs, as the surf raked the beach. The wind tattered the tops of the waves and within minutes the wool of the men's uniforms was soaked in the salty spray.

"Damn it, Jack! Let's get past these first breakers!" Keeper Smyth shouted from the stern of the boat.

Johnson glared at his keeper from the deep water next to the bow. The towering waves crashed just ahead of him, and it was difficult to keep his footing on the sand beneath the swirling water.

"Jesus Christ, Smyth, I'm workin' on it," he shouted in return. Easy for him to say, still up on the beach. "Harry, John, git in 'afore we wash sideways again."

Unsteadily, the men of Kinnakeet scrambled into their surfboat. As the bow edged into deeper water, the little boat porpoised into a heavy wave. Like a steer shying from the slaughtering pen, the bow swung sharply away from the onslaught toward the safety of the beach, and the wood planks groaned under the strain.

"Pull, damn you, pull!" A Kinnakeet man screamed as he toppled into the stern. Landing astride the splintered tiller arm, it punched deeply through the thick wool of his pants leg into his thigh. The man howled in pain, and his blood mixed with the black water that sloshed heavily over the men's boots in the bottom of the boat.

Johnson cuffed a surfman behind the ear. "Pull! We've got to get past this first line of breakers or we'll be over. Pull!"

The small boat struggled to answer the efforts of the oarsmen. Lurching over the next breaker, it smashed its bow onto the sea beyond. Johnson was knee deep in water and bailing for all he was worth. His chest heaved with effort, and the fog from his breath clouded his face.

Johnson glared around the surfboat, his mean, close-set eyes cursing silently at the men. "The next set's bigger. We gotta pull hard, you worthless curs." In the distance he could see the men of Hatteras Station down the beach. He shifted his eyes seaward to face the monster. The surfboat dug deeply into the next set of waves over the second bar as the men of Kinnakeet strained into the oars.

"They gotta straighten out," Elijah murmured from behind his upturned collar. The blue of his uniform had blackened with water, and the whites of his eyes rolled apprehensively.

Hooper's eyes narrowed at Elijah's statement. The big man was right. The Kinnakeet boat was at a steep angle as it plunged into the second set of breakers. The bow and the first few men disappeared under the towering wave as the boat struggled to break up and over.

Charlie glanced at his brother. His whisper was hoarse and voiced the thoughts of all. "They ain't gonna make it."

The stricken surfboat's bow broke free of the water, but the wave was cresting. The boat and the sea wrestled silently, and even the wind seemed to pause in anticipation. Suspended diagonally up the wave as the surfboat was, the Hatteras men could plainly see its deck. The men of Kinnakeet were all leaning low and forward in an effort to keep the bow from climbing out of the water.

The last thing Thomas saw before the boat went over was Keeper Smyth. He'd turned his head shoreward, and Thomas felt the man's desperation punch him in the stomach.

The wave balled up the surfboat and flung it back toward the beach.

"No!" Thomas shrieked above the storm and sprinted across the beach. The ship in the distance was forgotten in the immediacy of the tragedy close at hand. The men of Hatteras at his heels, Thomas plunged into the surf. The surfboat rolled past on the waves, its oars flung wide, its back splintered and broken.

Dodging the tumbling boat, Seamus grabbed the back of the first cork jacket he saw. The man sputtered and was struggling to get his feet under him. Unceremoniously, Seamus grabbed the man's collar and stumbled back toward the beach. The man coughed water, and Seamus left him retching on the sands to plunge back into the surf. He swept past Charlie and Jon, who were carrying a Kinnakeet man between them, and grabbed another man by the hair.

Thomas found Smyth in the deeper water right at the waves. He ducked through the green curtain and grabbed the man as he tumbled by, hauling him to the surface as he went. The other Keeper's eyes were wide with shock, but at least he was breathing.

Sparrow found Johnson first. The man was face down in shallow water. He could see the greasy hair fanned out around his head. Sparrow's step faltered, and he stared at the man's back for a fraction of an instant. Served the bastard right. He chewed his moustache in thought. It was Eli that decided for him. The big man shouldered past Sparrow, staggering in the waist-deep water. Sparrow caught the big man's eye, and Eli winked at him in the rain. With a quick grin, Sparrow leapt to help drag the unconscious Johnson to shore.

Flipping Johnson onto his back, Eli rudely wrenched the man's head sideways and shoved a finger down his throat. They'd trained on rescue breathing. Sparrow put his hand on Eli's shoulder as he bent his mouth to Johnson.

"You'd better let me, Eli," Sparrow said with a slight smile.

Eli's lips parted in a half-smile, and he squatted back on his haunches. Johnson might never be able to live with a Negro's kiss. Sparrow leaned in, canting the man's head back gently to allow his breaths into Johnson's mouth unrestricted. After two quick breaths, Johnson sputtered and gasped. A spray of salt water and lung juice splattered Sparrow's face as the man stirred and his eyes flared open.

Johnson's eyes widened in shock at the two men that bent over him. "Maybe we should nickname you Lucky, Johnson," Sparrow sneered, and Eli threw his head back to the rain and roared with laughter.

Thomas broke the moment as he hurried past on the beach, shouting. "Eli, pick the spot, now!"

Seamus's voice rose over the wind, "Hatteras, to our boat."

The men of Hatteras Station nodded as one, and turned their backs on the beaten men of Kinnakeet Station.

CHAPTER 39

December 1878
The Beach at Cape Hatteras

The men of Hatteras gathered around the surfboat at the edge of the swirling torrent. Thomas glanced seaward and grimaced. Evan was in all their thoughts. The surf was unyielding. He gathered the men's eyes solemnly like a stage driver gathered the reins.

"Men of Hatteras Station," Thomas began quietly, his voice barely audible against the crashing surf and roaring wind, "It's our turn. Lest we forget, we are surfmen. We have trained for this fight, and it's a fight we've got to make." Seamus swallowed hard, his pronounced Adam's apple bobbing against his collar, and the Mahigans shared a hard look. "I miss him, too, boys, but if Evan were standing among us, how would he react? Would he face the surf?" Thomas eyes roved among them, and he was greeted with hesitant nods. Thomas continued, "I believe he would. He wanted to be a surfman in ways we can barely understand. He sought us, to fulfill that dream. And fulfill it he did." Thomas voice rose above the wind. "How will we honor his memory? Do we honor Evan by cowing at the very surf that took his life?"

No one responded.

Thomas roared, "Well, do we?!"

"No, sir, Cap'n!" Seamus shook his head emphatically and his stringy wet red hair flailed violently. The other men added their voices to his own.

"Well then, I say, damn the surf—damn the Kinnakeet men —damn this storm. We've work to do! Who are we?" Thomas's eyes snapped, and, as if to punctuate his thoughts, the clouds raced behind him across the sea and lightning crackled in the distance.

"The surfmen of Cape Hatteras Station!" Sparrow yelled, and spat for emphasis.

Thomas nodded wildly. "You're goddamn right that's who we are! *Who are we?*"

The men of Hatteras howled as one; their keeper's fire kindled in their hearts. "The surfmen of Cape Hatteras Station!"

Thomas met each man's eyes in turn as thunder rolled out across the sea. "We've made an oath to the Service, but more importantly to ourselves, and most importantly to each other. With my brothers at my back, this bitch," he swept a dismissive hand out at the water, "does not scare me. We are the surfmen of Hatteras Station. We jest that we have to go out, but we don't have to come back. That is bullshit! We are going out and we all *are* coming back." He stared at each man. "And so are they." He pointed at the distant ship, his voice ending in a broken shout. "Today we remember Evan Thatcher and the sacrifice he's made! No man will drown this day!"

The men felt the surge of blood in their ears and, without orders, shoved the surfboat into the waves.

Seamus scrambled into the bow. "Eli! You've the call."

Elijah centered his bulk on the bench, his immense strength rowing for both himself and the missing Evan. He bent his back into the middle set of oars, with his head turned to watch the waves. "Pull heavy, port," he roared deeply.

With steady confident commands, Eli pulled the Hatteras boat through the first set of breakers. Thomas marveled at the big man's skill, for the tiller needed little adjustment under his hand. Elijah was steering the boat with his own back, and willing it forward with grim determination.

"Steady, men!" Thomas shouted as the boat nosed into the second set of breakers.

"Straight up, Keep," Eli glanced back at the keeper as the bow began to rise. The heavy muscles of his shoulders strained under his heavy coat and cork jacket.

The bow shot up the swell. Seamus threw himself hard against the bow, leaning far over, and the Mahigan brothers leapt to his side. The weight of the three men pushed to keep the bow from flipping over. For a fleeting instant, each man thought of Evan.

"Stay at it, Eli! Put her over!" Seamus screeched from the bow. He had little air as the Mahigans crushed into his back, mashing him against the forward gunwale.

The heavy surfboat paused, and the wave below began to curl amidships. Sparrow scrambled from his seat and threw himself against the Mahigans. A heavy coil of line flipped out of the bow from beneath his scrambling feet and caught Keeper Hooper across the face as he leaned forward at the tiller. Hooper blinked hard from the sting of the rope as the bow slammed hard down into the water beyond the crest.

Elijah roared in satisfaction, his voice lost in the triumphant tumult from his brothers.

Thomas grinned maniacally in the stern, "Steady, surfmen. To stations. Pull!"

The surfboat straightened as the men bent to task and plowed onward. Each oar brought the distant ship closer and more into focus.

Keeper Hooper turned his head skyward, looking past the rolling clouds and storm. "Thank you, Evan," he mouthed into the wind.

Chapter 40
December 1878
The Surf at Cape Hatteras

The crew of the *Fearless* pounded what was left of the rail in triumph, and Jubbs hugged a crewman, happily swinging the man in a swift circle before turning to his captain.

"They've made it, Cap! Help is on the way!" Jubbs cried to Captain Logan.

Logan squatted on the tilting deck, his back braced against what was left of the quarterdeck. He squinted up at the first mate and allowed himself a wan grin. He'd captained the *Fearless* for twenty years, and he felt her loss like that of a father losing a child.

"Very well, Mr. Jubbs. Make ready to abandon ship," he ordered around the stem of his pipe.

"Aye, bloody aye, Cap," Jubbs grinned. The crew needed no such orders; it was all he could do to get them to stay aboard at this point.

"Hallooo," Seamus screamed into the wind, and Jubbs fought through the seamen crowding the rail.

"Halloo, yourself!" Jubbs cried in return.

"Back water, boys," Thomas said quietly, his eyes fixed on the floating flotsam around the ship. "Steady..."

The surfmen backed their oars, but Jon's was trapped in rigging beneath the surface. The surfboat struggled against the anchor. With an oath, Elijah swept the oar from Jon's hand and hauled it forcibly from the pull of the heavy lines.

The surfboat bumped alongside the stranded ship. They'd approached from the beach side, and the towering ship blocked out the wind and sea. The water below was relatively calm.

Seamus leaned his head back to better see the seamen above. "Steady, lads. How many aboard?"

Jubbs leaned out over the rail. "Nine of us."

Thomas and Seamus exchanged a look. The surfboat was built to handle twelve to fourteen men, and Eli would count for two... at least. They'd be overloaded. The *Fearless* shuddered visibly, and Thomas' lips tightened in apprehension. It was now or never.

Thomas nodded to the men above. "Right, then. Toss the ladder; we'll bring you all at once. Come down one at a time or we're all done for!" he shouted, cupping a hand to his mouth.

Jubbs shoved the ladder over the splintered rail and glared around at the crewmen of the *Fearless*. "You heard the man! Jones," he pointed at the cabin boy, "you first."

Thomas studied the sea and the ship as the men descended the rope ladder. They needed to hurry. The ship was coming apart before their eyes. Even as the thought entered his mind, a large portion of the bowsprit broke away and nearly clipped the surfboat.

His eyes found Seamus and locked on. His Number One nodded, *I know...I know.* "Hurry lads, or we're goners!" he screamed up to the men above. Tar from the side of the ship covered his hands from fending off the surfboat.

Jubbs was the last crewman left aboard, and he turned to Captain Logan. "Skip?"

Logan looked up through pipe smoke at his Number One.

"Time to go," Jubbs said gently.

Logan drew on his pipe and studied the first mate calmly. "You go ahead, Jubbs. I'll be along." He drew a wet letter from the inside pocket of his heavy coat and held it up to Jubbs. "Pass this along to my wife, old friend."

Jubbs looked at the dripping paper in the captain's hand and his frown deepened.

Logan smiled but made no move to rise from his squatted position. "Go along, Jubbs. That's an order."

Jubbs reached for the paper as he searched the captain's guarded eyes. Then instead, he snatched the skipper's wrist, heaving him unsteadily to his feet. The captain staggered in surprise and his face ended up inches from the first mate's.

"Like hell," Jubbs snarled. "You swore to be home for Christmas, Cap. Now get off the goddamn boat." Unceremoniously, Jubbs shoved the captain against the rail and the ladder to salvation.

Logan's eyebrows arched in surprise. Jubbs had never disobeyed an order. Ever.

He straightened his torn jacket, having lost his pipe in his stumble to his feet. He smiled at the first mate. "My duty lies with the *Fearless*, Jubbs, as does my fate."

Jubbs stared at the captain in disbelief. "Captain, either you're going down that ladder or I'm shoving you down it!" he shouted darkly.

The two men stared at each other in the storm, and the moment held. Logan's eyes broke away first. "Damned if you're not the most contrary first mate, Jubbs." He bowed graciously. "After you."

Jubbs dark eyes narrowed. "Your word, Skip," he demanded.

Captain Logan smiled again. "Fine then," he said quietly. "My word."

Without another word, Jubbs swung over the rail and scrambled down the ladder to the waiting surfboat. A short man with flaming red hair pulled him aboard, and he glanced at the rail above. Captain Logan had a leg over the rail searching for a foothold on the unsteady rope ladder.

"Shove off, Seamus! Eli, back water!" Thomas shouted from his position at the tiller.

The ship above splintered and cracked. A tremendous rent tore through the hull alongside the surfboat, and a wave from within the ship itself nearly capsized the surfboat as its bow nosed away from the dying ship.

Jubbs watched the captain fight for balance on the rail as the surfboat swung away. The *Fearless* was breaking in half. Logan windmilled his arms, but lost his footing. He plunged into the sea. The smack of him hitting the water was lost in the creaks and groans of the ship above.

Jubbs stared at the sea where Logan had splashed down. His mouth opened and closed, but the words wouldn't come. He looked quickly to the man in the stern of the little boat. The man was staring at the water where Logan had gone in as well.

"There, Eli!" Thomas shouted, shoving the rudder hard over with all his weight. Eli glimpsed an outstretched arm above the waves and leaned into the oars. The other surfmen followed suit.

Logan coughed beneath the water. He kicked free of rigging around his left leg. He coughed again, fighting for the surface. Green water churned around him on every side. He thought of the Christmas goose and the fine white tablecloth in Gloucester.

He was at the surface. He sputtered water, gasping ragged breaths. His hair felt on fire, and he could feel strong fingers interlaced in it.

"Sorry, my friend, but I promised my men, the living and the dead, that no man would drown this day," the voice spoke from above, and Logan blinked hard at the saltwater that stung his eyes to see the speaker, as many sets of hands hauled him up out of the water. The captain of the *Fearless* stared at his rescuer between ragged coughs, seeing the blue uniform and gold etching of the Lifesaving Service.

The man grinned at the captain as he hauled him over the gunwale. "Just who might you be, Cap?"

Logan sputtered. His throat felt as if he'd swallowed hot coals. "Nathaniel," he managed weakly, "Nathaniel Logan, captain of the *Fearless*."

Thomas continued grinning at the shipwrecked Captain. "Well Nathaniel Logan, captain of the *Fearless*, I'm Thomas

Hooper with the Lifesaving Service." His grin took a wicked cast. "Welcome to Cape Hatteras."

CHAPTER 41
June 1879
Hatteras, North Carolina

"That's it, just ahead." Sumner nodded to the Hooper fish house with its twin piers running into the Pamlico Sound.

Sunset Cox patted Jesse Yeates on the knee and craned his neck to see the indistinct fish house buried in the marsh grass. "Just like you remember, eh, J.J.?"

Congressman Yeates grinned at his counterpart. "More or less, Sunset...more or less." He pulled the stub of cigar from his mouth and fixed an eye on Sumner Kimball. "Why didn't he come, Sumner?"

Kimball smoothed his large moustache self-consciously before replying. "Well, sir, he sent a letter up with his men, with his regrets. He just couldn't find the time, having spent the better part of a year away from his business with the Lifesaving Service."

Sunset's eyes twinkled. "Damnest thing, eh, Kimball? Not every day a man gets invited to be given a gold medal by the President of the United States." Sunset rubbed his hands together in anticipation. "Can't wait to meet him."

J.J. shook his head at the little man in disbelief. He'd been personally approached by President Hayes regarding the keeper's absence from the ceremony. He didn't like that kind of attention from the president.

Sumner read Yeates's thoughts. "Well, he sure saved those men on the *Fearless*. The eyewitness accounts claim that he succeeded where others failed despite horrific odds."

Yeates nodded and looked at Sumner coolly. "Yeah, well, Cape Hatteras was manned by Tarheels, wasn't it?"

Sunset Cox laughed and slapped Yeates a ringing blow across the back. "Well said, J.J."

Congressman Yeates grinned at the pair. "Just pointing out it was a Carolina crew that received gold service medals for bravery, that's all."

Sumner chuckled nervously and turned his eyes toward the fish house. He snuck a finger inside his shirt collar; damned Carolina summer heat. The skiff bumped along the pier as their hired boatman dragged the little boat up under the low-hanging roof of the house itself.

Yeates hopped out of the skiff and, turning, extended a hand to Congressman Cox. Sunset grinned at his younger counterpart and hopped out on his own, ignoring the outstretched hand. Kimball followed suit, and the three government men walked up the pier. Sunset was whistling "Camptown Races". The dull thud of a wooden mallet echoed in the large structure, and they could hear a murmur of voices from the wide platform.

Sumner paused to look around. Little had changed in a year.

"Well, I'll be damned." Seamus stood at the rail leading to the platform. "Lookee what the cat dragged in."

Sumner nodded to the grinning Scotsman. "Mr. Pennycuik, is Captain Hooper in?"

Seamus vaulted over the railing and landed lightly in front of the three men. He extended a hand to Sumner first. "I'll bet he is, Mr. Kimball. It's good to see you again."

Sumner shook the offered hand and smiled back at the Number One of Cape Hatteras Station. Turning slightly he said, "I'd like to introduce Congressman Jesse Yeates and Congressman Samuel Cox."

Seamus bowed, wiped his hand on his pants, and offered it to J.J. Yeates. "Good to see you again, Mr. Yeates. We met last year, I believe."

J.J. grinned at the memory and shook the Scotsman's hand. "I believe we did, Mr. Pennycuik. Glad to see another year's found you still in one piece."

The Scotsman returned the grin with a crooked grin of his own. "God willing, Congressman."

Sunset stepped forward. "Mr. Pennycuik, I'm—"

"Congressman Cox," Seamus interrupted, still grinning. "We met when I brought the Hatteras crew north for the medal ceremony in Washington." He shook the man's hand. "Glad to see you again."

Cox smiled, deepening the wrinkles at the corners of his eyes. "Right, then. Is Mr. Hooper about?"

Seamus whistled sharply, and a man appeared at the top of the short flight of stairs leading to the warehouse. "You lads remember Jon Mahigan?"

"What is it, Seamus?" Jon asked, regarding the newcomers in the dim light.

"Run and get the captain, would you?" Seamus jerked a thumb at the waiting men. "He's got guests."

"Aye." Jon disappeared into the dim interior.

Seamus gestured for the men to follow and walked up the short stairs. The men glanced at each other and followed the Scotsman.

Thomas Hooper appeared, pulling a shirt over his head. Sweat beaded his brow and he ruffled his unruly long hair, forcing it into some semblance of presentability. "Well, I'll be damned. To what do I owe this honor, gentlemen?"

He stepped forward, extending a hand in greeting, and continued, "Mr. Kimball." He shook the superintendent's hand and nodded crisply to Jesse. "Congressman Yeates."

He turned to the other man, and Sunset felt himself straighten under the force of the gaze. Sunset grinned at his own involuntary response. "Mr. Hooper, I'm Samuel Cox."

Thomas shook the offered hand. "Congressman Cox." He glanced at Sumner Kimball. "Damn, Sumner, two Congressmen this trip. You've outdone yourself."

Sumner squirmed, uncomfortable with the keeper's quick attention. "Yes, well, uh..."

"I believe our good superintendent is trying to say that I wouldn't be left behind, Mr. Hooper." Sunset grinned.

Thomas couldn't help but return the little man's smile. It was infectious. Stuffing his pipe absently, Thomas toed a wooden crate around in front of the trio. "Light and set, gentlemen. I'm sure that there's a story that comes along with this visit."

They had done so when beautiful woman emerged from the depths of the fish house holding a silver tea service. Her shirt was stretched tightly over the bulge of a child within.

"Tea, gentlemen?" she asked courteously and the three men scrambled to their feet.

Thomas smiled at Kimball. "I don't believe that you've met my wife, gentlemen. May I present Mrs. Della Hooper."

Yeates and Kimball shared a quick glance, but Sunset bounded forward, taking the service from her hands. "Truly an honor, Mrs. Hooper. I'm Sunset Cox. Please sit and relax."

Yeates extended a hand to Della, "I echo the words of my esteemed colleague, Mrs. Hooper. An honor, indeed."

Della glanced at Sumner Kimball. "Mr. Kimball. A pleasure to finally meet you." She turned to the other men. "A pleasure to meet you all. Tom, I'll leave you men to it."

As she walked away, Yeates whistled softly with a wry grin. "I guess I can figure what kept you in Carolina, Hooper."

Sunset chuckled and swung a leg over the crate. "Beautiful woman, Hooper, and congratulations. Got a name picked out yet?"

Hooper smiled. "If it's a boy, his name will be Evan, Mr. Cox."

Sumner mopped his face with a handkerchief. "Fine namesake, Mr. Hooper." He smiled sadly at the keeper.

Sumner started again after clearing his throat, "Well, it is my pleasure, on behalf of President Rutherford B. Hayes, to present you with the Gold Lifesaving Medal of Honor." Sumner drew a flat black case from his inside coat pocket and, flipping it open, held it out to Thomas.

Thomas lit his pipe with a match struck from the wooden floorboards and drew deeply. He made no move to reach out and take the medal. Exhaling pipe smoke through his nose, he locked eyes with Sumner Kimball.

Kimball shifted his feet under the direct gaze and carefully placed the medal box on the railing before continuing. "It was my direct recommendation for gold service medals for the keeper and crew of Cape Hatteras Station, based on the heroism and selflessness displayed by the men of Hatteras Station in the rescue of nine souls from the *Fearless* last December. Your men came north to accept their medals, but you did not. So..."

"So, we brought it to you, Keeper Hooper," Sunset Cox finished for the Superintendent as he ran out of steam.

Thomas stoked his pipe before removing it and rubbing his unshaven jaw with the back of his hand. "Gentlemen," he began quietly, "I didn't accept the keepership of Hatteras Station with the goal of glory or fame, with the intent of meeting President Hayes, or with the intent of being awarded the Gold Medal of Honor by the United States Lifesaving Service." Thomas met each of the three government men's eyes. "I accepted the keepership because it needed to be done, and no one else would." Thomas looked at the flat black box on the railing, the gleaming gold of the medal itself cradled on black velvet, before glancing back at Sumner Kimball. "Mr. Kimball, keep the medal. I've received all the thanks I'd ever need."

"Sir?" Sumner's expression was perplexed.

Without saying a word, Thomas dug into his tobacco pouch and removed a scratchy photograph from its depths. Wordlessly, he handed the worn picture to Sumner Kimball. As Sumner unfolded it, Congressmen Yeates and Cox leaned over his shoulder to get a better look.

The picture showed a Christmas table with all the trimmings. A smiling man, a radiant wife, two beautiful little girls, and three handsome boys in Sunday dress. Sumner turned over the photo. Scrawled across the back in a smooth hand was written, "Merry Christmas. Forever in your debt, the Logan Family, Gloucester, Massachusetts."

Thomas Hooper gazed out across the sound at the setting sun and blew smoke into the Carolina summer air. All the thanks he'd ever need.

THE END

AFTERWARD

"The Fact Behind the Fiction"

I thank you for taking the time to delve into the story of Thomas Hooper and the United States Lifesaving Service. As the editing process continued for this book, more than one reader asked me what was real and what was fiction. The following pages are dedicated to answering them. If the story of the United States Lifesaving Service intrigues you, I'd strongly suggest checking out non-fiction titles on the subject. Far better historians than I could ever hope to be have written at length on the subject.

The Numbers

The United States Lifesaving Service has been largely ignored by history. A shame. Over the course of 44 years (1871-1915) the lifesaving service assisted 28,121 shipwrecks and disasters at sea, resulting in the rescue of 174,682 lives in peril. That's more lives saved than were lost in WW1 and the Korean War **COMBINED**, and truly represents a tremendous impact on not only the coasts of the United States but the entire country.

The Timeline

As early as 1848, The United States Government recognized a need for active lifesaving efforts for shipwrecked victims on the East Coast. That same year, The Newell Act, introduced by New Jersey Representative William A. Newell, passed Congressional approval and subsequently provided the first organized lifesaving efforts to be undertaken by the federal government. This fledgling service established unmanned lifesaving stations on the coast of New Jersey. These first stations stored lines and flares and were to be serviced by volunteers from the local communities. The United States Revenue Marine Division, a division of the Treasury Department, built and serviced these far flung stations.

Newell's idea was well intended but poorly executed. The first scattered stations were rarely provisioned, and if they were, were often left empty by theft or misappropriation.

In 1854, on the heels of a fierce Category 4 hurricane that came to be known as the Great Carolina Hurricane, Congress made the very first provisions to staff the stations in an effort to more effectively help vessels in need. However, one deciding factor undermined this effort and caused the Lifesaving Service to fall into the political doldrums. The Civil War. The efforts of both the North and the South were concentrated on the war effort, and saving lives of the men of the sea fell to the wayside as saving lives of the soldiers on the battlefields of the Mid-Atlantic came sharply into focus.

In 1871, Sumner Increase Kimball was appointed Chief of the Revenue Marine Division. While Mr. Kimball had other duties with Revenue Marine, he fought tirelessly as an advocate of lifesaving efforts. His dedication and determination led to the first full time crews of Stations up and down the East Coast, and by 1874 the Lifesaving Service was beginning to take shape as an entity unto itself.

Through Kimball's individual effort, and the help of several key Congressmen and Representatives, including Jesse Yeates of North Carolina and Samuel Sunset Cox of New York, the United States Lifesaving Service was formally established in 1878 as a separate division of the United States Department of Treasury.

Sumner Increase Kimball

I cannot stress how important Sumner Kimball was to the establishment of the United States Lifesaving Service. Arguably, had it not been for the fierce individual efforts of Mr. Kimball, The United States Lifesaving Service would never have existed.

Mr. Kimball served as the one and only Chief Superintendent of the Lifesaving Service until 1915, when the Lifesaving Service was merged with the Revenue Cutter Service to create the United States Coast Guard by President Woodrow Wilson.

Despite my characterization, I sincerely doubt that Mr. Kimball was as nervous or unsure as I have portrayed. I apologize to historians everywhere.

Conflict within the Service

Surfmen puts the crews of Hatteras Station and Big Kinnakeet Station at odds. I doubt the validity of this characterization as late as 1878-1879, and I certainly have no intent of marginalizing the efforts of any lifesaving crews. However, many historians agree that there was severe incompetence within the service that came to light in the late 1870's as a result of several high profile tragic shipwrecks. The first appointments to the original manned lifesaving stations were often political in nature, and there are records of Keepers and Surfmen that couldn't even swim.

The Carolina Coast

The waters off the Outer Banks of North Carolina was given the monicker the Graveyard of the Atlantic in the Early 20th Century. Historians agree that well over 1000 ships lie at rest on the bottom along the Carolina Coast.

The area surrounding the Cape is perhaps the most treacherous stretch of water along the Atlantic Coast for a variety of reasons. The warm waters of the Florida Current flow North and meet the cold waters of the Labrador Current flowing South at this very location, and, subsequently, churn into a perfect storm beneath the sea. We all have seen weather maps on morning television depicting a cold front running into a warm front and the storms that are created as the two masses meet. A similar situation occurs every minute of every day beneath the sea at Cape Hatteras. These turbulent waters were only part of the problem for early seafarers. Geographically speaking, Cape Hatteras is the most southeasterly point of the United States. Thousands of years of erosion and turbulence have created dangerous shoals that lie in waiting to shatter the unwary vessel that strays too far inland.

The shipwrecks along the Carolina Coast are a testament to the treacherous nature of the Carolina sea. The *Fearless* is a fictitious ship; however, its fate is based on fact. Throughout history Captains have been wary of the sea along the Outer Banks; nevertheless, many a ship has tried to cut the corner running close to the Cape in an effort to save precious time on a run to the major ports in the Northern States. If you ask why they would take such a risk, I challenge you to look at your speedometer next time you're running late. I'd be willing to bet that you're exceeding the safe posted speed limit despite the risk...right?

Please consider visiting The Graveyard of the Atlantic Museum in Hatteras, NC the next time you find yourself on the Outer Banks. You will not be disappointed.

The wreck of the *Ephriam Williams*

Surfmen was originally conceived based on the short historical account of the shipwreck of the 487 ton barkentine, *Ephriam Williams,* and the subsequent lifesaving efforts to save the crew on December 22, 1884 by the men of Cape Hatteras Station. While Keeper Hooper, Seamus, Elijah, Sparrow, Jon and Charlie Mahigan, and Evan are fictitious characters, there were very real heroes that did receive the Gold Medal of Honor for their efforts. Their names were Keeper Benjamin B. Dailey, Isaac L. Jennett, Thomas Gray, John H. Midgett, Jabez B. Jennett, Charles Fulcher, and Patrick H. Etheridge.

Negroes and Racism

In the book, we see racism on the Outer Banks on a variety of levels. Remember that the Outer Banks served as a coastal mishmash of people. There were indigenous Indians, settled sailors of every possible color, white settlers, etc. Most historians agree that there was little racism in the area as a whole prior to the Civil War. This was not an agrarian society, and subsequently there were few slaves. As the sons of North Carolina returned from the ranks of Confederate soldiers, however, racism toward the black man escalated, due in large part to exposure to mainland Southerners' personal convictions. Coastal Carolina natives that had never been exposed to racial hatred had just fought for a number of years alongside men that weaned on just such hatred in a fight that was based in part on freedom for the black man. In such an environment, I can easily understand how such prejudice would manifest.

The allusion in **Surfmen** to the burning of Pea Island Station in 1879 is a true account. Keeper Richard Etheridge was the first black Keeper with the Lifesaving Service, and the crew of Pea Island were all black men. Arsonists burned the Station to the ground 5 months after Etheridge's appointment, and racial hatred was thought to be the motive. Incidentally, black men were employed by the Lifesaving Service from its inception. They received the exact same pay and benefits as their white counterparts, and several of the stations were mixed black and white.

In characterizing Elijah, I alluded to his service with the Confederate Army. Historians have argued for years as to the nature of black troops within the Confederate forces. Some argue that there were no black soldiers in uniform, and others argue that there were black men that had been pressed into service. A minority of historians argue that there were black volunteers that actively fought in Confederate uniform. This last group includes a whole contingent of folks that are Sons of the Confederacy and are black. Of course, the existence of black Confederate soldiers is an unpopular opinion. The Civil War of the history books was fought over slavery. Period. That's what we learned in Junior High. Historians of today are poking holes in this theory. I'm not suggesting that the abolishment of slavery was not a huge factor in the Civil War, but I am saying that rarely are wars fought for a single reason.

The Lumbee

Jon and Charlie Mahigan are Indian, most specifically Lumbee. The Lumbee were one of the original indigenous tribes of Coastal Carolina, and part of the overall Croatan Indian group. The United States government officially recognized the Lumbee as an independent tribe in 1956, but has never approved for the tribe any of the federal services that are usually accorded to recognized indigenous Indian tribes of the United States. This is an unusual set of circumstances, the driving factor behind which is the belief that the Lumbee do not have an independent culture or language, due in large part to early assimilation with mainstream English settlers. In the story, Hooper speaks to the Mahigans in Algonquin; it is thought that the Croatan/Lumbee were part of the overall Algonquin nation that stretched from New York to South Carolina.

The Croatan Indian tribes are still alive and well in Coastal Carolina, and the early assimilation that I speak of is reenacted throughout the summer on Roanoke Island in a performance known as The Lost Colony. The story of the Lost Colony is fascinating and has haunted historians since 1587. One of the first English colonies established on the East Coast by agents of Sir Walter Raleigh was the colony on Roanoke Island. In 1587, the governor of the colony, Governor White, returned to England for supplies and provisions. On his return, the colony was deserted. The only evidence of the English settlers was the word "Croatan" carved into a tree. The colony was lost and only questions remained. Did the settlers die off to disease or malnutrition? Did the Croatan/Lumbee/Hatteras tribes of indigenous Indians slaughter the settlers? Or...did the settlers assimilate with the indigenous tribes? The most compelling evidence for the assimilation theory occurred in 1719 when explorers located a tribe of Indians in the hills of mainland Carolina that were of mixed race: brown hair and brown eyes were mixed up with blond hair and blue and green eyes, fair skin was mixed with dark. The most unique part of the discovery was that the Indians spoke Elizabethan English!

Hooper and Seamus go to find the Mahigans at their fish camp in The Alligator Swamp. The Alligator Swamp and Alligator River are still in place between Roanoke Island and mainland North Carolina, and, if anything, it's gloomier and more forbidding than I could have possibly conveyed. Based on my personal observations, there may still be Lumbee back in there. The Alligator River National Wildlife Refuge was established in 1984 and encompasses 154,000 acres in Dare and Hyde County North Carolina. Definitely worth a visit.

Colloquialisms

I tried to use local vernaculars and nautical terms as much as possible without becoming too weighty, in an effort to make the work as readable as possible without losing its authentic feel.

Final Thoughts

If you find yourself on the Outer Banks of North Carolina, take the time to visit The Chicamacomico Lifesaving Station Historic Site in Roadanthe, North Carolina. This station is the most complete site in North Carolina, and one of the few remaining sites on the entire Eastern Seaboard. It is open from mid April through November, and, during the summer months, Coast Guard Station Hatteras still performs the Breeches Buoy rescue for the public. It is one of the last stations in the United States where this style of rescue is still demonstrated, and will give you a strong appreciation on rescues in general. Perhaps you too will have a chance to feel what it was like to be a Surfman of the United States Lifesaving Service.

About the Author

C.T. Marshall

C.T. Marshall writes from his native Maryland. Having spent a lifetime in the woods and on the water, Mr. Marshall has lived and worked among the characters in his stories, common men and women with scarred, callous-stitched hands. He lives on the family farm in a log home of his own design and construction with his wife and three children.

If You Enjoyed This Book
You'll Love Everything
That Has Ever Been Printed
Or Ever Will Be Printed
by

FIRESHIP PRESS

www.fireshippress.com

All Fireship Press books are available directly through
our website, amazon.com, Barnes and Noble and Nook,
Sony Reader, Apple iTunes, Kobo books and via leading
bookshops across the United States, Canada, the UK,
Australia and Europe.

Hail Columbia

by

Jack Martin

In 1869, four years after the Civil War has ended, Southerners bristle under the authority of a military government. Embittered Confederate veterans secretly form the Ku Klux Klan to fight what they perceive as their unjust oppression by the North. However, President Ulysses S. Grant views the Klan as a dangerous organization, one using arson and murder to destroy the newly won rights of former slaves and sabotage Washington's authority in the South. Seeking to break the back of the Klan without returning the country to the destruction of the Civil War, Grant turns to his most trusted agent, Major Alphonso Brutus Clay, to find a way to end the clan's violent activities in the South.

Aided by his friend, the writer Ambrose Bierce, and by his lovely, terrifying mistress Teresa Duval, Clay embarks on his greatest challenge yet. Not just to prevent a second presidential assassination, not just to preserve the unity of the country, but to prevent a secret cabal of corrupt financiers from gaining control of the United States, and to save the world from the designs of an organization far older than the United States itself.

Fireship Press
www.FireshipPress.com

WWW.FIRESHIPPRESS.COM

HISTORICAL FICTION AND NONFICTION
PAPERBACKS AVAILABLE FOR ORDER ON LINE
AND AS EBOOKS WITH ALL MAJOR DISTRIBUTERS

"OLD IRONSIDES" AND HMS JAVA
A STORY OF 1812

A highly recommended must-read for every naval enthusiast—indeed, for every American!

Stephen Coonts
NY Times best-selling author

HMS *Java* and the USS *Constitution* (the famous "Old Ironsides") face off in the War of 1812's most spectacular blue-water frigate action. Their separate stories begin in August 1812—one in England and the other in New England. Then, the tension and suspense rise, week-by-week, as the ships cruise the Atlantic, slowly and inevitably coming together for the final life-and-death climax.

The Perfect Wreck is not only the first full-length book ever written about the battle between the USS *Constitution* and HMS *Java*, it is a gem of Creative Nonfiction. It has the exhaustive research of a scholarly history book; but it is beautifully presented in the form of a novel.

WWW.FIRESHIPPRESS.COM
Interesting • Informative • Authoritative

**For the Finest in
Nautical and Historical
Fiction and Nonfiction**

WWW.FIRESHIPPRESS.COM

Interesting • Informative • Authoritative

All Fireship Press books are now available
directly through www.FireshipPress.com, Amazon.com
and as electronic downloads.

CPSIA information can be obtained at www.ICGtesting.com
Printed in the USA
BVOW08s1653040614

355396BV00011B/754/P

9 781611 792874